A Quest for Orion

by the same author

THE MOON IN THE CLOUD
(awarded the Library Association's Carnegie Medal)
THE SHADOW ON THE SUN
THE BRIGHT AND MORNING STAR
THE SEAL-SINGING
THE LOTUS AND THE GRAIL

for younger children

THE LITTLE DOG OF FO
THE FLYING SHIP
THE KING'S WHITE ELEPHANT
THE CHILD IN THE BAMBOO GROVE

for adults

THREE CANDLES FOR THE DARK
THE DOUBLE SNARE
THE SUMMER HOUSE
ALL MY ENEMIES
THE NICE GIRL'S STORY

✻ A Quest for Orion

ROSEMARY HARRIS

FABER AND FABER
London and Boston

First published in 1978
by Faber and Faber Limited
3 Queen Square London WC1
Printed in Great Britain by
Latimer Trend & Company Ltd Plymouth

British Library Cataloguing in Publication Data

Harris, Rosemary
   A quest for Orion.
   I. Title
   823'.9'1F   PZ7.H2437

   ISBN 0-571-11203-X

❦ Contents

1 § Stars Against Us

The wind was blowing off the sea, and bending the blonde summer-dried grasses as it swept from hollow to hollow of the crested downs; a warm scent was carried with it, of salt and gorse, and the honey-smell of small flowers scattering the turf—bee-orchid and thrift, and waxy yellow toadflax; and it carried too the gulls' wailing, complaining cries, a dismal and primeval sound as if the sea itself had found a voice to comment on disaster.

Matt Harvester, moving cautiously up the landward side of the humpbacked ridge, felt the wind's thrust thrumming against his eardrums, and paused in the shelter of a hawthorn, screwing up his eyes against the violence of the light. His head was aching, and he was sick at heart, and the relentless drum-drumming of the sea wind, which would usually have given him fierce pleasure, was now nothing more than a brutal reminder of the traditional sounds of war. De-rumm. De-rumm. Derum-rumm-rummm . . .

Up here it was as English a scene as any he could remember, the wide skies and cloud-shadowed downland still gave him some illusory sense of freedom. Well, these things were free, after all, and it was an historic strip of land, with its ancient, gale-lashed, summer-honeyed hills—on this very one a flaming beacon had once flared warning to all Sussex men during that spectacular Year of Grace 1588 . . .

"Capten, art tha sleepin' there below?"

Yes—Drake was sleeping now, all right, thought Matt

savagely. Sleeping soundly, wherever he'd slung his hammock in this Year of Disgrace 1999—the sod! No helpful quitting the port of heaven to come drumming up the Channel, or anything like that. And England's fortunes had slid too far for saving, modern aggression had proved too swift and savage. The bombardment via satellite—after the defenders' morale had been weakened by selective virus warfare—and even that old-fashioned last stage of glider-borne parachutists, were a far cry from the aborted threat of Philip's lumbering Armada. So England had gone down, neither grandly nor valiantly, but rotten with fear, and decades of industry's greedy bickering; and above the crash of that fall rose the self-justifying whine of some eager collaborators, who speedily joined hands with the invaders to help them round up slave-labour for other stricken zones in Europe.

And now he, Matt, could be called a collaborator too. Hadn't Tom called him that very thing last night?

He shifted the heavy rucksack on his shoulders, and heard Bill's voice just behind him, an echo of his bitter thoughts.

"Matt—collaboration won't help anyone. It's just stupid. Change your mind—Matt, please. Don't go. Don't give yourself up. It's too late—they'll enslave you with the others. That's all. At least while we're still on the run you're—we're—half-free—And it's just stupid to think you can worm your way into their confidence now—Just stupid to think anyone will do any freedom-fighting from inside that lot—Just *stupid*."

"Ah, shut it!" said Matt wearily. No more arguments. At least he wouldn't have those to bear, once he'd crossed this last hillcrest to join the crowds of people on the road below, who were being shepherded towards embarkation at the nearest Sussex jetfoil-port.

No more arguments. And no more heartrending scenes with Jan, who was standing with bent head, absorbed in unhappy thoughts as though she'd retreated into shadow. The rows had been as shaking as real family ones. (Not that he left any family behind him—his parents were dead, thank God: he couldn't imagine them caught in the earth-quaking events of this modern wilderness.) It was strange, he thought, to have formed such strong ties with a group of people known so briefly, none of them formerly aware of each other's existence; all of them on the run. Maybe it was the rule of terror that had this forcing effect on love, on dislike. Jan. Tom.

God, how his head ached. He felt muzzy, too. Perhaps it was this infernal wind blowing at them out of the sun. Or the weeks of semi-starvation. Or—had Marburg X caught up with him at last? The ugly bug that had been the enemy's first insidious weapon. Matt shivered. What a time and place to be caught by it . . . Then he thought: it's more likely plain cowardice. And the parting from Jan—

He felt a touch on his hand, and turned to find her closer to him. The wind was blowing her long pale hair straight out behind her like a comet's tail; the trail of freckles across her nose was a little more golden than the sunlight on the pallor of her upturned face.

"Matt—"

"No—Jan! Not you too, please."

His face was very white, greenish-white with strain; and she saw him as all black and white against the sun, eyes screwed up tensely, heavy black hair framing that unhappy face. She felt a dull pang of misery, and thought too: I can't believe we've only known each other a few weeks—

She shook her head. No more pleading; it was useless. And she hadn't Bill Mackenzie's pure Scottish tenacity that would make him continue arguing till Matt was over the ridge and walking away to join the enemy on the road below. But she'd meant to say words of comfort and encouragement—they wouldn't come. How could they? They'd be unreal, almost insulting. It was crazy what Matt was doing, of course. It was far too late for pretence collaboration. No one would be fooled, no one looking at him could ever imagine he was one of those soft people of the type that had smoothed the paths of conquering Roman legionaries or Nazi stormtroopers, oiling the

11

mechanics of defeat by their ingratiating help. But was Matt crazier than she and Bill, Tom—and Charlie—who were on the run here at home, sleeping rough, foodless and homeless, without papers and subject to the severest penalties if they were caught?

"You could still chance it and come with me, Jan," Matt said softly. "It takes more than one to start resistance."

"No, she couldn't—don't deceive yourself there, at least! One thing's sure, we know what happens to the girls—specially one who looks like Jan." Unhappiness made Bill almost brutally curt. "And you'd best forget any specious promises those bastards are handing out. They won't give you any form of training abroad in some 'compliant students' centre', whatever you may think. And you won't get back here again."

Matt winced. For a moment he hated Bill: kind, good-tempered Bill, who surely hadn't meant to make him feel a louse; who'd been with him longer than the others. A lifetime, as one counted it these days: it was almost two months since they'd met up in the shambles of Bill's medical school, attached to the hospital at Canterbury where Matt's guardian had died of Marburg X. They had helped surviving students bury the dead, and then got the hell out as parachutists landed all along the coast. For a time everyone had hoped the bug would be impartial—then it dawned on them that the enemy troops must be immunised. And so many collaborators survived too, thought Matt sardonically; till some of them were no longer needed . . . What a lot of underground preparation there must have been.

Perhaps there were other people, over there on the Continent, ready and willing to help him start a different sort of underground?

"Well, say goodbye and get on with it." Tom's voice broke in harshly, with the underlying scorn that had been absent from Bill's. "Can't hang around too long, even for your sweet sake. Jan. Bill. Hurry up."

"We'll watch him to the road," said Jan stubbornly.

"Too dangerous."

"There's trees."

No one argued. They were all too sick of arguing. If Matt felt that it would make things harder for him, he didn't say so. He led, the others followed, as they worked their way along the ridge towards the sheltering trees. Here the down fell away in spurs of chalk above empty houses by the embarkation road. And here the wind brought with it other sounds than gulls' cries: a sort of murmuring, ceaseless lamentation from crowds of people, mostly young men and women, now shuffling down the road; the relentless rumbling of a tank, close to the procession's end; and—now clear, now distorted by capricious gusts—words mouthed in heavily accented English through loudspeakers mounted on a slowly-crawling van: "—the Free Association—of Kindred States—and Nations—" (Freaks, the British Press had dubbed them before the collapse) "—assures the people of England— they have—nothing to fear. Obedience and constructive— labour will be—" The wind whooped up over the hill and bore away the final lying words.

"Matt, how can you be a *fool?*" burst from Jan, in defiance of herself. Following Tom's example she threw herself down in the trees' shelter, and her tears dripped steadily on to the grass. Somewhere nearby a lark was singing, tossing on the wind. Behind the spur of land the downs rolled backward into haze—mile upon mile, dotted with empty houses, empty farms, and traversed by almost empty roads. Only the land and the larks, thought Jan, are still the same; and somewhere close by an enemy jetfoil's waiting to take Matt away from me across the Channel . . .

"Lie down, Bill," Tom was saying. "Unless you want soldiers up here after us—They've got laser guns. Bill!"

When Bill obeyed, Matt was left standing in isolation on the chalk brink above a descending path. When he spoke his voice croaked like a raven's. "Jan. Take care of yourself."

13

The futility of words! She tried to smile at him. "No—*you* take care of yourself."

"I'm only acting how I feel—"

"I know. I understand."

"Well—" He reached across, touched her hair above her forehead. And said again, hopelessly, "You take care. Goodbye, Bill."

" 'Bye, Matt."

Tom said nothing.

They watched Matt set off along the descending path. Children should have been running down it towards the summer sea, but there was only Matt walking away to join the shuffling crowd below.

The rumble of the tank grew very loud.

"Don't look any more, Jan," said Bill quietly. "You won't see, anyway. And it's safer to lie flat."

"I know." She lay on her face, aching. She couldn't cry now. The hard earth felt like the body of a rejecting mother. There was no comfort anywhere. Matt, she thought. Matt . . . And against her will remembered their most painful argument, last night.

"You'll have to give in, soon," he'd said finally, "and how will you ever get in touch with me again?"

They'd looked at each other in silence; until she answered defiantly, with deliberate lightness: "Carrier pigeon!"

"Oh Jan! Don't joke, now. But if either of us ever get a chance of sending word—We ought to have a codeword, maybe. Suppose you end up in some place like that Northumberland valley you kept talking of—That one you showed me on Tom's map."

"Golden Valley—that's what I called it; lovely summer camping times we—my family—had there." She sighed, thinking: even Golden Valley may be changed, in this appallingly changed world. What hasn't altered? Stars, maybe—constellations?

"Codeword Orion. Golden Valley, or whatever. And signed Orion, Matt."

"Fine. Make it Orion."

Now, hearing the crescendo rumbling of that tank, their interchange seemed too pathetic. Children playing with bathtoys, while a great ship foundered under them . . .

A shout, followed by a soldier's challenge.

"In the bag," said Tom. He glanced at Jan. "Come on. Best be getting back to Charlie. And pray heaven she's stayed quiet in the barn like we told her to . . . But don't get careless," he added, as Jan stood up blindly.

The tank's roar was decreasing towards the quay.

"Now."

They began cautiously retracing their steps across the downs. A little way, and Jan's foot struck against a pebble, bullseye striped. She recalled Matt kicking it on their way out, and stooped for it, to tuck it surreptitiously away in her pocket.

"We shouldn't have come," said Bill suddenly. "It didn't help Jan or Matt. And we shouldn't have left Charlie all alone. After all, even though she's been on the run as long as we have, she is only thirteen."

"We could have brought her with us," said Jan dully.

"No we couldn't, she's too—" Bill groped for words.

"You're dead right," said Tom, "she is."

As they descended towards the valley, the wind dropped, and the larks stood higher, singing. There was a sweet, hot smell of wild thyme. The still heat might have made anyone drowsy, but Bill and Tom were alert, scowling, scanning the sky and distant roads for anyone or anything that moved.

"Plague, sword, exodus," said Bill abruptly. "Book of Revelation come to life, that's what it is. Sword: that's what *we* need, though—Where's Arthur's, or whatsisname's, Roland's?"

"What Europe needed was another Charlemagne, Matt said," murmured Jan, rousing herself to speak of him.

15

"Oh, Matt—he didn't know he was living in this century at all," snorted Tom. "That's what comes of being an historian. Well, he'll wake up now all right. Face to face with modern man at his worst—those bastard neo-Stalinists from all over the place, grouping themselves together in Central Europe!"

"He's just as much a modern man as you are, Tom! A maths man like you, too, he—He had a double first."

Tom's face darkened. "*He* said. You're easily impressed, Jan. My hero!"

"Now stop squabbling, you two. Gods and heroes, they're all dead, anyway."

"That's right," agreed Tom. "Light of common day, we're living in. Not much longer either, unless we scrounge some food soon. We don't need maths—we need some way of making meat out of grass."

Jan heard him as though he were far off. Everything seemed to be happening in a vacuum. She stared away over the empty landscape lying deceptively golden in the heat, and hugged herself as though cold. Bill put an arm round her. "A year or two ago who could ever have believed all this would happen?"

Charlie was careful to be back first. Like the others she kept watch before she moved, and scanned the sky. A very fragile blue it was today—blackbirds' eggs. Gingerly cradling something in her scarf she skirted a corner of the deserted manor house, pursued her way across straw-scattered yards towards the farm buildings, and mounted stone steps into the great barn's loft. Tom had declared it the safest place on the estate, and since he'd been first discoverer and occupier of the barn, no one had objected, except Charlie who was yearning to try the old manor house instead.

"Real beds, up there."

"And creaking floors. And it's attracted looters already."

"But there's only two ways out of here, Tom. Steps and that high-up window."

"Three. We can jump off the loft end, if we're pushed."

Charlie had thought this hilarious, and rolled about on the boards spluttering "if we're *pushed*".

"What Charlie needs is the opposite of elocution," Bill had said. "Shut up, Char—every soldier left in Sussex will be down on us."

There were shadows in the arched roof. Swallows flew in and out of small open spaces near the eaves. Each time one reached its nest there was a high, sweet, urgent twittering. True that beds would be nice, thought Charlie, but swallows were better. She put down her bundle, then stretched herself out on the floor, sniffing. Lovely woody, meally barn smells. Strange, exciting new life. Like being born again. Yes, that's when I really was born—That day Jan and Matt and Bill found me eating stolen cherries in a ditch, just a week after I got clean away from Auntie and Albert . . . She sighed with nostalgic pleasure, remembering: "Auntie", clutching at Albert in a Bognor street, head thrown back, staring at the sky; the little silvery-green forms dropping beneath dandelion-puffs of parachute; the sirens joining Auntie's wailing, and then outdoing it, as everyone dived for cover—or just ran.

And was I right to run! I must be the only person in England pleased about what's happened. And the barn's terrific. I love it. I'm so glad we found it . . . Pity we had to find Tom already in it, though. Tom Jay—what a name! Suits him. She turned on her back, and stared upwards at the roof.

Swallows . . . Jays . . . Seagulls. Matt on the sea . . .

After a while she woke, and peered at her battered watch. Start the fire? Never mind what Tom says.

She took twigs from behind a beam where Matt had hidden them. Matt . . . Best not think of him. Yet she did. How could anyone give up their freedom? But Matt didn't know what fostering was like. Seven years of seven foster homes. "Lotty, help Auntie with the washing up—those are Albert's books, don't you touch them. You say 'get lost' again, and I'll tell the Welfare on you."

Auntie. Albert. Lost for good, now. And on that awful Bognor visit too. Charlie's lips twisted to a happy grin. Then she turned quickly, head tilted. Nothing? Maybe a rat, somewhere below. I'm still alone. Gorgeous freedom, gorgeous aloneness. Only bad if—if—Longish time now: after two. Suppose someone did trap them? Suppose they're all way out on the Channel—

Her lips wobbled. Get that fire ready, they'll be back soon. Four large flat stones in a square, small twigs first, cone, like Tom said. Then one log. Looks good. Only half a box of matches left, and mustn't chance smoke through those open spaces near the eaves, not while alone, not even for a short time. Count the matches . . .

She was counting them for the seventh time when she heard Tom and the others coming; not that they didn't move cautiously, but Jan had given her imitation of a thrush, which wasn't guaranteed to send another thrush out of its mind. Charlie felt relief all over her: a tingling, like bubbles rising in ginger beer. But she arranged herself crosslegged, nonchalant, yawning. Her thick braids were full of meally dust. Bill, first up, glanced at the round fresh face and guileless dark eyes.

"Been asleep?"

"Uh-huh." Charlie threw back her head, stretching her arms wide. "Seen Matt off, have you?"

Heartless little beast, thought Jan. Tom followed her in, scowling. He knocked his elbow on a beam end, and swore. Charlie eyed his thin length warily. Moody—near as bad as Albert.

Jan stood, hands in pockets, staring up at the swallows, but all she saw was a jetfoil moving out above a heavy swell; there were white faces lining the sides, Matt's among them. She said sharply to Charlie: "Hasn't Tom told you again and again never to get fires ready till there's food? Suppose you'd had to run? Giveaway."

Charlie rocked gently, smiling.

"You're positive you dug the very last potato, Bill?"

"Yah—that green one; made you sick, Jan. I've told you twice."

"Then we'd better tighten our belts till morning, and try mushrooming again." She sat down, looking defeated. (Wish I'd gone with Matt—I might have been with Matt now.)

"Try not to be a nit in future, Charlie," she heard Tom say crossly.

"I'll try." Charlie was carefully arranging her scarf bundle on the floor; untying the knot, smoothing out its ends. Three pairs of eyes focused sharply.

"Two—four—six—nine *plovers'* eggs?" Bill whistled softly. "Plovers! So you followed us, after all. Well, it's food, at least—but you know, Char, you did promise—"

"Tom made me, and it wasn't fair. Wow!"

"Oh don't, Tom," implored Jan; for his heavy-handed slap had brought the blood surging to Charlie's cheek.

"She simply must learn not to endanger everyone."

"But if we don't eat, we'll die," intervened Bill mildly. "And we don't want to try and start up Fascism, you know. *I* think she's done very well, if no one saw her."

"I'm not a fool. And I hate you, Tom!" One precious egg went hurtling Tomwards, but spattered the wall instead. Charlie leaped up furiously, slipped between Jan and Bill, charged down the steps, and disappeared.

"Oh Char, do come back!" called Jan after her; too loudly for their safety.

Bill went outside, scanned the scene, and returned.

"Dramatics! Gone into hiding. Where's our pan—shall I start the cooking? And Jan—you go and bring the infant warrior home. On its shield."

But Charlie was nowhere to be seen, in farmyard, gardens, or the orchard; then at last Jan ran her to earth in the hall of the deserted manor house. "Do come on back, Char," she said again. "And do stop crying. You know you always fight with Tom."

"I'm not crying," said Charlie, outraged. "'M sniffing. I've always said there's food here, hidden somewhere. Hoarded."

"We combed the place, you know that. Those eggs will be horrible cold—Bill's cooked them." Jan sighed longingly.

"Tell him to hardboil mine."

"You know Tom said keep away from the house!"

"Oh—Tom! There's something funny about him—why's he always angry?"

"Char, how should *I* know?" Jan shook her head miserably, sensing trouble everywhere. It was a crazy situation, anyway; she couldn't imagine why they'd opted to stay on. And as she retraced her steps barnwards, without Charlie, she was thinking: Matt's right; we really are insane.

A small, determined hand was tugging at her shoulder.

"Jan! Wake, can't you!"

"*Don't*—Wanna sleep," she mumbled. Then sat up, suddenly alert, her heart beating rapidly, like a startled hare's. "Char! Something wrong?"

"Hush, you idiot! Don't wake the others. Come outside." Charlie crept back through the loft, and Jan, yawning and pulling straw from her hair, followed reluctantly.

"Lazy things—you can't have been all *that* tired. And you can't have overeaten on those eggs. And you didn't set a watch."

Jan yawned again. "I know . . . Don't go on about it, Char. Oh—whatever's that?"

Triumphantly Charlie handed her a jar, covered in dust. "Dried milk. Oh Jan—I've found a whole hoard." Her voice sounded ecstatic. "Come and see."

"You've not—really—"

"*Yes.* Come on, quickly!"

"Set a watch, first?"

"*No.* We won't be a minute. Let's surprise them."

Stifling misgivings, and still half disbelieving, Jan followed her through the yards and gardens. Inside the watchful-feeling house Charlie muttered in tense, excited tones: "It's in a sort of airing-cupboard place, near the attics."

"I thought we searched everywhere. However did you find it?" asked Jan, as they climbed the stairs.

"Mouse-droppings," said Charlie briefly.

On the top landing the linen-cupboard door was open and inside, a hole showed black against dimness. Charlie had pulled out some removable shelves and pushed up the back panel.

"We never looked here properly by daylight," she said over her shoulder, as she clambered into the cupboard and leaned forward into darkness. "What was it, d'you think?"

"Priesthole, maybe."

"What's that?" Charlie began pulling out a heavy tin.

"Where Catholic priests hid, in the days when they were persecuted."

"Oh—" Charlie thought food more interesting than priests, any day; but Jan was thrilled. It made England seem a little less lost, this reminder of a long, historic past.

"Pots, tins, and more pots," Charlie reported. She was like a hunt terrier, wild with excitement.

"Don't drag any more out," said Jan urgently. "Somebody might come! Let's just take two over to the barn."

Charlie yielded with surprising docility. They closed up the linen-cupboard and, carrying their finds, trudged back through the gardens. On the barn steps they paused, grinned at each other, and then made their entrance. Bill had just woken, and he sat up, staring. Tom was still sleeping, curled in straw. Charlie stirred him none too gently with her foot. He woke, glowering, and she dumped her tin squarely in his lap.

"Father Christmas, yum-yum."

"Lord almighty," exclaimed Bill, as she tugged off the tape that sealed the lid. The open tin gave off a heavy, sweet smell of fruit.

"And there's more too, much more. These are runner beans,

stored in salt, I think," said Jan, examining her pot, and then handing it to Bill. Tom seemed speechless.

"Genius! How did you find it?" asked Bill.

"She didn't," said Charlie, outraged. "It was all me again. It was in the house, behind the panelling."

"Well, clever Char," said Tom at last. "You've done quite well." He sniffed gluttonously at the pungent smell of dried apricots and raisins. "Think of eating twice in one day."

Jan was thinking of it. And of her family. "Christmas," Charlie had said. Christmas and dried fruit together reminded her of making puddings, baking cakes; her mother and sister stirring the mixture, making wishes for luck. Her eyes filled with tears.

"Gone all broody, Jan? What's up?" asked Bill kindly.

"Nothing." (To upset anyone else by mourning one's lost family was taboo.) "My eyes are watering instead of my mouth, that's all. Come on, let's have a second feast. There's dried milk outside, too. Has anyone filled our can from the stream just lately?"

It was awful—as Tom said later—how greedy they were getting. After they'd finished eating, Charlie began begging for a third examination of the cupboard. But she was over-ruled, and Bill went out instead to do a routine checking of the farm and neighbourhood. Soon he returned, rather shaken, to report seeing figures on the skyline of the nearest hill: a sturdy-looking man, carrying a gun, and someone slighter and smaller, who might have been a young man or a boy.

"They didn't see you, I hope? We'd better lie low for a while—that means no more fires today," decreed Tom. "We can get more of that food out at dawn tomorrow. Listen—I've a hunch about moving on soon; specially if we've collaborators nearby. In the meantime we'd better keep watch and snooze in turns. And let's have a proper conference tonight."

"No, Tom, not Wales. Scotland," said Bill.

"That's just nostalgia, you Scot—Wales is nearer."

"Char, back me—you'll like Scotland."

"Is it terrible rainy?"

"Well—not East Scotland. But we mustn't go east, since we may need an escape route: Ireland, America."

"Don't want to escape." Charlie's lips thrust out mutinously. "I want to be the first English woman guerrilla."

"We might have to go—if we could," said Tom. "But *I* still say Wales."

"East Scotland," said Charlie immediately.

"Jan?"

"Scotland's an awful long way. Freezing winters, too. Isn't Wales easier for Ireland? Wales, then."

"Two against two, even split, and Jan's right, it's a long way," said Bill resignedly. "Okay, Tom, Wales it is."

"But how?" Jan cupped her chin in her hands, and looked anxious. "You know what Matt picked up from that soldier's slave the other day—when he risked foraging near the embarkation camp: there's a regular hedge of armaments, all the way from Southampton to London, while the Freaks drive everyone in the south-east to their embarkation points."

"We must cross it somewhere; that's when the crunch comes."

"Feint east?" Bill suggested. "Look for a small boat on the Kent coast?"

"Sail round London?"

"Is that crazier than anything else? Say we land in Suffolk, trek across the Midlands—"

"There may be other 'hedges' up there," said Tom. "And first build your boat, Noah. Think the Freaks'll lend you one?"

Bill looked crestfallen. There was a silence while everyone considered their dilemma; Jan apprehensively, Charlie with rising excitement that cramped her stomach muscles.

"That hedge," said Bill. "It encircles London, too. Remember?"

They remembered: Matt's voice, relating, "—then this fella told me, 'It's a wasteland now, partly burnt: a lot of it's

23

flatter than your hand. The docks are open—slave labour, and enemy troops. But the City and the rest—It's sealed. Doomed. Rats and ruins, and everyone the Freaks have written off scrounging on what remains till it gives out. The gang boys are hell's own, they say; some out of prison. Very few girls, most of 'em with the junks—and then more savage than you'd think possible. Yes—it's a nasty mess up there, all right.' "

"At least we're not going through London," said Jan thankfully.

"I am," said Tom. "And I hope you're coming too."

In the following silence the swallows' twittering sounded raucous.

Jan felt as though a hole had been blown in the pit of her stomach. Charlie and Bill simply sat and stared.

"You can't—we couldn't," squeaked Jan at last. "It's altogether mad. *Through* London? We'd have to get in—and then out."

"And why?" asked Bill suddenly. "It's not just dangerous, it's hopeless. We'd never make it."

Tom's silence was stubborn till, borne down by their fierce, accusing gaze, he muttered, "It's Alastair. You needn't come—we can have a rendezvous, if you like, somewhere outside Oxford. Then head for, say, Glastonbury." He made it all sound calm and reasonable: a day out, such as anyone might have fixed with friends before the terrible days of the collapse; before distant food wars in India, Africa and South America, and minor ideological clashes between declining Eurostates, had led to the steady, subtle—finally swift and shocking—rise to power of the Neo-Stalinist Free Association of Kindred States and Nations, whose Asiatic Section had their head-quarters in New Bohemia; from where they had launched their murderous attack against what was now renamed—rechristened was scarcely the word—the Western European Zone. Rumour had it that the Freak-States of Columbia and Venezuela were already causing headaches to neutral America;

while the setting up of neutron-warhead rockets in Freak-affiliated Scandinavia hardly promised well for peaceful, almost unarmed Canada, backdoor to the U.S.A.

Against this background it was scarcely surprising that Bill's response to Tom's airy suggestion was: "Tom, you're raving! You can't go it alone. And just how—supposing we all survive so far—do you expect to find your young brother now? If he's alive, he's in central Europe, somewhere. Matt's more likely to stumble on him."

"I have to look," said Tom quietly, coldly. "That's all."

"But—but we swore we *wouldn't*." Jan's voice was husky with terror. "I mean, w-wouldn't break up any more, after—after Matt. We said we wouldn't endanger each other searching for anyone, didn't we, because it's hopeless, and—" She couldn't finish, or she'd cry. For Matt, for herself, for her family, living or dead. Oh—it wasn't treachery, was it, to form a group and stick with it? And now Tom, Tom of all people, usually so repudiating of sentiment, was denying the whole creed of sworn survival at any cost—

In the darkness Bill's comforting hand closed over hers.

Charlie wasn't upset. She was outraged. "You've gone soft!"

"Glad to see the last of your lot, weren't you? But Alastair's —different." Tom's voice sounded unlike any of them had heard it before: pleading. "To start with he's alone, unlike your family, Jan. And you say yours was visiting Australia, Bill. Anyway, I keep thinking about him, like it or not. So I'm going. Whatever any of you feel."

"Never said all this before!"

"Don't tell you all my thoughts, do I?"

"Suppose he never stayed on there, anyway? You said he was at some special school, with other—If they weren't killed maybe they went north, people did, before they were brought back and—"

"If Alastair survived—" Tom's voice sounded oddly remote —"he'd most likely be left in London. Anyone—anyone like Alastair—was just jettisoned there."

"But he was only spastic—legs, you said."

"Legs, mainly. But he was always a bit—different."

"Retarded?" asked Bill, with an embryo doctor's interest.

"Just—different. Not retarded, at all." Tom hesitated. Then he said rather reluctantly, as if ashamed of it: "He's—Well— our mother," his voice stumbled on the word, "always had a name for it: she called him 'a sensitive'. Hard to explain, really. He—he was open to things, in a way most people aren't."

"Soft—or crazy?" asked Charlie, with deep interest.

Tom looked at her darkly, and Jan hurried to smooth things over with, "Don't be silly, Char. I think Tom means ultra-intuitive; sort of psychic—ESP, and all that."

"Well, that *is* crazy." Charlie wasn't to be quenched. "What a family. Jay, Jay, they put them away."

"You'll be put away in a moment," said Bill, "if you're not careful. Tom—all this about finding Alastair is really since Matt heard things about London?"

"Well—yes."

Bill and Charlie accepted this. Jan's intuition made her doubt it. She considered Tom's increasing dark moods, his bitter carping at Matt. Tom doubts himself. He's got to prove something.

" . . . can't argue me out of it. Thing is, are you coming or not?"

"Bill, are we?" whispered Jan. If only Bill would come out against it; go with her and Charlie. She clasped her hands, to keep them steady; and with a sick heart heard his reply.

"Better all stick together, even if it's London. There's not much hope, either way."

"There's the question of Charlie, though," said Tom. "She's a mere child. Can't take her into London."

"I'm not a child!" Charlie's voice quivered with indignation. "I'm a guerrilla, and—"

"Gorilla," murmured Bill. "Wait for it: going to beat her chest. But listen, Tom: if we're doing something crazy for

26

you, you'll have to take the crazy consequences. All or nobody for London."

Good, good, thought Charlie. Good for you, Bill. She hugged herself, rocking to and fro.

"If that's all settled, shall we sleep?" Tom's voice was cold. He turned on to his face and pulled some straw over him, deliberately shutting himself off from the others. But memories weren't so easily excluded: that last fearful row with his father, before the Freaks invaded; Alastair's frantic phone call begging to be fetched—and his own failure to pass on the message. He'd been stewing in sullen, jealous anger—yes, he'd admit to jealousy of the affection between Dad and Alastair. But he'd not meant to hold the message up for ever—things had gone too fast, that was all: his father's unit ordered to the coast; his mother's death when their house was destroyed by flamethrowers; his own last-minute escape. Well, thought Tom, I'll make amends, if possible—and if Alastair's not dead. Though of course he might just as easily have died in Sussex, if Dad *had* sent for him. The whole thing's their fault, anyway—why did they always make me feel so miserably shut out?

He shoved pieces of straw away from his hot face, and heard Jan saying: "Bill and Char, you rest too. I'm not sleepy yet—I'll wake someone later."

"Come on then, Gorilla. Snuggle up," said Bill. "Good circulation, haven't you? It's like clutching a hot water bottle."

Charlie bumped Bill in a friendly way, and slept at once, like the child that Tom had called her.

Nothing stranger, thought Jan, than to be awake when everyone else is sleeping. Huddled on the stone steps she shivered slightly, even though muffled in two old sweaters and her anorak. Heavy dew after warmth made the ground mist thick as cottonwool, so that she seemed to be floating through it, as on the prow of a ship. The moon was a pale tangerine circle, hung like a Chinese lantern among a small company of stars.

Is Matt star-watching as well? Orion . . . Is Matt thinking of Orion? We won't see the real one till December . . . December. When one couldn't even say "tomorrow"! Tomorrow will be stranger than fiction, anyway. Hang on, hide, work, pray for a turning tide. But what hope is there of *that*?

Her eyes ranged the misty yard and shadowed buildings beside the house, until strain made them smart and blur. She pressed the palms of her hands against her eyelids, and at first saw darkness. And then, as usual, scenes—with herself at the centre of them.

She came out of her room, ready for her younger sister's birthday supper—Lydia, who was three years younger than she was, the same age as Charlie. ("Friends to supper?" her mother had exclaimed. "Now?" and "Might as well put a face on things as long as possible," their father had replied.) Her parents stood side by side, their faces stone-white, their mouths open. Her sister was huddled on the settle. The front door was open—a spray of leaves nodded just outside. The cat Cuthbert Four-paws twined hopefully around the legs of a stalwart soldier, who held a laser gun.

The soldier didn't speak. He simply jerked the gun sideways, meaning "outside".

She'd wanted to move, run down and join them. But she felt paralysed, and she could neither speak nor scream. If the soldier would only look up, if anyone would—

They didn't. It wasn't till the lorry started up that she was released from the frozen sense of unreality. Then she ran, shouting, to the door. Too late. There was only the empty drive, and the sound of an engine thrumming as the lorry turned out of it and up the hill. She'd run a little way, then gone back, dazed, into the house. No one had come to Lyddy's supper. She remembered little of the next three days, only Cuthbert's disappearance; he was probably stolen for meat. And then Matt and Bill, who had met up in the nearby village, wandered in, and she'd shared her last loaf, and gone off with them.

Stop this, thought Jan.

She stared at the misty sky again, and put her cold hands in her pockets, touching a smooth roundness in the right one. Oh, that stone—That one Matt had kicked. She weighed it in her hand, thinking it a pleasant thing simply because Matt had touched it. Comforting. And it had been in the world so long, but the sea hadn't destroyed it, only polished it to an acceptable shape. The white part glowed faintly, the black was like ebony and absorbed the moonlight. Somewhere else I've seen coloured shapes interlocking like this, into a whole . . .

This stone's a symbol. It's all I've got of Matt now.

She threw back her head to look upward. Those stars. Not Orion. But the same we used to watch when I was little.

On the Continent Matt watched the stars as well. They looked clear and enormous, unshrouded by Sussex mist. The cattletruck was jolting slowly eastward. Matt and his fellow deportees, chained together, were crammed so tight that they could barely move. A woman was sobbing. When she quieted there was nothing but the rattle, rattle of the trucks crawling through the night, past isolated houses, crossings, sudden groups of trees.

"They say a few people are resisting everywhere," a man was muttering.

"They say anything."

"Explosions, farther south—Derailments."

"Chap told me, on the platform."

"*Agent provocateur.*"

Matt wasn't listening, he was thinking savagely of his own foolishness. No one could say Tom and the others hadn't warned him. "Who hath done this deed?" "Nobody; I myself. Farewell." All he had now was a memory crammed with education, the fine words of a literary heritage, his double first in history and maths. Some use, in this fearful new world! All we needed were survival courses. What price the sodding Idylls of the King now—and all the hero myths? Where's my be-your-own-legend kit?

He continued staring at the stars, his mouth grimly set, and thought achingly of escape, and other things. Pity it's the wrong time of year for Orion—

Then Jan's face swam across the stars, her long pale hair mingling with the Milky Way, and for a moment blotted out his loneliness.

It still felt like the middle of the night when Tom roused them, though the birds were already trying their first notes. At the manor there was whispered discussion about who should be left on guard.

"Tom took the early morning watch, so I'll stay," said Jan. "It's Char's hoard, anyway."

The house had an eerie atmosphere at this hour. Even Tom and Bill glanced over their shoulders now and then, as they pulled out the linen-cupboard's shelves for Charlie to go in like a ferret and begin handing out tins and jars. By brief flares of matchlight Bill examined them in the passage. Jam and chutney; bottled fruit and dried apple rings; more dried milk, and instant coffee; cocoa, tea, sugar; cans of beer and cider. The larger tins contained oats, flour, rice, broken-up macaroni and spaghetti, packets of chocolate, and matches. There were also multivitamins, and aspirin, and a whole tin of grain.

"That's it." Charlie backed from the cupboard brandishing a dozen or so packets of seeds.

"Pathetic! Carrots and parsley for health, and sweet peas for prettiness," said Bill. "Poor old hoarders. I wonder what happened to them. Killed? Deported? Died of Marburg X?"

A nasty cold sensation gripped Charlie's stomach, and she yelped: "But we've eaten things already! Can it—you know, hang about?"

"Yes, is that likely?" asked Tom. Bill had his first medical exams behind him, and so had been elected their adviser.

30

"The Freaks don't seem to worry. But we know they're immunised. It could become endemic, I suppose."

"Whatever's that?" asked Charlie, nervously clutching at her throat.

"Suspended animation. Then flares up again. That means some sort of host, though; or the ground. If that food were affected you'd probably be dead by now. Our real immediate problem is what to do with all this stuff."

"Choose what we want, keep the rest here? But some were sealed—how can we do them up again?"

Bill held out a reel of sticky tape. "Here, in among the rice! Canny fellows, our hoarders. We'd better hurry—Jan will be getting cold."

She was. When they rejoined her outside, her face was pale in the dawn light. "You've been an age," she whispered. "Kept thinking I heard people—but no birds flew up suddenly, or anything. Brr—" She shivered.

"Come on, then. We've some cocoa here, you'll warm up on that. Or a nice cuppa."

"Cuppa," she said lovingly.

The birds were singing with joyous abandon. Sometimes it seemed to Jan as if this riotous birdsong were an encouraging chain linking present to past and future; at others it seemed to emphasize the bitter contrasts between today and yesterday. But now it merely heralded the almost forgotten pleasure of hot tea. It was while they were waiting for the pan to boil that she suddenly exclaimed: "This hoard—it's muddled things."

"*Muddled*," snorted Charlie.

"Jan's right. Risk staying here to eat it, or lose most of it," said Tom. "We'd need a small van to shift it with us."

Charlie sighed. A heavy, greedy sigh.

"Carried, Char." But Bill looked serious. "It's almost July, isn't it?"

"Exactly," said Tom. "And you know what September can be. And we've to go a long journey and get dug in somewhere else. Find food for the winter—grow it, if possible, late though it is. Get thicker clothes, somehow. Who'll last without them?" He stared accusingly at Jan. "You don't look very strong. Are you?"

"Like whipcord," lied poor Jan.

"Had any major illnesses?" inquired Bill.

She shook her head. (Forget pneumonia.) "Bit chesty, that's all. Tom looks pretty tough," she added quickly.

"Measly complaints, and one broken toe. What about our indestructible little treasure?"

"If you mean me," said Charlie with dignity, "I've had measles too. Whooping cough, scarlet fever, and meningitis."

"That accounts for it, then."

"Pay no attention, Char. Tom's teasing you. *I* only claim one lost appendix. And—Marburg X."

"Bill! Marburg X?"

"Why, man, you must be the half of one per cent or whatever who actually recovered." Tom reached over to pat Bill on the back. "What a find. He can doctor us if the nasty bug's endemic."

"Was it horrible?" breathed Charlie.

"Like terrible 'flu, with delirium. My temperature went soaring till I saw green giraffes. As for doctoring—One of the latest drugs worked, but only on a few people like me."

"Oh, very helpful," said Tom. "And there was only aspirin in Charlie's hoard, anyway. Listen, though: to leave all that is heartbreaking. But we ought to go. And as for Alastair, the longer I stay, the less likely I am to catch up with him, alive or dead. Any comments?"

Everyone had some. Till comment developed into argument, which only ended when Bill pointed out that they'd have to be clairvoyant to choose rightly. "So let's stay two more days as a worthwhile risk—then take everything we can." Tom nodded reluctantly.

"Gimme more to eat on watch, then," demanded Charlie urgently. "'Cos Bill, we haven't set one! That shows we're slipping. Tea—chocolate slab, more oatcakes. Thanks, Jan."

"Don't get sleepy, Char."

"Not me. And it's my turn. You kip, I'll wake Bill later."

She picked up her mug and went out on to the steps. A flight of birds crossed the clear, light sky in a prickly cross-stitch pattern. Free. Charlie gave a great sigh of pleasure, and sipped. The hot tea warmed her through and through. She patted her stomach lovingly. More oatcake and chocolate coming down. Like that? No Auntie, and a full meal inside: wonderful. She put down her mug, and stared dreamily across the yard.

They were shaking her awake.

"Stop it. Leggo—"

The ungentle fingers pressed harder, and she stared up into a stranger's face. A large hand silenced her startled squawk. She bit, trying to struggle free. She kicked too, but her captor sidestepped, dragging her upright.

"Ugh, glug—" mouthed Charlie.

Beside the steps stood a boy aged about seventeen, carrying a gun. Another lay at his feet.

"Do something, Geoff! She'll bite through me in a minute. Gag her."

"How can I, with your great fist in her mouth? Here—" The boy pulled out a handkerchief and brought it close to Charlie's contorted face. "Shift a bit, Dad: hold her nose."

Charlie tried to scream out a warning, but they were too quick for her. She choked and went plum-colour as the gag was knotted behind her head.

"Drawn blood," said the man, aggrieved. He shook his arm, and redness stained Charlie's shirt. "Grab her wrists, lad, can't you? Pin them behind her back . . . Now, gimme my gun, and get round and stop the barn's other end, like for ratting. *Now*, missy, in we go."

Tom and Bill were sprawled untidily in the straw, both

33

softly snoring. Jan had her head burrowed against Bill's side, and was curled shrimpwise, heels close to her rump. It was a peaceful scene. Charlie's tears overflowed, and she made gulping sounds deep in her throat.

"Ready, Geoff?" hissed the man behind her.

A cocky whistle answered beyond the loft's far end.

"Leo, too?"

"Both here, Dad."

"Wakey, wakey!"

Tom rolled over, yawning. It took him seconds to realise what had happened, but Bill came to at once, glaring helplessly at the gun. Jan wriggled round, and gave a little shriek.

"Charlie, you oaf!" said Tom bitterly. His glance flicked to the drop at the loft's other end.

"None of that, lad. Geoff!"

"Yup?"

"Come on up. C'n you climb it? Pretty harmless-looking bunch, but you can't be sure." He sounded edgy. Perhaps he'd expected something worse—a tough gang on the run.

"Do you have to rough up a child?" asked Bill coldly. "She's not all that dangerous."

The man looked him over in an unpleasant way. "You're on my land."

"*Yours?*"

"Under licence." The man reddened slightly.

There was an awkward silence, while his two boys scrambled up into the loft. Charlie, squinting angrily above her gag, thought the one called Leo looked quite pleasant—he had a better-tempered mouth than that other one. Wouldn't drown kittens for pleasure, she summed him up. That swine Geoff had enjoyed gagging her—She retched, and Jan implored: "Please—let her go."

"Get on over to your friends, then." The man prodded Charlie with his gun. "But as for not being dangerous—" And he raised his other hand to show the toothmarks.

"Oh Jan," sobbed Charlie, once ungagged, "I just dozed,

and then they—they—" She burrowed her head against Jan's shoulder, and tried to control her humiliating tears.

"Brace up, Char—could have happened to any of us," said Bill. Tom looked sour.

"By rights I ought to turn you all in." The man balanced on his heels, gun across his knees. "Boys said there was someone up at the old place, nights ago, but I was too busy to investigate. At the new moon it was, when Geoff first came back saying he'd seen two lads skulking in the orchard."

Charlie wiped the back of her hand across her eyes. Oh, this was better—it was probably the night Tom and Matt had gone foraging. So they must have been careless too.

"Well-provided, aren't you?" Suspicion flared again as the man noticed their empty tea mugs, sugar and powdered milk. "Geoff, get on down to the yard, sharp. Maybe there's more of 'em about."

"Why me, always—an' not Leo?"

"Do as I say. You're sharper. Yes, sharp's a weasel is my son Geoff," he told them with pride.

"Looks like one, too," muttered Charlie.

"Your tongue will land you in trouble soon, young lady; like your teeth. And now maybe you'll explain yourselves? Whole family lying up in someone else's barn! Takes wits even to stay alive these days, and—" He stared harder at the food.

Charlie was just opening her mouth to say they weren't one family, when Jan pinched her, hard. A family would seem more innocent, less like the nucleus of a gang. "Our parents died—of the Sickness," she improvised hurriedly. "Then we were bombed out—"

"Bombed—where?"

"Dover," said Bill, quickly picking up his cue.

"The military sent all youngsters to the Continent."

"Not your two sons," put in Tom.

"Not discussing us, are we? Far cry from Dover, here."

"We—we drifted. Had to—to find food."

35

"And succeeded." Again that roving look. "But it's no use hiding, lad. Got to go some time, haven't you? Longer you hang around, the angrier someone's bound to be, eh?"

He sounded more reasonable, and Jan wondered if they could possibly win him over. "Would you like a cup of tea?" She smiled at him, too sweetly.

"Tea, now! That'd be something, wouldn't it, Dad?" Leo grinned uncertainly at her, and his father looked annoyed.

"Well, make it, if you want to; or rather, let her! But they're not talking themselves out of this. Living on sufferance ourselves."

"Can't we let them go, Dad? I mean, s'not as if they're dangerous. Why should anyone know we saw them?"

"Things get out. We're too close to trouble, here. Remember what's happening tomorrow, don't you?"

"What's happening?" asked Tom; cold and still.

"Soldiers' summer camp moving in. They'll use this old place for target practice."

"Cripes!" Jan's stomach cramped. She visualised the four of them taken unawares, and the first laser fire tearing through the roof.

"Yes. Then if someone gets to hear we let you go, what happens to *our* rations, eh? Food's scarce enough *with* forms, but without—"

Trying to persuade himself; worried. Maybe he's not too bad a type underneath, thought Jan. Shouts, then dithers . . .

"Just forget us," said Tom suddenly, "and we'll never tell a soul you saw us. We swear. And we can get you food— quite a lot." He saw Charlie's anguished expression, and shook his head at her.

"*You* can?" The man's eyes narrowed. "You've been stealing from a camp!"

"Wouldn't dare," said Bill.

"Up at the old manor, is it, then?" He was too acute. "You give it another look, Leo, when we've dealt with these."

36

"The Freaks will like that, won't they?" said Tom. "Find food, and keep it for yourselves? Have to tell them, wouldn't we? They might be grateful."

"Don't get too clever, sonny. Easier, on balance, if you just—vanished. Eh? No questions asked."

Bill put his arm round Jan. "Four shots? Won't be lonely long, will you?"

"We can't, Dad! I'm not shooting anyone."

"Rotten shot, anyway," said Leo's father angrily. "Not like Geoff. Well—where were you off to, may I ask?"

"Scotland," lied Bill.

"Long way. No point, as I can see."

"There is!" Charlie sat up and glared. "Up there, might get left alone. Bill's got—we got relatives."

"If they're still there." The man was wavering, Jan thought, and she pushed a mug of tea his way. She gave Leo one too; he said, "Thanks" appreciatively, and didn't offer to take one to his brother.

"And how were you going?"

"On our feet. Through London."

"Load of old tripe. London's sealed off."

"We heard that," said Tom very sweetly. "Your—friends have decided it's expendable."

Jan saw their captor's hands clench on his gun. She looked away from him to the boy Leo. He's ashamed, she thought; probably talked into it all. What would she have done for her family's sake? But there'd been no choice, only that revealing moment when she'd stood frozen on the staircase.

"So it's Mr High-and-Mighty, who can afford to choose his friends?"

"Tom—" murmured Bill warningly.

"Perhaps he'll explain how the feeble likes of us can afford to do what most of Western Europe didn't manage?"

"Tom can't explain anything," said Charlie. "But he does want to find his brother Alastair. In London."

"London. Well, now. *His* brother, missy? Not yours?"

"She's adopted—family mascot," said Jan swiftly, giving Charlie a warning look.

"Lucky, aren't you? Well, what's to be done with you all, anyway?" The man stood up, with an air of decision. "Leo—nip back to the lane and bring that van down. Quick, lad. We'll just hold them for the present." A hard blue glance raked them. "You girls tidy up your bits and pieces: leave this place just as you found it. Don't want soldiers thinking I've let runaways hole up for shelter in *my* barn."

Charlie was in despair. "The food, Jan—the food!" she muttered. But Jan hissed back, "Schoosh—he'd simply take it." Bitterness almost choked her, as she started fluffing up the straw and collecting things.

"We might just as well have gone with Matt," mourned Charlie in a whisper. Jan, who'd been thinking the same thing, made no reply.

Imprisoned in a gloomy farm attic they couldn't see the sun, but by Bill's watch they knew it was past midday.

"I'm ravening," sighed Charlie. "And—"

"Listen! Someone's coming—"

There were footsteps on the twisting attic stairs, and a key rattled in the lock. When the door was flung open Leo stood there, holding a jug of water and a bowl. Behind him lurked Geoff, inseparable from a gun.

"Porridge. Those oats you had."

"How good of you! Did you put the salt in?" asked Tom.

"Salt—in porridge?"

"It's horrid without it," said Charlie. "Are we eating with our hands?"

"Eat mud with your feet, for all we care." Geoff caressed his gun.

Leo glowered at him, and said, "I forgot the spoons—I'll fetch them."

"Just hurry, then. Dad always says you've a mind like a sieve," growled Geoff, pointing the gun at Tom's stomach.

38

"In the guts it hurts," he warned, "so don't try anything on."

"Enjoy yourself, don't you?" muttered Bill, as they waited tensely for Leo's return.

"Someone might as well. Are those girls strong? Dad needs some household help, and I wouldn't mind a woman round the place. We might ask for 'em—put 'em in overalls, cut their hair; slap a brand on 'em, too." He grinned at Jan. She felt sick with horror, and then thought of Matt. Matt: what mightn't have happened to him, already?

When Leo returned he shouldered roughly past his brother, holding out some spoons. As Bill took them he felt something else thrust into his palm, and glanced up, startled; but Leo was already turning back to Geoff, and saying: "C'm on— forget playing soldiers. Dad wants us down Swallowfield, hedging."

The door slammed, the key rattled, and the two brothers went clattering downstairs.

"Sod them," said Tom.

"Sl-slavery!"

"Don't cry, Jan—oh please don't cry!" Charlie flung her arms round Jan, weeping herself. "I know it's awful—it's all my stupid fault."

"Let's starve. Let's not eat their filthy porridge—"

"Stop gulping, Jan. Silver spoons may have silver linings." Bill held out a piece of crumpled paper. "I don't think Leo's exactly fond of gruesome Geoff. He's written: 'See you later, because I want to talk—alone. Dad's busy today, can't take action till tomorrow. Keep quiet tonight when you hear me unlock the door.' "

"Oh, good for lovely Leo," cried Charlie. She threw a caper, and tripped herself up.

"Gorilla, be your age," said Tom. "This may sound all right, but what's he up to? Is it that old chestnut of the sympathetic guy you trust with all your secrets?"

"Well, somehow I'm in favour of this Leo," murmured Bill. "So let's wait and see. Not much choice, anyway, have we?"

It was past midnight when the four of them, huddled together on a pile of aged carpets, heard soft footsteps outside the door. There was a pattering sound too, and a quickly-silenced whine. Trusted collaborators were sometimes given wolf-hounds as protection; and Jan, who had a horror of large dogs since one had tried to savage her in childhood, clutched at Charlie, while Tom and Bill slid to their feet.

"It's all right, Jan," whispered Charlie, feeling unexpectedly maternal. "If it tries anything on, I've a good strong kick."

When Leo unlocked the door he found himself facing four hostile pairs of eyes. He backed, holding the dog's collar. It *was* a wolfhound, and Jan's flesh crept.

"He won't hurt you," whispered Leo, seeing her face. "We mustn't talk loudly, Dad 'n Geoff don't know I'm here."

"So you say," said Tom.

"You two go and stand against the wall." Leo shut the door and leaned against it, still holding the dog. "Now come over here one by one, and let him sniff you. Don't rush me—or he'll attack. You first," he told Tom. "Hold out your hand. That's right. He's a friend, Hoppo."

"Hoppo? Odd name," muttered Tom, trying to cover some disquiet as the dog sniffed him over in a critical way.

"Geoff named him. A hoppo's some kind of Eastern customs officer."

"Lick equals chalk? What happens when he finds something to declare?"

"One reason for this visit is to make sure he knows you're friends."

"So we're friends, are we? What's the other reason?"

"Well—that's really what I've come about." Hoppo had finished with Tom, and was regarding Bill with an approving air. The lick was a perfunctory dab, which missed. Jan was next, but she shrank back against the carpets.

"I'm frightened of large dogs. They know it." Her subconscious was imprinted with memories of a huge shape hurtling forward to bite her in the neck. There was still a scar beneath her chin.

"Don't be silly, Jan," muttered Tom. "It's boring."

"She can't help it. She's got a thing—haven't you?" Charlie put her arm round Jan's shoulders. "Let Leo send him over—and I'll bite him if he does something bad."

"Just let him sniff you," Leo said, releasing the dog. But Jan's outstretched hand shook and gave off a smell of fear. Hoppo cocked an ear backward, as though perplexed, and began to make a noise like the whine of an overcharged engine.

"Hoppo!" muttered Leo severely.

"*Hoppo*," said Charlie simultaneously, and clasped his muzzle with her free hand. "Don't make such a horrid noise, you stupid beast." Hoppo was so surprised that the growl abruptly stopped. He was squinting.

"Ugly, isn't he?" Charlie shook him a bit. "But he's quite sweet, really." She removed her arm from Jan's shoulders, seized her hand, and pressed it on Hoppo's head so violently that his legs gave way and he sank floorward, looking embarrassed. "Now you know us both, don't you? And you love us." She began fiddling with Hoppo's ears while Jan, sure he was merely overcome by shock, contented herself with allowing him to smell her hand.

"If the animal-taming's over, let's know why you're here," said Bill quietly to Leo.

"Want to get to London, don't you?" Leo glanced back over his shoulder, as though afraid.

"What's that to you?"

"Well, one of us goes up there on the farm produce run. Weekly. Dad supplies a south-west garrison. Tomorrow's my turn, with the van: leave before dawn, about four. On these empty roads I'm there by half five. That's roughly when Dad gets up."

"Offering us a lift?" Tom sounded frankly sceptical.

"In exchange."

"Thought there'd be a snag. Well, we've nothing to give, man. Nothing we want to, anyway."

"You have." Again Leo gave that quick glance over his shoulder. "Company. Freedom from all this."

"Make up a better one," said Bill. "We're not free; are we? You're free. Relatively."

"I'm not," insisted Leo. "But what can one person do alone? Dad and Geoff see nothing wrong with what they're doing."

"Gone along with them so far, haven't you?"

"Tom, listen to him," put in Jan, remembering Matt. "What else could he do, really?"

Leo looked at her gratefully. "Got some scheme, haven't you? Not Scotland, either—wouldn't have told Dad. If we could reach London with no one searching us, there might be a slim chance of getting in—together."

"So you want to join us?"

"All the way."

"Don't tell him anything!" said Tom. "How can we trust him? You guess what's coming: we'll need food, won't we? And they've failed to find it, so he'll need to know just where it is, won't he? Am I right?"

Leo flushed. "I can't take food from here! Don't—don't hold with what Dad's done, but still can't let the Freaks think he helped us if—if things go wrong."

"Why not? Prize collaborator like him. Get what he deserves."

"Oh stop it, Tom! It's difficult for Leo. You don't understand how things—go wrong, and—" But Jan wondered suddenly if he understood too well. People who couldn't trust themselves never trusted others.

"It's a put up job between him and those skints. They want that food before they turn us in. And we couldn't prove anything against them—there's no written tally."

Leo looked so furious that Charlie thought he might slam out of the attic, condemning them to slavery; Auntie and Albert would be nothing to it.

"Don't, Tom—Jan's right, and I believe Leo. It's my hoard anyway, 'cos I found it. I say he can go and get it, and take us all to London. If I'm wrong we can't be worse off than we are, can we? Don't you want to find your precious Alastair?"

"Gorillas are practical creatures," murmured Bill. "Do as you please, Char. Can't think anyone could stop you, anyway."

"Of course I want to find Alastair," muttered Tom sullenly, "but—"

"Then you'd better start trusting Leo, and shut up," said Charlie; so vigorously that they had to hush her. "Are we all going to the manor?" she asked Leo, but he shook his head.

"The longer you're here, the safer. Someone could wake— Geoff might even come to check up. Now look: I'll fetch some old curtains from our lumber room opposite, and you start tying them together. We'll dangle a rope of them from this window when I come back for you: takes care of how you got out, see, if you're missed too early. With any luck he'll think you found them here. The one thing that mustn't happen is for *him*"—it wasn't "Dad" any more—"to think you've gone with me. He'd ring the garrison."

"His own son?" asked Bill incredulously. "He wouldn't."

"Don't you see, he'd have to?" Leo sounded both defiant and miserable. Everyone was silent, pitying him. "I'll put the barn ladder up against this window when I get back from the manor. The curtains won't be too safe—rotting. So don't try anything rash! Now, you—Charlie: where's this food?" And when she'd told him, he asked: "Does anyone's watch go?"

"Bill's is best."

"Good. You'll be able to time me, then. I'll have to be careful how and when I take the van—might rouse someone. Look for me around two, or maybe three. I'll do my best to be on time."

But he wasn't; it was some while after three that he returned, and Tom was already saying, "Told you so" when they heard light scraping sounds outside, and the top rung of a ladder showed against the stars. The attic window was high in the slanting roof, and they had to pile the carpets beneath it, since not even Bill, the tallest, could reach it otherwise. The escape was still none too easy.

"Don't drop me, ow!"

"Shut up, Char, you goose—you'll be heard. Who'd have thought you'd weigh so much?"

Struggling and panting, Charlie's sturdy form was forced up and through the window. The ladder's top vibrated alarmingly as she fought for balance. Then it was Jan's turn.

"Don't forget to throw that curtain rope out after you."

"Not us. Do hurry."

Soon all four were standing outside with Leo, while Hoppo licked their ankles fondly.

"Wait by those bushes," whispered Leo. "Putting the ladder back. Someone flatten out any marks."

He was gone. Charlie, Jan and Tom ran for the bushes, while Bill scrabbled up the earth, then followed. The moon and stars shone tonight undimmed by any cloud, and they felt very conspicuous. Jan was too aware of Hoppo pressed against her legs, and wished she were more like Charlie— loving the thrill of this escape. *Her* imagination hadn't already got to London. But Char's never had it soft . . . Poor Char. Maybe that's why she's good at living in the present—

It seemed ages before Leo returned.

"Come on, van's behind those sheds." He flitted ahead of them, from shadow to shadow. Stopped.

"Here—In you go, get down under anything you find. There's sacks, and stores. Shelves, too. Our food's up that end. No talking—there's sometimes patrols; don't let that child chatter." He sounded worried. "I'll be back in about an hour." He was gone.

"Child! Chatter! Why can't we start now?" complained Charlie.

"Too early, I expect. Mustn't act unusual."

A cock crowed suddenly, startling them. "You go back to startling henny-penny," murmured Tom, cautiously pulling down the van's back hatch. "Hey, Charlie—don't grab all that chocolate."

By quarter to five they were many kilometres away, and the moon was pale, low in a paling sky. The van's headlights were less effectual than by darkness. From the road's verges rose strong grassy scents, fresh with dew. When they drove through empty suburban towns the good smells gave place to dusty ones: pavements and tarmac. The van was stopped twice by patrols, but each time was waved on after the yawning soldiers had given Leo's cards a perfunctory look.

When it pulled up for the third time, everybody held their breath again. The hatch was raised suddenly, letting in early daylight, and Charlie squawked.

"Shush!" Leo clambered up. "Whoever heard of vegetables yelping? Whatever happens, keep quiet."

"Where are we?"

Leo heard the suspicion in Tom's voice, and hastened to explain: "Twenty minutes from checkpoint. We're off the direct route, on a deserted housing estate. I always stop here to eat something. Nice and quiet. Now look—" a pencil of torchbeam glowed—"here's a map. And here we are—and here's the checkpoint: straight ahead on that road. This is where I turn off, right—an' there's the garrison. This cross is where I unload. They're quite—friendly."

Silence.

With a slight effort he resumed: "There's a sort of— swathe cut down all round central London, as if it was the middle of a cornfield being reaped."

"Very poetic," said Tom. "Don't you mean raped?"

"Rows of houses blasted flat, nothing but rubble. That's so they can see people trying to get out. Searchlights on it at night. Guns trained on—"

"Wire? Wall?" asked Bill intently.

"Not yet. Rumour says it's started, on the North Circular, but there's none this side. Or wasn't, last week. The—ring's about fifty metres wide, hundred in some places. Not so wide by this garrison, an' opposite there's the remains of a road running straight in, mazes of little streets. Used to be the meanest bit of Battersea. They've moved in closer, stage by stage. It's all planned."

"The centre must be getting quite full," said Tom grimly.

"You're right, except that—oh, forget it." Leo looked from one to the other, and pulled a pair of scissors from his pocket. Tom stared at it as if it were a dagger. Leo saw his expression, grinned uncertainly, and said: "It's all right, I'm not mad! If she'll agree, I'm clipping Charlie's hair—"

"Funny time to play at hairdressing, if you're not mad," remarked Bill.

"Ah, there's reason in it. Now: here's my plan—"

2 ❦ Alastair in London

Two nights before Matt's embarkation, Alastair was half
lying in a sort of nest beside an open window. The nest was
made of two old sleeping-bags slung between poles propped
on orange-boxes. The window was open because half the wall
was open too, where it didn't still tower precariously to
support the floorboards of an upper storey, now destroyed by
bombing. Here and there the sky peered through in a friendly
fashion; although not so friendly when it rained. Luckily the
summer had been dry.

Alastair sighed, and stared up at one indistinct star. In his
own corner Hercules brooded. Nice if Hercules would show
affection, thought Alastair; if he'd share the nest, for instance.
But he sat all huffled up, just waiting to sail out of the wall
over the ruined city and go hunting. Before Hercules' arrival
Alastair had had a tame mouse. That mouse's end had taken
some forgiving. But at least Hercules, with his soft feathered
beauty, large eyes, cruel beak and terrible pounce, was very
much a part of life. And he could be talked to—

"I wish Wolf would come. I'm sure he's late. That star's
been there a long time."

Alastair's stomach gurgled, and he patted it, trying to keep
it quiet. Suppose Wolf never comes again—

Fear uncurled at the bottom of his spine. In the evening it
was always possible to let go, to allow hope and courage to be
swamped by terror . . .

With a great effort he withdrew his thoughts into a kind of

closed centre. He didn't know if it was just his thing, or if other people understood about it too; nor did he remember exactly when he'd learned the knack of it, nor how, but it was certainly a long time ago, when he was first in hospital. It gave him a timeless sense of being Alastair in a place where nothing could harm or frighten him. He breathed deeply, evenly, as the increasing inner light flooded his being, making him aware he wasn't crippled, but strong and wise and ageless. In this state he looked into strange pools of light, with shifting reflections, out of which pictures formed: Wolf came loping out from the jumble of pillars and blocks of fallen stone where collapsed St Paul's spilled over into Ludgate. He was drawing shuddering breaths, and his face wore its cynical post-battle look. But before light and picture faded Alastair had time to notice with satisfaction that he carried his old torn and bulging plastic bag.

"Food's coming, Hercules." And he began to chant: "One, two, three, four, Wolf is coming to the door—"

Just then Hercules took to the air with his effortless sweep of wings. Alastair forgot Wolf in the sheer pleasure of watching as Hercules circled the room, then floated out over the ruined wall, wings spread so wide that one of them brushed against his face. Owl into owl-light, soft ghost of steely intentions, gliding out over the city with a ringing whooooooo that was enough to curdle any mouse's blood.

"Hi!" Wolf spoke in the doorway. "Old flipper gone?"

"He doesn't get friendlier," said Alastair sadly.

"Survival, that's his game. Same as us. You hungry, kid?" Wolf squatted on the floor, and spread out the bag's contents. Alastair gave a sigh that was more than words.

There was an odd-shaped black loaf, still warm. A mixture of dried split peas and lentils, with chopped mint and dandelion leaves mixed together with pigeon's egg into a kind of mealy mess. And two small roasted birds on rough wooden skewers. They were scorched one side, pinkish on the other, but the smell of them was grand.

"Wolf, I'm awful thirsty."

"Can't you wait? I'm awful hungry."

"No," said Alastair apologetically. "Mouth's like sandpaper. Couldn't swallow."

"Getting spoilt," said Wolf over his shoulder, as he got up reluctantly to cross the room. Thames water was all they had these days when it didn't rain, since their looted soda water had run out. They dripped it into a bowl through layers of charcoal rigged up in old sink strainers, one above the other, propped in the hooks of a Victorian hatstand. (Hercules was fond of the highest hook—which endangered the water supply.) Wolf had made the charcoal, piling pieces of driftwood together on the beach near Tower Hill, and fighting off anyone who tried to steal it. Even after the bottled water had dripped through charcoal several times Wolf thought it probably unsafe. However—

"Couldn't you have got it for yourself?" he asked Alastair severely.

"Not since I turned my ankle, too."

"I forgot. Here you are, then."

Alastair drank contentedly. It was all right when Wolf was here; sometimes he would curl up in a corner and sleep there; sometimes one of his gang would come to fetch him, whispering just out of Alastair's earshot, while Wolf stared at the ground, frowning, or played absently with his flick-knife. On those evenings Wolf might tell Ox to stay; and Ox would obey, though he'd cast sullen glances at Alastair and refuse to speak. It wasn't comfortable when Ox stayed, though it did mean that Alastair needn't dread marauders from another gang.

"Eat up." Wolf dug sharp white teeth into a pigeon wing. "You're brooding. Who'd have thought these old birds would come in handy? Lot of damage, they caused. Know what? There's a patch of ground inside the dome gets morning sun. An' Grouse has dug and hoed it, an' planted lettuce." He laughed, juice trickling down his chin. "Good old Paul's. Dome makes a terrific greenhouse."

49

"Wolf," said Alastair—timidly, since though Wolf had more or less adopted him after finding him semi-conscious in the ruins of the school, one never knew, these days—"we can't—can't go on living like this always, can we? I mean, here?"

"Where else?"

"Well—always! *Wolf?*"

"Now listen, son. Want to stop worrying, see?" Wolf gestured with a gnawed bone. "This is how it is: we're living logical. People before, they were always pretending. Holidays, businesses, learning—all for the big bright gaudy future, and then—pffft! Something fused, an' they didn't know what hit them. Now you an' me—Another day, another minute. To think I might have been living it up as a Post Office clerk for sixty glorious years!" He wiped the back of a wiry arm across his mouth, and muttered: "Sometimes this don't seem so hot, neither, but at least it's for real. Each morning another bleeding, exhilarating day trying to keep alive in spite of Freaks. Come on, smile."

But Alastair couldn't smile, and Wolf said sharply, "Brooding on your parents. S'no use, better face it."

Alastair had faced it. He knew he'd never see them again—at least, not as he'd known them; for in one of those moments of total withdrawal he'd looked into the pool of light and seen them staring up at him, and had known they were gone out of touch or time into another world. But Tom—Tom's state he couldn't fathom: somewhere both dark and light at once. Also, Tom's face wore a familiar look, like the time when someone had accused him of stealing things at school. Father swore Tom hadn't, and the Head had apologised, yet—

"Sorry, Wolf." He crunched—"This is a good pigeon"—then added, "No, it's my brother. Keep seeming to see his face. He's always looking this way, towards me. Sometimes I want him to find me, and sometimes I think he mustn't, and—"

"*What's that?*" Wolf was on his feet, and the curved knife

50

looted from an Indian shop glinted between his fingers. Alastair stared at it, always amazed by Wolf's swift reactions. But his own ears were sharp, and picked up the distant ringing of blade on blade.

"Beyond the dome?"

Wolf interrupted tensely: "No! Quiet."

They listened. The room was so dusky now, it was only possible to see by bars of moonlight shining through the wall, and Alastair and Wolf looked down a bright beam towards the black hole of the door. There was a shuffling, dragging sound beyond it.

Alastair clawed himself round on to one elbow.

They waited.

Wolf's knife hand rose slowly till it was poised like a spear-thrower's above his head.

"Wolf," muttered Alastair.

"Ssssh!"

The shuffling stopped, paused, distanced itself as fast as it could go.

Wolf was over at the broken wall in a flash, leaning to look out. "Yah! There he goes—" He held the knife by its handle, point downward.

"Wolf, please, Wolf."

"All right. An' it's my best. Mustn't lose it."

Alastair swallowed. "Who—what—" And Wolf responded, "From Bart's, I shouldn't wonder. They've moved their camp up Cheapside. Smelt our food."

"Wolf, he couldn't."

"Developed noses like truffle hounds, they have."

"Oh Wolf, he's coming back—"

"No. S'Ox." And Ox it was, vast and slow, moving with astounding lightness in the shadows, and glancing at Alastair with brooding distaste.

Wolf stared coldly, standing in the moonlight. Ox's eyes were drawn round to him as though on string. "Sent again," he said. "Still want to join us. 'Least, combine."

"Who came?"

"Old redhead—Skullcap himself. Seems they're talking with other groups, too."

Wolf sniffed. "Which?"

"From the Scrubs. An' Junks from Denmark Street. But Skullcap says all groups or nothing. He most partic'larly wants ours."

"And then what?" asked Wolf; cold as ice.

"Says we'd be stronger."

"Stronger . . . " Wolf's voice grew soft. "*You* think we'd be stronger, Ox? You do?"

Ox shifted uncomfortably. "Well. Makes sense. And Fox says—"

"Makes sense. To the Freaks? Or might it—be upsetting?"

"Parley with them then, maybe," suggested Ox.

Wolf flung back his head and laughed. A strange cracked sound.

"Don't!" cried Alastair involuntarily.

"You do as you're told, Ox, see, an' leave the thinking to me."

"But if Fox says—"

"Fox says!" Wolf thrust his knife back into its sheath. "*I* say nope. Get on back, an' tell Skullcap to keep his ugly mug out of my manor."

Ox stood, head weaving; and suddenly the knife was back in Wolf's hand. He hissed like a snake, and Ox turned to go clattering downstairs, not bothering to move quietly.

Alastair was sweating. He clenched his hands together and mumbled: "It—it was Skullcap wanted to finish the—the weak—so there'd be no one to—be a drag, and—"

"Listen, kid. No one's going to finish anyone while I'm around. As for joining with that orange cannibal . . . Forget it."

"Maybe—maybe he wants to storm a guard-post? Break out?"

Wolf snorted. "Crazy enough. Out of sight, that's our act, now. You all right, kid, till I send Ox back?"

Remembering Ox's look, Alastair felt as if a hole threatened to swallow him. "Wolf—don't send Ox back. Please. I'm okay." He tried to smile. His legs had never felt so useless.

Wolf moved over to him and stood looking down. Alastair saw he understood. It made his blood chill to see that Wolf couldn't deny Ox might be uncertain. Instead he held out the curved knife and dropped it on Alastair's chest. "Here. If you have to, it's upwards, see? Like this." He sketched a quick gesture.

"What'll you do?" asked Alastair. Scared but proud.

"Me? I'll—" Again that cracking laugh. "Never seen me fight, have you? I've plenty of knives, but I don't need 'em." He retrieved the plastic bag, and moved purposefully towards the door. Alastair didn't envy the erring Fox.

"See you, kid." Moonlight touched the steel tabs on his leather jacket, and turned the painted yellow dragon to fire. Wolf's Hellers wore the old gear of the sixties, a fashion which had returned just before the collapse, but their designs were all their own.

Listening to the pad of Wolf's departing footsteps, Alastair lay fingering the knife. If I were like other people, he thought sadly, I'd be thrilled. But with almost useless legs—Lack of co-ordination, doctors had called it.

Here in this ruined room it was very lonely, with night's darkness increasing, and mists gathering outside about the fallen dome of Paul's.

A sudden disturbance of the air. A sepia and moonlight-striped ghost rocked over the broken wall to make a perfect landing in one corner. Hercules had returned . . .

But his presence was little comfort in the cold hours of early morning when the moon was a bleak roundel low in the misty sky. Alastair was half dozing, clutching the knife. He jerked awake, and shot up in bed with a suddenness that made Hercules unfurl his wings and beat the air as though it were a drum.

Light shone on the stairs. The rotten door shot open with

a crash. Torchlight—a blazing swab of tarred and twisted rag wrapped round a piece of driftwood—illumined the wrecked room with bewildering stabs and flashes of orange fire as the leader twirled it aloft.

Alastair, cowering on the bed, knife stuck to his sweating palms, peered upward, and knew this was Skullcap's gang. What other was arrogant enough to advertise their presence? And they all wore Skullcap's sign chalked, painted, or sewn on to their jackets and torn shirts.

"Yah, cripple! Wolf cub—*Wolf's* cub, hah . . . "

"Bring him, then." They surged forward. Alastair's hands wavered upward before his face.

"Look out, got a knife."

The line surged backward in the centre. Hercules spread his wings ready for flight.

"Strewth, got a ruddy owl too."

"Kin you eat 'em?"

"Have a try." Three knives flashed by torchlight.

Alastair, forgetting terror and his legs, launched himself sideways to the owl's defence. Hercules! (Despite the mouse.)

"Look out—the cub!"

A stream of curses. Alastair's wrists were seized as he fell writhing. There was a yelp, and Wolf's special knife clattered to the floor, while the leader stared awestruck at a thin red line that split his leather jeans from groin to knee and dribbled blood. In the turmoil a shadow drifted across the room and broken sill, and strong flight feathers precipitated it into the safety of the air.

"Flay you alive, cub! Split you like a sodding kipper—"

"You forgotten Skull wants him?"

There was an ugly moment while Skullcap's authority was silently questioned. Then the leader moaned dramatically, and clutched at himself.

"S'not that bad! 'Sa scratch!" They stood round him, jeering. He straightened up sullenly, wiped an arm across a dirty, tear-dribbled face, and muttered, "Get that cripple outer here. I'll give him knives."

Alastair, with bare hands, was helpless. His arms dangled like a puppet's when they picked him up and flooded through the doorway bearing him like a trophy. The torch scarred the woodwork as they went.

He was borne beneath an arch calcined by fires of the long ago forties blitz, and through a wide stone porch into an ancient church that was now the Skullgang's headquarters. They had reached it by a tortuous way, past buildings old and modern slung in heaps of rubble across steep streets or open courts. Here were the Inns of Court, the former seat of Law, now harbouring the lawless.

Cold seemed to clamp itself about Alastair's bones. He didn't think "This place is haunted", yet he was aware of presences, anger; and power that tried to ripple out at him across some invisible boundary. He could sense its fingers feeling towards him as a tide fingers its way towards a shore.

He stared about him. "This bit's—round!" he said, surprised; and then regretted drawing the predators' attention: six pairs of eyes, scornful or hating.

"Round!" They laughed, put him on the ground, kicked him, and laughed again to see him curl like a hedgehog to protect himself. "He's round!" They yelled to each other, and fell upon him, bowling him from one to the other, a new sport. Alastair was spun like a football between pillars and tombs, fending off stone, yelping, bruised, dizzy, till one last kick sent him sprawling up the triple-arched nave.

Whimpering, gulping, he watched them turn from him towards a side door as Skullcap came in, banging it behind him, and swearing with brilliant profanity. Alastair, crouching in the nave, felt invisible presences draw together in disapproval. Skullcap looked like a parody of the stone-carved knights upon the tombs, with his cyclist's crash-helmet instead of their battle helms. His gang held pride of place because they were the only motorcyclists left in London. Their cache of petrol was guarded jealously except when pride or display made them choose to roar through the summer's evening, leaping the smashed rubble and pavements like crazy acrobats, screaming and yelling as they rode.

"Got him?"

"Yah, got him for you, Skull."

"Ah—now we'll finish off that lone-Wolf stuff." He watched Alastair painfully drawing himself into the shelter of a pew. "You beaten him already? After what I said?"

His anger scorched them. The thin white face, narrow eyes and flaming hair intimidated. They scuffled, backed away.

"Put him in the freezer." He slouched down the aisle and stirred Alastair with a booted foot.

"Hurt you, have they?"

"Not—much," whimpered Alastair.

"That's right. Going to sign something for me, aren't you? Something for Wolf." He snickered, jerked his head, snapped his fingers. Alastair was bundled up again, carted hurriedly to a small stair, half-pushed, half-dragged up it, head bumping against stone.

"Someone was starved to death in here," they told him, lugging him over a threshold. "Some old knight. Know what this place is? Templars' church. Seems this was where they got theirs for disobeying orders. See through those slits? C'n see the whole place, like old starver did. Sweet dreams!" They shut him in and went louting down the stairs again.

The darkness was horrible, and smelt. Might there be—bones—? He scrabbled his way across the cell, got his fingers in a slit, pulled himself up.

The light was cold and grey. One way he could see the altar, and stained-glass windows cracked and broken. In the round part, half hidden by a pillar, Skullcap was sitting on a tomb, his gang crouched round him. He was writing on a scrap of paper. Once he looked up to where Alastair was imprisoned. He spat on the tomb, and continued scribbling.

56

Alastair watched, fingers gripped cold on stone, but conscious of a familiar sense of becoming Alastair in a different way: warmed and lighter, assured against all harm. Still gazing through the slit—though now it felt like an inner form of looking, not quite real—he saw something just above Skullcap's head, suspended in mid-air. It was moving downward, black and white, a sort of rippling—

Chequers of black and white. A shield. An eight-pointed cross—

Alastair stared, eyes wide and fixed. Skullcap looked up and caught a thin whiteness in the slit of window. He waved mockingly. Alastair's throat was dry. Didn't Skullcap know what was happening? He was blotted out suddenly by a shadow. The sword sliced right through him, and then was drawn away into darkness, barely seen, dissolving, like the hand that wielded it. There were three ringing knocks on stone, the last echoing into silence.

"In three days!" Alastair fell groaning to the floor.

Skullcap leaped up and spun round, peering into shadows. "Who's there? Who—"

"Cub cried out."

"'Twasn't him knocked, though. Down here."

They hunted through the church, and came scuttering up the stairs again.

"Playing tricks, eh?" Skullcap's booted foot was drawn back, ready. "Don't you play with me, son." The tone was soft, but bit. The nailed boot stroked the air.

"Doom. For—you," gasped Alastair, eyeing it.

"What's he say?" Skullcap looked round uneasily, then back. "Don't know what you're saying, do you? See anyone down there?"

"Yes—no!"

The boot stung his side, a nailed hornet.

Alastair wept, but this time no one laughed. He pulled his sleeve across his eyes, and muttered: "You won't—understand. I—Something came, blotted you out. Then the knocking." He raised his head and looked almost compassionately into Skullcap's ugly eyes. "Three days left. For you."

There was silence, as if the walls encased them in a giant tomb. Even the cruelty and the meanness seemed to have drained from Skullcap. Everyone backed from Alastair, as though he'd said "Marburg X." He heard them whispering uneasily as they bunched together and trooped downstairs.

"Cub's odd. Nothing in it."

"No one in the old place, though. Guard set."

Skullcap sat apart, legs astride a tomb, head bent. After a while he began whistling a tune between his teeth, but it died.

Dawn light filled the nave through broken windows. Then Skullcap came up the stairs again, a twist of paper and stick of charcoal in his hand. He held them out at arm's length as though not wanting to touch Alastair.

"Sign it."

Alastair read as he wrote: "They've got me. Skullcap says you better join his gang, *or else* . . . "

"'M' foot hurts. Where it touched you." Skullcap was regarding him with barely cloaked suspicion, and Alastair, though he was so terrified himself, almost laughed. What would Tom have said? Psycho-something. Yes—Maybe I could use it . . . What *does* he think I am?

Tom. Wolf. Skullcap's veiled threats. But I hardly know Wolf really, there's no reason why Skullcap's gamble should pay off. Bringing food, helping a cripple—different from crippling yourself and your gang . . .

"Three days c'n seem an awful long time," threatened Skullcap, recovering bravado. "Grapple's delivering this today—n' your Wolf had better come."

But Wolf, that natural survivor, was wary. The empty room, the blood, the charred wood where the torch had touched it, told their own story. He thought Alastair dead till Grouse came with tales of the Skullgang heading for their quarters with a prisoner. Wolf put two and two together and, like a canny debtor, got himself out of range of writs. Word went out that no one in his gang was to put himself in the position of receiving notes from Skullcap. No parley.

"Can't blackmail you, if they can't find you," he told Fox. "And won't hurt the kid till he can put the pressure on. Redhead needs him alive till then."

Fox shook his head; but he favoured collaboration anyway, and Wolf eyed him fiercely. "He'll wait till he finds us," he insisted. His eyes raked Fox, and he said, very sweetly, "*If* they find us you'll know what's coming to you, won't you, Foxy? I'll make it my personal pleasure."

The Hellers went to ground, infiltrating up Holborn and into Jockey's Fields, a scattered gang's abandoned manor which Wolf had had his eye on for some while as a possible reserve ground if anything threatened their pitch at Paul's. As they went, Grouse kept up a soft lament about his wasted lettuces burgeoning in the dome greenhouse.

"Oh, dry up, or I'll stop your grousing for you. Did someone bring the pigeon net? Water's the worst, since bombing." Wolf eyed the sky. "Might get rain—put the plastic sheet out. If not, river patrol when it's dark."

"I'll go," said Fox, too eagerly.

Wolf fingered his knife. "No—Ox."

"All this for that Alastair?"

"You, then," Wolf told another boy: the gentler, sleepily-smiling Mule, who was of West Indian descent.

Wolf himself didn't know why he allowed softness towards Alastair to influence his decisions. It made him uneasy. Harshness had kept them going, until now. He couldn't fit a need to help someone into the new frame of things; but it was there, like an insistent murmur beyond the threshold of logical thought, insisting that it was what you took with you into survival that mattered.

"Hell, why?" snorted Wolf, angry with himself for listening.

"Why what, Wolf?"

"Nothing. Kept us all alive till now, haven't I? Free even of the Skullgang. Anyone wants to quit, better go now." No one moved.

"We trust you, Wolf," said Fox plaintively.

"*Do* you?" He looked round, nodded, began to trot again; wishing that his mind would ease off worry about Alastair—undoubtedly too close-guarded for any rescue—and if Skullcap really would stay his hand.

Alastair was uncomfortable, but safe. At present. They brought him water; the food was nearly garbage. They wouldn't let him out, not for anything, and soon he only sipped the water and lay in misery. Sometimes he felt lightheaded, and then it seemed as if he shared his prison with someone else, who had suffered as he was suffering, maybe worse. The closeness was a sort of company. At times in the half-light he managed to free his thoughts and send them winging above the city with Hercules. Soft feathers, freedom, sweet smell of the air. No diesel now, and the lilacs had survived.

On the evening of his third day's imprisonment Skullcap went out angrily into the dusk, swearing he'd bring back Wolf himself. Or else.

"Get a fire lit, by that altar," he called to Grapple, who was keeping watch up in the gallery. And, "Hear that?" called Grapple in his turn towards Alastair's prison. "Hear that, hear that"; the words beat from wall to wall in a shuddering echo that gained in menace each time they reached Alastair's ears.

It was a night of drenching summer rain, falling in black sheets from a thunderous sky. On and on, an unbearable rattling on the roof like endless sinister applause. Alastair tried not to think of Wolf, and watched the flickering reflection from Grapple's fire.

It must have been around midnight when Skullcap returned, evil-tempered. He was carrying his crash-helmet, and the water streamed off him and turned his red hair to a sleek black cap.

He looked at the fire, then upwards to Alastair's prison, and laughed.

"Okay, so Wolf's not playing. Just vanished. Bring that cub down here." He lounged back on a crusader's tomb and crossed his legs in unconscious parody of the stone knights. His left hand stroked the figure. "Bet our friend here saw a sight or two like this."

Quaking Alastair, trying not to cry, was brought downstairs, propped almost tenderly between two Skullgangers.

"Got any ideas for a rousing start, anyone? Don't all speak at once."

But they were silent, sheepish. Only the rain beat furiously on the roof like a reply. Skullcap eyed them disapprovingly.

"Yah feeble nits. Someone get cracking, then."

He lounged; the gang disposed themselves in the pews. It might have been a theatre. Alastair, whimpering, was lugged towards the fire. Someone held his hand above the flames. He screamed, Skullcap laughed, the gang sniggered dutifully. Rain hammered.

"Choir practice! Get a great solo from you, kid, I will. Hear the rain? Sounds like a ruddy organ. Come on, sing!"

There was a flash, a roar of thunder, a sudden calamitous pelting of stone from the round church's tower. Alastair's captors swung round, releasing him; blocks of wood and stone lay scattered among the tombs. Now it was they who whimpered.

"Oh—gorblimey, Skullcap!"

"Is he—?" They approached gingerly.

He was. The wet black hair was red again, and seemed to flow across his face. He lay sprawled along the knight's carved length, hands spread wide as if trying to ward off the rain of stone. The true rain dwindled to a gentle hissing on the roof. Only Alastair, licking his smarting hand, thought he saw blurred shadows like rows of crossed blades dazzle in the air.

Grapple let out a yelp of accusation and terror. He pointed

61

at Alastair. "*He* done it! Remember? Three days he says—an', an'—th' instant he touched the fire—"

For a moment they hesitated. Action, fear, and anger, were equally impeded while the balance swung: then it came down on the side of panic and, howling, they fled, scrabbling at the great door, fighting to escape. Behind Alastair the fire's flames dwindled. It was barely possible to distinguish where the stone knights lay silent on their tombs, and one was piled high with a double burden. Beyond, the porch door was open on to greater darkness. A stone fell, sharply. Then silence.

"Dear God," moaned Alastair; dragged himself into the nearest pew, and slid from semi-consciousness into an exhausted sleep.

The light had come back. It fell in gentle golden waterfalls from roof and windows.

"Waking. Watch out!"

There was movement away from him. He raised his head and stared. Three pairs of eyes stared back, pleadingly.

"Don't kill us."

"Food, see?"

A charred fish, on a plate of leaves. Half a can of beer. Alastair looked towards the tombs, and gulped. The figure of Skullcap had gone. "Where—?"

"Outside." They crawled closer as though fascinated. "There's a sort of—of place—"

"Don't tell me. Keep away."

He looked down at the fish, and his gorge rose. Instincts of survival said, "eat". He chewed a little, and sipped the beer. Both were disgusting, though nothing like so bad as what they'd given him before.

Silent, they watched. There was a quality to their silence which puzzled him.

"Help me up."

A test, both of his courage and theirs. They weren't eager,

and their hands trembled. Alastair was deposited on a pew. He gained confidence enough to ask their names.

"Skullgangers don't have names. Just words, see."

"But you're not Skullgangers any more."

"Oh no," they said quickly; but looked reticent.

"In prison, weren't you? Who cares now?" These three who'd returned weren't the worst, so far as he could judge. At least they hadn't pushed to the front in last night's ugly business. Yet he would have liked to send them packing, with threats to help them on their way.

Can't do without them, though. Not yet.

"Where's the rest of you? Grapple?"

"They gone—ran."

"Ran where?"

One made a vague gesture; another gave a silly, high-pitched laugh, quickly silenced when Alastair looked at him.

"What's so funny?"

"Nothing. But Grapple met another gang, didn't he?"

Evidently Grapple's popularity wasn't high.

"Only Grapple?"

"The—some others. Didn't see. We hid. No one—came back."

"They might have linked together?"

They shuffled. "Not ruddy likely. If you've no one to look smart for you—plan for you—see ahead, like." Three pairs of eyes peered at Alastair. "Knew what was coming to old Skullcap, didn't you?"

He almost laughed. Alastair the priest-king! He said soberly, "I'll use a different gang-name."

"That's right."

"Templars, maybe." Bit risky? He glanced up: no crossed blades, anyhow. But there were troubles ahead of a strictly mundane kind. To start with, he mustn't sound hesitant: orders were the thing. But he'd never told anyone to do anything in his life.

"Get Wolf for me—I want Wolf."

They eyed each other.

Alastair glanced at the tomb where Skullcap died, and put more fervour into it: "You get me—*Wolf*."

They weren't eager. "You give us names, first," suggested one.

Alastair eyed him. "You're nothing. Garbage. Couldn't even get yourselves killed! Fetch Wolf."

"Well, where's he, then?"

Alastair coughed. Three pairs of eyes narrowed. Three minds, such as they were, considered coincidence.

Then Alastair closed *his* eyes, linked his hands behind his head, and leaned back, trying to ignore the probing minds. Wolf . . . Where would he go? Why had he gone? If it was to avoid blackmail . . . yet why should he, Alastair, weigh so heavily in anyone's plans; and if there were some other reason, if Wolf lay dead in some dark runnel . . .

He opened his eyes. "You still got your bikes? All of them?"

"We got 'em, yah. They ran, see, didn't ride."

"You ought to be guarding them," said Alastair sternly. "Now. Suppose this other lot's stolen them?"

"Couldn't stop 'em, anyhow."

"You could try to fetch your own three, couldn't you? Change their place. And tonight, tonight—" He folded his arms, glared, "you can take me to Wolf. We'll all go. Ride."

"Know where he is now, don't you?" Placatingly.

"None of your business. Go hide those bikes, fast. Find food, get water. Help me up into that pulpit place. Give me a knife."

Once they'd gone, leaving him hidden, semi-secure, he set his mind to ranging over memories of Wolf and Wolf's brief, pungent conversations. Casting wide, into a dark net, he tried to make contact . . . Names, *names*.

Not south of the river, Wolf had said. It's bad there; worked out . . . Kensington? You name it, kid, they've got it . . . Denmark Street? Junks there are worse than mambas, I'm warning you. And as for their girls!

It was afternoon before Alastair got nearer it. Wolf speaking thoughtfully of somewhere up near Holborn. Not been properly milked out yet, he'd said. Bet there's still food there, if you knew where to look. If we're ever flushed out of Paul's . . .

The only trouble was, Alastair couldn't get the name. Odd one, to do with horses. Try as he would, it eluded him; but at least these mind-threshings kept him from wondering if the newly-christened Templars had slipped away to leave him here for good.

3 ❦ Over No-Man's Land

The soldier emerged from the guardroom just as Leo swung the van round and pulled up by the unloading chute. He was sloppily dressed, and his face wore an expression of hostile boredom. The London Rat Run wasn't a popular posting.

"Late." He kicked sideways at the van, marking the paint. "Unload. See Post Commander."

Leo stiffened. "Why? The stuff's all here and correct. I—I had a puncture."

"Post Commander say: check stuff quick. Take down load. Someone from farm, ring; then line break, no good. Mending now."

Leo's legs felt wooden, but he walked slowly round behind the van. The four inside gripped each other's hands.

"Oh glory," breathed Jan. "Done for—"

"Ssss—"

The hatch was lifted. "Don't come too near," Leo was saying. "Got our dog with me. Last time someone tried to hold me up." The soldier edged away.

"Hold?" he queried, looking vaguely interested.

"Attack."

The man spat. "All English, very stupid. Next time, shoot, see? Bang, bang." He gestured with his gun in the direction of crumbling Battersea. "English there; fight, kill." (Spit.) "Yesterday, one come running." He smirked. "Cry 'help, help!' Say 'Weirdo! Weirdo makes magic.' Very powerful, maybe." Now the man wasn't smirking, he looked scared. "Say

'Magic', say 'temple'! Post Commander order beating, find why man run. All English stupid, allsame something happen."

"I thought you shot people who escaped," said Leo, lifting out a box.

"Shot, yes; shot. Beat, shot." The soldier strayed nearer, picking his teeth with a grimy fingernail, and mumbling on about why the boy had run and what he'd told. But Leo was barely listening, for it was time to give Bill their prearranged signal to set Hoppo free.

This was Charlie's cue. She crawled from the van, wincing away as Leo aimed a cuff towards her freshly-cropped head.

"Hoh!" The soldier raised his gun.

"Our slave," explained Leo hurriedly. "Got two now, I'm training this one. You! Get those sacks out," he commanded Charlie. "Quick." Hoppo growled—at Leo.

"Train dog first, maybe." The soldier roared at his own wit, and lowered his gun. "Beat slave, work more. Beat hard, work more hard."

"Got our own brandmark, too." Leo tried to sound brutal and, seizing Charlie's ear, turned her face so the soldier could examine it: beet juice and earth together had done an efficient job. All the time he was thinking, what did Dad want, will he get through again? A better Post Commander would have come out to look into things himself; the soldier's dirt and slackness reflected the fact that London was a low-graded posting, which was something to be thankful for—it meant there were no laser weapons at the garrisons, whatever else they had.

Hoppo's presence was having the effect they'd hoped for, the man was giving him a wide berth, and the van; but he did rouse himself enough to check the number of sacks and boxes going down the chute.

"Twenty, good," he said at last. "Finish. You turn van. I tell Post Commander. You come see." He slouched away, and Leo touched Charlie's shoulder warningly as he moved towards the driver's door.

She ran. Her rubbersoled shoes made no sound but Hoppo, bounding at her heels, let out a yelp. Leo cursed, and the soldier spun round. He yelled a warning, "Slave! Slave escape!"

"It's all right. My dog's after her." Leo climbed into the driver's seat, and swung the van in a wide sweep. He didn't even glance towards the fleeing Charlie, but pulled up just short of no-man's-land, where he waited looking the picture of lazy unconcern.

The soldier came plodding after him. "English bastard—you fetch! Not one go—slave not go—that *not* place slave go—" Brandishing his rifle he became more incoherent. Leo stared at him with deliberate lack of comprehension.

A window in the guardroom opened; someone leaned out, shouting angrily, and the soldier ran a few yards into the cleared space, and almost danced with rage as Leo stared, boneheaded. He raised his hand like a traffic policeman, and in the small gun turret fifty metres to their right a muzzle swivelled.

Time, thought Leo. "Tell them not shoot—I'll go fetch slave," he yelled. He switched on and drove slowly forward. Charlie was halfway across the cleared ring, running flat out, Hoppo loping behind her. The three in the back of the van held hands and prayed, as it bumped forward.

"Flat!" hissed Tom. "Wish we had sandbags in here."

They lay trying not to imagine the feel of flesh stopping bullets. Charlie and Hoppo were now almost three-quarters of the way across. The van gained on them, not too quickly. The gun turret was still silent.

"Too good to be true," muttered Bill. "Caught them bending."

They could see nothing, only wait. The noise, when it came, was like bees swarming. The van jolted, zig-zagged; was Leo hit?

"You, Jan?"

"I'm—oh!"

Holes sprang all along the van's side a few inches above their heads.

Charlie, almost home, never looked back, but bent double and ran plover-fashion with her arms spread to keep balance. Hoppo yowled, and streaked past her with his tail clapped to his hindlegs.

The van shuddered, slewed, sprang more holes, jolted forward twice as fast.

"Are they using arrows?"

"Oh Bill—don't joke—"

Shells of half-ruined houses were leaning over them. They drove into a welcome tunnel of early-morning shadow. They overtook and then ran level with Charlie. Leo leaned across to open her door and pull her in.

"Quickly."

"H-Hoppo!"

"Can't stop—they should have dirtier weapons than— Hold on."

"Leo, you're hurt."

"Shoulder. Cripes, what a go—"

"Oughtn't we—look inside?"

"May have missiles."

"Leo, *please.*"

"Wait."

The van bumped, slewed, almost flew past one, two, three more rows of ruined houses. Then Leo braked, gripping his shoulder where red flowered against his shirt.

"Now. Quickly." He started heaving himself from the driver's seat, while Charlie was down in a flash.

"Hold it, kid, they mayn't be—"

"Jan—Tom—Bill?" She was hammering on the hatch. It was raised from inside, and Tom's white face looked down. "Three here okay. You, Char?"

"Yep. Leo's hurt. You'll have to drive, I think. Oh, where's poor Hoppo?"

Poor Hoppo was streaking ahead like a grey thunderbolt.

"Come up, Char." Jan pulled at her.

"No, going in front: with them."

The van moved forward again, Tom at the wheel. As they went there was a terrible hissing and crackling behind them, and two rows of houses melted into sheets of flame.

"Woken up. Thought we weren't—serious," gasped Leo. He slumped a little between Tom and Charlie.

"Your wound's pouring." Charlie's eyes popped like a pekinese's. "Bill must—Oh Tom, don't turn off."

"Best thing. Case they follow up. This road's too straight."

"But we won't catch Hoppo."

"Not trying to—Leggo the wheel, Char! Oh, very well."

"*Do* you mind?" said Leo. "That's my shoulder."

The streets were free of people, and the shopfronts wrecked or gutted. From one, some hairdresser's dummies gazed coyly, garnished with wigs. The white markings on the road controlled no traffic, the lights were sightless eyes, not flashing red or green. "Brit-Rail runabout tickets to Euroholidayland 199–" ran the message on a torn poster. Ferns and decorative ivy sprouted from basements, split doors led into silent halls.

"I feel we're being watched by thousands of hidden eyes," declared Charlie. "Look—Hoppo's stopped running."

"Char, he'll need feeding."

"Don't be such a pig. He saved us. If you pull up at that old Lectrostop, Bill can bandage Leo."

While their embryo doctor prodded the shoulder and then bound it with Leo's handkerchief, which was fortunately clean, a tremulous Hoppo was coaxed back into the van, where an equally tremulous Jan received him reluctantly.

"Pet him now and he's all yours," Charlie encouraged her. "Terror's made me terrible hungry."

"Surgery's over," said Tom. "And Bill suggests food and general rest-up somewhere."

"Food—oh yes. So let's go buy us a house!" Charlie's spirits were hysterically high, released from fear.

"But I do wish we had some guns," mourned anxious Jan.

"We've two. Leo brought them—he's a godsend. Dad must be up the wall."

Tom returned to the driving seat, and soon they were cruising along, looking out for something neither too derelict nor impregnably locked by fleeing owners.

Suddenly Charlie exclaimed: "Listen! What's that?"

Above the van's engine note hummed another: a distant angry buzzing like a giant hornet's.

Leo emerged from a haze of pain to mutter, "Helicopter. Didn't think we'd manage that easy."

"But we're in, not out." Tom's glance was raking the street, searching for shelter. The van, though—where to hide the van?

"Could be some routine dawn patrol. But they must be wondering what we want in here. Made fools of them, too."

"Never thought of that." Tom's face was drawn and anxious. Hell, he'd let them in for it, Jan, Bill and the others.

"Garages at the end, see? Concrete, too. Step on it, for the Lord's sake."

Tom accelerated. The van shot down the road, lurching over potholes.

"Far one's open," said Leo tersely.

They were only just in time. When Tom switched off, the sound of the helicopter increased to a vibrant snarl as it appeared from the south-west, hovering low over the roofs.

"Hope it's dark enough in here." Bill peered through a corner bullet-hole, and reported: "Still hovering."

The helicopter hung at an angle above the street, rotors churning. At last it rose to swing northwards.

Everyone let out sighs of relief.

"Let's try that end house," suggested Tom. "It looks suitable. And the van's well hidden."

"I'll put my belt through Hoppo's collar, shall I?" Charlie stroked him lovingly.

Tom gave another sigh. "Come on, then! But don't let's hang around here—better run for it."

They ran, looking nervously about them as if they expected walls and fences to burst into flames. But the house, when they reached it, seemed safe enough: dry and dusty, and no one had locked or looted it. The blind globe of a holovision eyed them blandly from the living room, and fibrous-looking settees and chairs offered more comfortable welcome than the Sussex barn—though Charlie muttered: "Alberts and Aunties."

A series of small thuds overhead caused Hoppo to quiver.

"Rats. Not so Auntie! Let him go, Gorilla—anything to feed him," said Tom hopefully. Hoppo went bounding upstairs while they began sharing out some food.

"Just coffee, if you can make it." Leo forced a smile.

"Dare we light a fire?"

From above came a flurry of barking, and a cry.

"What the—" Bill snatched up a gun and precipitated himself towards the stairs. "Keep watch down here," he yelled at Tom.

"I'm coming too," bellowed Charlie, and leapt after him.

Through a half open door Hoppo's tail could be seen moving in a subdued way, as though unsure of the correct signal. Bill pushed the door with his gun, and they peered into the room.

The bed had been shoved aside, and its rose-coloured quilt dragged on to the floor. Cherished family holograms looked primly down on the boy who lay sprawled across it, blackening it with dirty boots and hands. Bill noted professionally that he was almost fully grown. Whopper when he stands up, he thought. He trained his gun on the boy, who simply lay there as if anything that could happen was past preventing. Only when Hoppo made a grab at one ankle he cried out.

"Drop it, Hoppo. You hurt?"

"Man, do I look it?"

He did. One side of his face was contused to purple jelly,

the eye closed, the mouth swollen out of shape. The bruise spread down his neck over his collarbone, visible through the gashed leather of his jacket. There was dried blood on his hands, and in his hair.

"They beat me up, the dirty b's," he gasped. "Got away in the end, me an' Shrike. Had his bike, see, but it run out of juice in the next street. He got me here, anyway. Fireman's lift. But the b. ran off yesterday—said he'd find food and water." He licked his lips, and winced. "Guess he broke out alone, that's Shrike for you. Wow." He grimaced. "Can't breathe proper." He was panting.

"Broken rib, most likely. Here." Bill thrust the gun at saucer-eyed Charlie, and dropped on his knees to prod professionally. "This hurt?"

"Every ruddy thing hurts, mate." Sweat broke out on the boy's forehead. "Thought you was from that heli." He began to cry, silently. "S'game, for those Freaks. Sport. Like lion hunting."

"Very friendly." Bill gave him water from a jug that the deserting Shrike had left. Then he felt the swollen ankle. "Just severe bruising, I'd say."

"I'd say we're on the holo. You a doc, or something? Where'd you come from, if you don't know about the helis?"

"Just come into London.

"Come *in*? You must be joking." He bit his lip. "Stop prodding, I can't—"

"I say, Bill, you've made him faint."

"See that, can't I? Call Tom; we'd better get him down while he's unconscious. Can't just leave him here, can we?"

"If they're all knocked about like this we'll have to stop somewhere, won't we?" said practical Charlie. But she retreated, yelling, "Tom! Tom, there's a man with skulls and crossbones on up here, and he's hurt. Bill says could you come?"

The boy came round sweating and moaning as they placed

him on the sofa. He swore at Jan when she started cleaning up his face with a towel from the bathroom; and Hoppo swore back.

"That'll teach him," said Charlie. "Ugly customer. Don't be so nice to him, Jan, he's not worth it, I'm sure. Why would he get beaten up?"

The boy regarded her in a startled way. "S'easy to see you've not been in London long," he muttered. But he did say "Thanks" when Tom handed him cold coffee made with tinned milk. "It's for real," he said unbelievingly; and soon handed back the mug for more.

"Wish we'd some antiseptic for Leo, and this fella," said Bill.

"The bathroom cupboard?" suggested Jan; and soon returned triumphantly carrying a large bottle of Veedol. Meanwhile Tom had forced one of the locked windows, stuck the barrel of his gun in the gap, and was squinting down the sights.

"You know, this isn't a bad sort of pitch," he said. "Why don't we shack up here tonight?"

At his words they all recognised how tired they were. During the last few days tension and excitement had kept them going. Now, sheltered from immediate danger, the prospect of rest on ordinary beds was like paradise.

"I'll take first watch," said Tom handsomely. "After all, coming into London was my plan."

Everyone demurred, although not hard. Bill declared he'd doze downstairs, to keep one watchful and not entirely trusting eye upon his second patient; but the rest went off upstairs thankfully enough, and Hoppo returned with pleasure to the quilt.

"Helicopter!" reported Tom, about six o'clock.

And at seven he woke Bill again. "Better call the others for a meal—daren't show lights after dark."

74

It was while they were eating that Charlie said commandingly: "Come on, you, stranger; say something about yourself. What's your name?"

"His name's Clanger," said Bill. "Or so he says."

"I mean his real name. I'm not calling anyone Clanger, it's too stupid. Shrike and Clanger! Like some awful comic turn."

"We weren't comic turns, us Skullgangers." It would have been a sneer, if Clanger's swollen lip hadn't spoilt it. "Never used real names, seeing as we'd sort of mislaid 'em. In the clink."

"Oh, you're that sort of lost Londoner, are you?" Charlie was unimpressed. "Might have known."

"Why were you inside?" asked Tom.

"Me and Grapple got time for robbery; carrying arms," Clanger answered sullenly. "Two years. Wouldn't mind being back inside, sometimes. It was okay when Skullcap was looking out for us, but—An' Shrike's gone, or dead."

"Dead," said Bill. "Remember, Leo? That soldier kept going on about someone they brought in and shot? That was a funny thing too: seemed there were odd signs happening in London."

"Wasn't exactly listening. Too busy faking," said Leo, with a grin.

"I listened, all right. Ears to the vanside. Some kid who knew the future. He struck people down—this fella was running from him, more scared to stay in London than break out. A weirdo, he kept saying; and something about a temple. That soldier sounded scared too: uneasy. Afraid of primitive magic, maybe. And thought the English had reverted to it."

Clanger gave a painful snort. "Magic. More like witchcraft it was; ruddy witchcraft. Three days, he tells Skullcap; there's doom waiting—for you. Three raps on stone, we heard . . . an' three days later the tower goes an' falls on Skullcap, didn't it?" He brooded. "So Shrike's dead," he said at last. "Gone off, like I said. Fine old pal."

"He paid for it," said Jan sharply. "And if your fine old pal was another gunman, what d'you expect?"

She was raked by a blue-eyed glare. "Middle-class plum-in-your-mouth missy. We were human in there, same's you."

"And was Shrike frightened?" asked Tom. "Was that what you and he ran from?"

The boy moved restlessly.

"Didn't threaten us, but we were—were in trouble with him. Not like Grapple, mind. Grapple was right scared stupid when Skullcap died. That was the end of Skullganging, wasn't it?"

"Clear as ruddy daylight." Charlie licked apricot off her thumb. "Who beat you up, then?"

"N'other gang. Junks. They gotten instinct, junks has. Wouldn't have touched us with Skullcap. 'Course, most of us fled without our bikes—could be that alerted them." The boy shifted again, and sighed. "All that lovely juice, lost. Makes your heart bleed."

"Juice?" exclaimed Leo. "You mean petrol?"

"Sure I mean petrol—what else?"

"We'll need petrol for our van."

"Come in a van?" Clanger looked awestruck. "Over no-man's land?"

"What else?"

"An' *they* didn't mow you down?"

"They tried."

The boy pursed his lips to whistle; grimaced instead. "How many died?"

"All present and alive."

A sullen, suspicious look settled on Clanger's face, and he forgot to chew. "Why d'you come? Don't make sense. No one would. You're in league with Freaks. That's what. You've nothing on me, mate. An' I can't help you round anyone up. Jus' look at me."

"Shut it," said Tom. "Take a look at the van, if you don't believe us: mass of holes. No, what we came for was to find my brother Alastair. He's a spastic; crippled legs, so we—"

"What's wrong, Clanger?" put in Bill sharply. "Feeling faint again?"

"He goes sort of blue when he's faint, doesn't he?" said Charlie. "It's not very nice."

"Been stringing me along, an' all the time you was his mates! No wonder Shrike lit out, he's got instinct, Shrike has. Holes in the van—bet they went clean through you. Look, I never hurt him, I ruddy swear it. Never laid a finger on him. It was all Grapple, an' Skullcap, an'—an' one or two others. But I never hurt nobody, I'm not that type."

"Is he mad?" asked Jan anxiously. "Bill, he must be." Certainly Clanger's eyes looked quite wild; and Hoppo growled low in his throat, smelling fear.

"What's biting you, Clanger?"

"Hoppo will be, soon," muttered Charlie. And then, "It was when Bill mentioned *Alastair*."

Clanger's fingers clawed the sofa. "Don't! Jus' don't! If the mucking ceiling falls on me it gets you too, don't it?"

"Alastair," said Charlie; watching.

Clanger moaned.

"An interesting trauma—If I'd already done my trick-cycling, I'd—"

"Cut it out, Bill," said Tom violently. He gripped Clanger's shoulder, and demanded: "Was your weirdo Alastair spastic?"

"Was he what?"

"What Bill here said: half-helpless; wobbly legs."

"Having me on, aren't you? You know it. That's why you come, wasn't it? He called you—don't need bleeding radics, does he? Guides you in, doesn't he? Oh cripes, is he watching now?"

"Really fascinating. Reversion to a more—"

"Bill."

"You said Alastair wasn't quite like other people," murmured Jan.

Clanger rolled his eyes, and shuddered.

"What's that about hurting him?" said Tom fiercely.

"Just a game, see? I never—Don't wanna talk about him, 's unlucky. It—"

"Tom, *don't*," cried Jan; for he had snatched up a knife and was bearing down on the wretched Clanger; bringing the point close to his throat, pricking the skin.

"Talk. Go on. Say it all. From the beginning."

"I—I—Take that knife away! I never—"

"Stop lying, Clanger. Or what'll it be—the knife, or Alastair?"

"He'll be frothing soon," remarked Charlie, deeply enjoying herself.

The narrative wasn't too clear, because of Clanger's abject terror. Skullcap. Skullgang. An' that sneaking Wolf—ah Wolf, there's cunning for you. Paul's manor, but got Fox on our side; listen, Skullgang meant no harm, what choice? Get the Wolf's cub, Skull says, and so Wolf comes running— what harm? But it didn't work out, did it? And for why? Cos Wolf goes to ground instead, an' we're just landed with— Cripes, what we're landed with! Couldn't guess, Skullcap, could he? Kid seemed so helpless; an' natur'ly Skull gets mad, 'cos he's not patient, is he, an' when Wolf doesn't come—

Tom dropped the knife, seized Clanger by the shoulders again, and shook him. Clanger cried out in real pain.

"It wasn't me. I'm telling you, aren't I? Kept him in the Temple, didn't we? It's—"

"That soldier said a temple," remarked Bill.

"*The* Temple—sort of ruddy round church, with crummy tombs, an' a stone cell. That's where we kept this—kid."

"Who—hurt—him?"

Clanger swallowed. "Third night Wolf won't come, an' Skull says light a fire, see." Tom went very white.

"Steady, Tom," whispered Jan.

"Bring the cub down, he says. So Grapple, he puts the kid's hand in—near the fire, an'—an' Skull laughs; an' then the stones fall on him an'—kill him. So they drops the kid, an' runs. An' I run too; fast, I'm telling you. He's sudden death, that kid. We run like hens, squawking. That's when the Junks come. I never touched him, man." Clanger put his arm across his eyes, to shut out the fury in Tom's face. "It's Gospel: never touched him, not even when they brought him in."

Tom stood over him, drawn and stony; knowing he mustn't ask if Alastair was all right when Clanger ran; or pretty soon Clanger would overcome his subservient fear, and start asking himself questions.

He turned his back, muttering, "You make me sick," and jerked his head at the others. "Leo, will you watch him? And the street. Here's your gun."

The others crowded with Tom into the minute dining-room.

"Is it really your brother?"

"Two of the same would be a bit much, wouldn't it? But we *must* find out—and quickly. If they left him alone, God knows what's happened there."

"It sounds as though anyone would be terrified to go near him," said Bill.

"Then—if there was no food or water . . . "

"Bet they kept *some* stuff in this temple place. But could your brother really play tricks with stones and things like that?"

"Of course not, Char. But he might have sensed it would happen. He—he sort of had this intuition thing, even when he was a little kid."

"Why didn't you ask that wretched Clanger about the food?" asked Jan.

"Don't you see? He's thinking all sorts of things, such as: there's some weird communication between us, and Alastair really has black powers. Remember how uneasy that soldier was? It might give us some queer kind of advantage for people to go on thinking it. If I was really in league with Alastair I'd know he was all right. Come on, we must get things together and go on down into the City, now."

"No, Tom," said Bill firmly. "We've slept. You haven't. Leo needs rest too. And even if he's a louse we can't just dump Clanger here and leave him, can we?"

"One more night and Alastair could be dead of thirst. Why did we come to London, anyway?"

They thought that over. It was unanswerable.

"As far as Clanger goes, he's coming too. We'll need petrol, won't we? Besides, if Alastair's dead I'm going to string Clanger up myself. I can hold out without sleep, now—with more coffee inside me."

"Oh, poor Leo," murmured Jan. "It's so comfortable here." She thought achingly of the apricot blankets that had snuggled her into a day's sweet oblivion of the dreadful present.

"Leo will hold out too. He's tough—farmer's boy. He and Clanger can travel in the back, with Hoppo, Jan and Charlie; we'll show Char how to hold a gun if Leo's shoulder stiffens. It's just up her street."

Jan wasn't offended. She knew it wasn't up hers. "The Temple—you know it, Tom?"

"Yah—between the river an' the Law Courts."

Charlie's eyes sparkled. "Shall we have to fight, d'you think? Junks and so on?"

Jan shuddered. Junks! Meat and drink to Charlie, like wildness, freedom, the pitting of wits.

"You'll not try to provoke anything, Char," said Tom crushingly. "And Clanger's going to guide us through the hostile lines. Let's tell him the news, and get started."

Jan had been going to argue, but she saw that it was useless, and said sadly: "I'm taking that pink quilt, anyhow; and some blankets, too."

4 ❦ Wolf Territory

It was dusk when they set out; not dark enough to lose the way or need lights; too dark to be an easy target. Clanger was carried, protesting, to the van. "Shut up," Tom told him roughly. "Alastair won't hurt you if I'm with you. Want to stay and starve?"

"Could leave me food," said Clanger sullenly. "C'n tell you where the juice is."

"Think of lying there waiting for the ceiling to fall on you when Tom finds Alastair," said Charlie bracingly.

Clanger quieted.

There was no trouble south of the river. Occasionally they saw someone creeping along, who slid to cover as the van approached.

"They're frightened," said Jan pityingly.

"Don't get vans in London, see?"

Battersea Bridge was negotiable, though twisted and pitted with holes; but the lovely arch of Albert, with its painted and gilded span of towers, lay broken-backed across the river. Chelsea Old Church still stood, a landmark in the devastation; but the statue of St. Thomas More lay sideways. He was beheaded as in life, and his gilded face regarded them eerily from some bushes.

"It's funny—" Charlie peered out through her pet bullethole—"Those gulls are just the same, still. Swooping and guzzling. Selfish old couldn't-care-less—"

Clanger roused himself to interrupt: "You better tell 'em

up in front, real trouble starts at Pimlico. There's some sort of bunch lying up in Royal Hospital, but they're oldies, won't bother us. They're fond of road blocks in Pimlico. Had some nitro-glycerine too. Could be ambushed."

"But if they think we're Freaks?"

"More so. They're tough. Nothing to lose, see?"

"Which way, then?"

"Ask Alastair," said Clanger, greatly daring.

"Tom won't bother Alastair with things like that. Though if you didn't help us—"

"North, then," responded Clanger quickly. "Into Quitters, then down the Mall. There'll be trouble somewhere, anyway."

"Quitters?"

"Knightsbridge—where the bleeding Guards surrendered. Freaks cut 'em off, see—landed on Harrods' heli-dome. Was the old place looted later!" He sighed. "Set meself up with anything I fancied—but some Mick got it off me in a fight."

There was no trouble. The quiet felt threatening. The trees ahead in St. James's Park whispered by the lake. Stars pricked out above. The road was murky grey, dusk-dazzling.

As they swept round the ruined monument they could see the façade of Buckingham Palace, dark sky and occasional star looking through its windows. There was a smell of fire.

"End of stupid old history!" Charlie bounced up and down on her heels, jolting Clanger, who groaned. "Oh, what will happen next? Isn't it a thrill?"

"You've no sense of tradition, Char."

"She can be my woman when she's grown," said Clanger unexpectedly. "Never seen anything to beat her."

Charlie gave him a withering look; but Clanger was unquenched: "Better take my offer while it's open."

They were approaching the fallen rubble of Admiralty Arch. "Here we go," said Tom quietly. "Got the gun ready, Bill? Knock back to Leo, will you?" Three raps on the driver's partition was the pre-arranged signal for trouble. Two meant "Roll up the hatch and fire".

The four passengers turned towards each other.

"Told you, didn't I?" said Clanger with morose satisfaction.

Some sort of obstruction had been formed three-quarters of the way across the road: construction-workers' barriers, all piled together. There was a gap just wide enough for the van to negotiate—slowly.

"Think we ought—"

"Go on. We've no choice."

But as they approached, a dark figure slipped across the gap, dribbling something from a can. The road ahead flamed suddenly into fire.

Tom braked.

"You're meant to! Go *on*," gulped Bill, raising the gun.

"Petrol tank—"

"Risk it."

There was a scream from the back; a thudding sound as the hatch rose. Confused shouts, a shot.

"*Step on it*," howled Bill in Tom's ear, swivelling his gun sideways.

The van brushed through the gap, with flames spurting up around it; there was a horrible scraping noise, and an awful moment when it seemed they hung there unable to escape. Then, Bill saw a sight he was never to forget. Faces, he'd say. Just—faces; white, or coloured, but all starved and wolfish— gleeful in hope. And two girls like—Well, like nothing human.

But the van was through, with no explosion from the tank; scorched, it zig-zagged as Tom almost lost control, his damp hands slipping on the wheel. Then they had recovered, and were racing across the bottom of Trafalgar Square towards Charing Cross.

"Oughtn't we check . . . "

"Daren't stop."

Bill banged heavily on the partition; yelled, "Okay behind?"

A muffled shout from Leo answered him.

"What's he say?" asked Tom; weaving.

"He shot one. Had to—they got the hatch up."

"Oh cripes."

(Charlie, who had found it too thrilling, was being sick.)

"Strand's a mess. See the stones, or—"

"Weave harder."

They wove. Without lights it was perilous.

"Junks' territory now, I guess," said Clanger without relish. "They'll have moved in; this was our manor once. Oh well. Law Courts is still standing up. Temple Bar too."

"Will Tom know where to turn off?" asked Jan. She tried to sound practical, but her voice shook. Much more of this and she knew she'd jump screaming from the van, drive herself deliberately to danger, just to get it over.

"He's turning now—'bout right. Middle Temple Walk, or something. Cut down here, so—"

The van stopped.

"Ohhh," moaned Jan.

In the narrow lane two silent forms had catapulted from the dark on to either side of the driver's cab. Two razors threatened Tom's and Bill's throats. A roar of motorcycles started up behind.

"Get the hatch up," gasped Leo, fumbling with his gun; but someone was leaning down on it outside.

"Had it," groaned Clanger. "They got our bikes. What price Alastair?"

"Just act as you're told," the righthand captor was instructing Tom, "and make your friend drop his gun. That's right. Straight on down here—mind the mess."

Tom drove, cursing inwardly. The cyclists roared in their wake. It was a tortuous way, till they came out on to a wide paved space beside—

"Isn't that—" began Bill, staring.

"Shut your trap. Pull up, you."

"Why, what we got here?" A voice challenged from the semi-darkness of a porch. "You been busy, Ox."

"Some of *them*. Van an' all. Must be, mustn't it?"

84

"We're not—"

"Nark it. Go fetch Wolf—not taking on this lot alone."

"Wolf! He said *Wolf*?" In the back Clanger raised himself painfully on one elbow. "That's—I dunno—"

"Is it bad?" asked Jan anxiously.

"Wolf! I dunno. Better than Junks, maybe—"

Wolf came out of the porch, a slight figure in his leather jacket and tight black jeans. He looked Tom and Bill over in silence, observed the van, and said:

"Get out."

"They've got a gun, Wolf."

"Take it, you nit. Get their hands up. Are you covering the back?"

"Sure, Wolf."

Bill and Tom jumped down, hands high. Wolf regarded them coldly.

"What you doing here?"

Tom looked up at the round tower rising above them, and said boldly, "Searching for my brother. Name of Alastair."

"Do I believe you?" asked Wolf very softly.

"Have *you*—got him?" The anxiety in Tom's voice was obvious. "Oh—and we've wounded in the van. Girls too. And a dog. They're frightened."

Wolf gave a sudden yelp of laughter.

"Frightened. Who isn't?"

His knife prodded Tom in the breastbone.

"You come with me. Watch the others, Ox."

Tom, aware of that knifepoint now level with his liver, preceded him through the archway. Inside the Temple he stopped, and blinked. Two flaring torches lit the scene. Half-way up the nave Alastair was lying on sleeping bags, and playing dice with Fox. "Two pairs, six and five. You've done it again and—" He glanced up. "Tom!"

"This your brother, kid?"

"Tom—" Alastair wriggled forward like an otter, his face split into a beam of welcome. "Oh Tom, I always knew you'd come! Sort of felt you nearer, every day. Isn't it terrific, Wolf and I've got a gang, well it's his, really, but I made a bit of one too, so mine joined his, and we've got some motorcycles, petrol too, and I made my gang take me to find him, and it was Jockey's Fields, and even Ox is nicer to me now. Tom? Why, Tom, you're crying—"

"Kid's a wizard," said Wolf, with his sharp sideways smile. "Happy, too. 'Spite of all he been through. Like he's centred, somewhere. Unlike—" He glanced at Tom's shadowed features. "Here, have some." The proffered knife skewered a slice of duck.

Tom's lank hair fell forward to conceal his face. He chewed. He'd found Alastair. Hadn't deserted him. Had come into danger to find him, bringing others too. Would the account ever balance? No telling . . .

He longed for sleep. His eyelids blinked. He hunched forward, still chewing. Wolf's voice continued softly in his ear: "—they're all dead scared of us now. Bikes handed over, only had to ask. Word gone out—ripples in a pond—"

Tom's head jerked. "That so?"

"That's certainly so." Wolf hugged his knees, rocked on his haunches. They were crouching round a small fire where the cooking was done, in the former cloisters. Tarpaulin, looted from the riverside, gave shelter, and cover for the flames. Wolf had refused to allow cooking inside the church.

"Ask for a stone shower," he'd said; and: "The old knights'll give us shelter, if we treat 'em right."

Tom heard him talking now as if faraway: "—after we'd set up here in the Temple with the kid's gang, three more of Skullcap's lot came creeping back—we drove one off, a shocker *he* was, an' kept the others: made 'em swear obedience on pain of nasty ends. They don't know what the kid is, that's a fact—Well—" sharp glance at Tom, who grunted—"no more do I. Dunno why *I* started fending for him like his Daddy. You know what? Most think he's sudden death, but some thinks he brings protection. See the food his brother's brought us now, they're saying. Yah, make you laugh, don't it? But guess what Ox finds today: fish on a dock leaf, in the porch. 'What's this?' he asks. An' Grouse says: 'Someone brought it for Alastair. Sneaked up with it. Cos they're scared, see. An' they want his goodwill.' How we laughed."

"It's no good talking to Tom, Wolf," said Jan softly. "He's asleep."

The fact that the former Hellers lived and throve where Skullcap had been destroyed increased their reputation. They took the name Alastair had given—Templars—and their painted dragons gave place to the ancient Templar badge of two knights on one horse. Alastair had found the insignia when poring over old books in the ruins of the Master's house beyond. "Kid's whimsy," Wolf had called it; nevertheless, gave orders for a repainting of the jackets. "Tom—you have a bash. You've nothing much to do."

But Tom saw no reason why he should take orders from Wolf, just because he'd been surviving longer in London and had found Alastair first. Anyway, he himself was as busy as anyone else, wasn't he? "Not my line," he said. "Try Alastair —with some of your looted paint." There was an undertone in his voice which made Wolf look at him sharply and turn away, tucking in his lips.

So Alastair set to work. His knights rode in a spirited way upwards from left hip to right shoulder. Then he thought they should have something to aim for: a cluster of stars. He wasn't sure how the idea had entered his mind—it was as if someone had given it to him. But ever since that early discovery of his strange and puzzling gift, the one thing he had learned with certainty was to follow unquestioningly where intuition led.

"It's like a shoulder flash," Charlie said, looking on.

"It's what they're seeking—And they're us. In a way."

"Did you think of that before you started?"

"No. The knights were obvious—the stars seemed to suggest themselves. But that's the way it works. Sometimes."

"What does?" asked Charlie.

"Now don't start showing off, Alastair," said Tom.

Alastair answered neither of them, but continued working absorbedly. Wolf joined them.

"Put in one more, you'll have old Orion himself."

"What's Orion?" asked Grouse.

"Orion," murmured Alastair thoughtfully. He glanced up, and down, and painted in a star.

"Some say he was Nimrod, mighty hunter before the Lord," chanted Jan. "He ought to be a Freak-hunter, too!" And then flushed, fearing the others might laugh.

"Jan's romantic." Charlie flung wide her arms and pirouetted round the little group. "Isn't that right, Jan? You're always turning one thing into something else, as though you don't ever like them just as they are. But me, I like life. Life without Auntie and Albert. I'm happy. And Hoppo's happy—such fat rats. Alastair—are you happy?"

Jan put a sympathetic hand on his shoulder. She didn't think Alastair romantic, exactly, though he was certainly different. Wolf called him "kid", yet she wouldn't have shown her special black and white stone to someone who was still just a kid. Matt, she thought. I feel such a nullity without him . . . I'm sure the others must feel it about me . . . Much of the time they treat me as though I'm hardly here . . .

Can't answer Char, Alastair was thinking. Don't understand myself! Happy? Hardly. Parents dead. Freaks all round London. Defeat everywhere—no news out of anywhere. Nothing . . .

And yet sometimes he felt nothingness would be filled. How and with what he didn't know. Only it meant waiting. Not thinking too hard. Harking neither back nor forward, but being empty . . . He thought suddenly of Hercules, to whom time and disaster meant nothing at all, except mouse- or not-mouse time; sun-time, or star-time. Orion-time . . . And

88

again Alastair had that strange sensation, as if he was thinking someone else's thoughts. Orion-time. Something there—

"You know, Alastair, your mouth's open, and you look *distinctly* odd. You're often odd, did you realise?"

Wolf's grin flashed. "Aren't we all, Char? Just for surviving? We'll feel odder still if our store of gelignite ever goes up. Fox—I say, Fox; game of dice?"

"Busy," said Fox over his shoulder, from the round part of the church. "Come and look at this, everyone. Worth seeing."

"What is it?" Alastair did his otter wriggle down the aisle and the others followed him. "What you got there, Clanger? Let's see."

" 'S bit primitive." Clanger's hair fell forward over his flushed face, where the bruise was fading. He wrestled with pieces of plastic-covered wire.

"Old-type radio," said Fox. "He done a course, Clanger did. In clink. Going to be a nucleo-radic operator, Clang was. Like your Leo had his eye on planes and didn't fancy the farming bit. But the stuff they give Clang in clink come from the ape age. Sixties, he says."

"Why bother, then?" asked Jan unkindly. She couldn't like Clanger. And to see him there, a reasonably well-fed and accepted member of the gang, tore her heart. Remembering Matt . . .

Clanger's flush had increased.

"Where'd you find it?" asked Tom; ostentatiously idle, he propped himself against a pillar, arms crossed. Sunlight glanced through the windows, and lit the Temple with a peaceful light. The guards were out, and Leo with the food foragers. It seemed as if life had always gone on this way, and always would.

"Dug it up," muttered Clanger. "I'd need solder for this wire, see. Heating in a fire's a long job."

"How d'you know where to dig?" asked Wolf suddenly.

"Cos I hid it, didn't I?"

"And only just remembered? Interesting."

"Things mightn't have worked out."

"Got any more treasures, Clang?" asked Fox, grinning.

"Few."

"Oh, leave him alone. He'll show us, in time. And I think we'll need him," said Alastair suddenly; and, as he used to: "Wolf, I'm awful hungry."

"Tighten your belt, kid. Mustn't eat through Char's hoard too fast, must we? An' pigeons are thinning out." He dropped a hand lightly on Alastair's shoulder. "Offerings seem less, too—or something's stealing 'em. Not rats, either. Hoppo's had those."

"Oh, I know," said Alastair, "it's—"

"We're getting fat and easy, like penned beef for the killing," interrupted Fox.

"Time for another stone-fall, maybe?" Clanger's tone mocked them.

"Huh! Listen!" Wolf held up a warning hand.

"That's the third heli this morning," whispered Jan, sounding scared.

"Van's well hidden—*I* saw to that. But what about the bikes?" asked Tom.

"If anyone's forgotten, I'll—" Wolf slipped through the arch into the porch.

The helicopter hung above the wilderness of the Inner Temple gardens, buzzing inquisitively. It darted to and fro, but always returned, coming ever nearer. Wolf drew back, and watched.

Grouse, looking upward, rose out of ruins on the paved court's farther side. He began to pick his way from stone to stone towards the porch.

"Fool." Wolf's lips shaped the word, curling back in a snarl of disapproval.

The helicopter hung motionless. Grouse was uncertain, too obvious now for camouflage, and aware of error. He looked round, then back. "Back, back," mouthed Wolf. But Grouse's nerve snapped, and he came headlong, barely taking cover.

Wolf heard his sobbing breath, and stood aside to let him in. The helicopter rose like a gull on a thermal, skimmed the roof, and disappeared south-west.

"Wolf, I'm sorry, I got worried, see, an'—"

Wolf's look of iron fury was more painful than being hit. "Led him straight. *Get* inside—send Fox out on guard instead. Tell everyone: discussion, soon's I've mulled things over . . ."

"They didn't like the van getting in," said Tom. "But I thought they'd given up. Anyway, can't know it's hereabouts, can they?"

Wolf said nothing. He sat crosslegged, apparently withdrawn yet aware of a new grouping: Clanger and the five former Skullgangers, all their eyes on Alastair. He felt as though some inexplicable burden had descended on his shoulders, making him responsible for the unreadable future. An' why, I just don't know—

"Can they?" insisted Tom. But no one answered him. Leo, Jan, Charlie, Mule, Bill, and other Templars were looking to Wolf—and Alastair.

But where was Alastair looking? Neither at Clanger, Tom, nor Wolf. At the ground. Tracing patterns with a finger.

They want me to speak, thought Wolf. But let it build; wait for it . . . Kid's waiting.

Who betrayed us, an' why? What would those Freaks give in return? Nothing Ox nor Clanger want: power lads, both . . .

Acid. Dope. That fits. Kid scares the Junks, yes? An' fear brings hatred, an' hatred breeds informers . . .

Clanger had something when he said time for another stonefall. Yah, that's right. Otherwise, when the Freaks come, Junks'll help 'em. Not much time . . .

Tom glared at Wolf, and was swamped by a terrifying and shaming anger. Shaming, because it wasn't directed at the Freaks—and he knew it. Damn it, I led the others into London, didn't I? Successfully. And Alastair was glad enough to see me . . . Then, just because this Wolf has a knife or two, and a manner of using it, everybody starts acting as if . . .

He opened his mouth to say something, something forceful that would make everyone sit up and take notice. But the chance was lost, for Clanger was already saying: "Wolf. You called a meeting."

"Did I? Did I call one, Clanger? Want to say something, don't you? Well, say it."

"I say leave here. Fight another gang. Take their manor. An'—" he scowled. "Let those who fight best, lead. That's how Skullcap ran it. That's how we want it, now. Us Skullgangers reckon on force now, an' fear. You're gone soft, Wolf."

"No."

"No to what?" Clanger's head thrust forward.

"All of it. An' you're not Skullgangers. You sworn."

"The kid was leading us. 'Least, with you. Thought he knew things." He turned suddenly to Alastair. "Come on, kid, tell the truth. Accident, Skullcap, weren't it? We should laugh! Well, the game's over, see? Time to play different."

Alastair smiled. A slow, shy smile.

"The truth, kid."

"Wolf," said Alastair, not looking at Clanger. "Let's go north. I feel—something's—leading us that way."

"North, kid? Back to Jockey's Fields?"

"No, really north. Out of London. North of England."

Wolf sat nodding like a mandarin. "Well."

"Magic carpet?" asked Clanger with heavy irony. "Armoured train? Rocket?"

"How, kid?"

"London's finished for us . . . That's what I feel." Alastair looked at his pattern in the dust, and drew a finger thoughtfully through it, crosswise. "But in the north, somewhere—" His brows wrinkled, and he looked pleadingly at Wolf. "That's the place . . . The next stage."

"Oh, Alastair," said Tom wearily. "Do stop play-acting."

Jan glanced at him, and the ex-Skullgangers snickered.

Wolf's voice was very quiet, but still just held them.

"Tell us how, kid?"

Alastair shook his head; hesitated. "I think—helicopters."

"Sure, *they're* coming, kid," cried Clanger. "That's what. Several men to each. An' lasers—An'—"

"Wolf!" Fox broke in on them, holding Hoppo by the collar. "It's Junks. All of 'em. Quickly."

Split temporarily forgotten, they crowded to the entrance porch. Ox's outraged voice exclaimed: "They got our bikes."

"Only two of them," Wolf said calmly, stepping forward. "Get out my manor, you. An' stay out. Whatever scum stole those bikes can put 'em back where they belong."

A low jeering ripple of insult went up from the intruders, as they moved in closer: a wavering line of about fifty strong. Knives came out stealthily, on both sides. Only Wolf's hand stayed empty. He stood looking disdainful, and the line stopped about three metres off, uncertainly.

Tom, shoulder to shoulder with Bill and Leo, felt a hand tugging at his belt. He looked down. Alastair had wriggled forward. "You stay back, Alastair."

"Out there. Now. Oh Tom—help me. By those ferns."

"Do as the kid says, can't you," murmured Wolf sideways. But while Tom hesitated it was Bill who helped Alastair prop himself on a stone among the ferns, his back against the wall. His appearance led to renewed jeering.

"Skullcap, eh!"

"Weirdo . . . Cripple! Where's ya power, huh? Gonna bring the sky down, are you?"

The Junks' leader was a little fellow from Whitechapel, a former tailor, who was said to be a devil with a bodkin-sharp knife. They called him Bartlett. It was on Bartlett that Alastair fixed his gaze, smiling calmly. Bartlett glared at Wolf. Tom looked away. Whatever happens to Alastair now, he was thinking, it's all Wolf's fault.

"Hah! Put him there to scare us, have you?" growled

Bartlett. "But heard tales out of school, we have. Not been much fortune-telling lately, has there?"

Wolf heard slight movement behind him from a former Skullganger, and made an accurate guess at the talebearer's identity.

"Don't tell fortunes," Alastair's voice sounded young and clear. "That's silly, anyway."

"Silly? You'll look silly, soon. Clean you out, we will. Like a wasp's nest. Tonight."

"You won't like our sting," volunteered Wolf; and Hoppo, as if verifying this, let out a growl.

"They're sending in the helis?" asked Alastair.

There was an uneasy murmur down the line, and Bartlett looked nonplussed. "That's just your guess."

"Better not help the Freaks," said Alastair, "whatever they're expecting. You're going to obey Wolf instead . . . Because if you don't . . ."—he stared almost dreamily into the ferns—"you'll have something to reckon with, that's all."

Bartlett laughed, but looked uneasy. He glanced back at his wavering line, and saw his leadership was threatened anyway and, in such company, his life.

"Not going to accept that, neither. Not from a scrawny cripple kid, that needs a hiding." He groped behind him, and someone thrust a knobbly stick into his hand.

Tom made a sudden movement, but Alastair remained calm. "Don't you threaten me, Bartlett."

"Stop me, can you, weirdo? Magic contest, hah! C'mon, young Moses—see the staff?"

Laughter rippled down the Junks' line. They reeled, propping each other up. They jeered louder as Bartlett thrust the stick at Alastair, who raised his hands and grabbed it. Bartlett overbalanced, and let go. Alastair lowered it very gently into the ferns. Movement came to meet it. He sat quietly, turning a smiling face to Bartlett, who had recovered, and advanced again. Then Alastair thrust the stick forward in his turn. What hung there, close to Bartlett's face, was coiled, heavy, silver-grey and sinuous; a little forked tongue flickered in and out of its mouth in hungry fashion, as a triangular head reared—

"Moses, did you say?"

The choked scream from Jan was echoed down Bartlett's line. Tom's face went blank, rigid. Even Wolf's arrogant smile froze, while Clanger and his former Skullgangers fell over each other to get back inside the church. As for Bartlett and his Junks—they seemed to melt into the fallen masonry like shadows, laying about them in their haste. The two stolen bikes were left standing in the sun.

"Well, kid," said Wolf, shattered but essaying non-chalance.

"Alastair!" said Tom almost reprovingly.

"Meet Percy." Alastair was trying not to laugh. "Even Tom thought I'd conjured him, didn't he, Wolf? Someone's lost pet—or from the Zoo. Percy's been stealing my offerings for days. I didn't think you'd like it—but you'll let him have them now, won't you? He's so sweet-tempered."

"Kid, he can have 'em all. Don't you ever let Clanger know you didn't work it, will you?"

"Clanger's all right, really."

"You think so, kid?"

"Pretty sure. It was all that one who came and joined us last, I think."

"Maybe you're right, kid. Well, bring Percy, an' don't let Hoppo eat him—we'll have a little showdown before dark. Someone knows what Bartlett meant, all right."

"But suppose they send in more than two helis?" asked Jan for the twentieth time.

"Shouldn't need to—they've the best, like I told you," repeated Wolf patiently. "An' the Freaks think we were beat up by Junks today."

"Suppose Bartlett warns them, though?"

"Put your faith in fear of Percy's revenge," murmured Bill. "And Freaks don't like failure."

"Jan's made me go all gooseflesh," protested Charlie. She readjusted the rag that bound Hoppo's jaws together in case he gave an untimely bark.

"And Clanger: you keep with us." Leo's voice held a note of threat.

"He will." Wolf's was very gentle, caressing the words. " 'Cos he won't forget that little showdown we had, will he? Nor the way we dealt with that Judas Skullganging chum of his!"

Wolf's "little showdown" with the former Skullganger had brought to light a neat and lethal plan, hatched between Junks and Freaks: a pincers movement, operated from Strand and Embankment. Leo and Charlie were wanted alive, for questioning. But at the details Wolf could only guess. "If it was me I'd say: eight men from each heli, armed. An' a guard left with each pilot. Radi-comm, of course."

"Going to be tricky," Clanger had said lugubriously. "They'll be in touch with base, all the way."

"Got no choice, have we?" Wolf had snapped.

"Only scatter."

"Yah—an' be hunted down like rabbits? Now those Freaks have found us, they want us out. Kid says, go north, so that settles it. How much juice do these helis take, Leo?"

"Enough, I'd think. Probably self-fuelling."

"Then put your faith in the kid. An' Grouse an' good old-time gelignite." Grouse, whose task was both grim and tricky, had been allotted to Tom, at the Strand end.

" 'Cos I'm helping the girls get the goods on board, so Grouse is your goods, see?" Tom had nodded his assent. Underlying differences had not so much been forgotten as put aside in the face of imminent, horrific danger. And getting Grouse back to base in this hair-raising scheme would be bad enough, yet he also had Alastair to think of: should he be entrusted to Ox? But Alastair when consulted said he'd sooner have two of his original gang.

"They're pathetic, really. But they're good survivors, and

96

that's all I'll need. And Clanger can teach them how to cope with radi-comm."

So now, all plans made and details settled, Wolf's little party crouched waiting at the Embankment end.

"*Listen!*" said Jan at last.

The sound was faint, but ominous. At first no more than a trembling on the air—yet enough to make Charlie forget she was the strong one, and clutch Jan's hand.

"Wish we hadn't split up. Suppose one half gets away with it, while the other doesn't? Suppose Tom's lot—"

"Be quiet, Jan, you Cassandra," murmured Bill.

"Wish you looked more Junk-like, Wolf," complained Charlie uneasily, as the buzzing grew, and two dragonfly shapes, a little darker than the sky, neared from the south.

"Done my best, haven't I?"

"You don't look sick enough."

"Do I feel it!"

And at the same moment Alastair, crouched behind fallen masonry in the Strand, was saying urgently to Tom: "Take care, won't you—"

Fox's ears pricked. "Kid, you don't think—"

"Think nothing. Just feel there might be some sort of hitch. Don't relax, Tom—specially when Grouse—"

"Relax! You're joking—" Tom's voice sounded half-strangled. "Now, wait for it—Here they come . . . ."

"You sent the messages?" The Post Captain's words were clipped and correct, his manner briskly efficient, his laser gun wicked, though small as a toy. The heli crews were a very different breed from the garrison ground staff; all of them spoke good English, which was still often used, even by Freaks, as an international flight language.

"Not me." Tom's voice was hoarse. He stood there, in his Junk's rags, trying not to shake. He jerked his head southward. "Leader done it—Embankment side. I'm his second."

"Fair enough." The officer raised a hand to wave his

men out. Seven. So Wolf guessed right. Half got those guns, too.

"Where's your three hostages?"

"Here: my brother, he's—he's crippled, an' these two."

"On board with them, then. No tricks. I'm leaving a guard with the pilot, understand?"

"Yes, sir, I do." An abject eager-to-please whine, clothing arrogance. Well rehearsed.

Alastair was helped into the heli. The men stood round watching, their eyes expressionless as robots'.

"Captain—"

"Hurry, there."

"You—you brought the fixes?"

"Find out, won't you?"

"They promised!" Indignation and whining fear mixed.

"Get into line, there. You first." The gun threatened.

"Sure, sure, Captain, sir. That Temple gang, they're not— in much shape."

"Beat them up properly, did you? Kept to your orders?"

"Oh, they're still alive. *We* don't—"

"Only rat, eh?" The Post Captain had a walkie: a little round radi-comm button, on his belt. He pressed the top, spoke: "Landing 1, in. North positioned. Guide and hostages all set. Over." Another voice answered: "Landing 2 in. South positioned. Our hostages include two girls. Guide says van stored arches, right; gang holed up in Temple, most injured. Confirm meet rendezvous."

"Confirm," snapped the Post Captain. A third voice came in distantly. "Base 20. Hearing you, North and South. Keep contact."

"Girls!" The officer waved Tom ahead with his gun. "Girls and fixes. Luxury—for now." And smiled: a grim, secretive smile.

Half-way down Middle Temple Walk, Tom said: "Through here. Shall I—" And wriggled first through piles of rubble supported by blocks of stone. The tunnel was black and narrow, with only width for one. It twisted, joined other tunnels, and confused the soldiers.

"Close together, men." The Captain floundered. His voice was low, edgy. "Hey, you there, guide—"

"I'm here," muttered Tom, just ahead. "M'lot should be, too—" He acted puzzlement. "There's the church, see?"

An open space. The church, dark and looming. The van parked under nearby arches.

"There's my lot, now." Tom pointed at approaching shadows.

"That's ours."

"No. There." Tom waved an arm vaguely towards a stone block's shadow. "Late."

"Trust junks," muttered the Post Captain, outraged, as the North and South parties converged, and their guides Tom and Wolf seemed to melt suddenly into thin air. "Don't fire," he adjured his men. "We've got their hostages." South's lieutenant saluted. "Think they'll get fixes—I'll fix them. Deploy your men, recce."

Some twenty metres away, behind a broken wall, Grouse lay waiting, tense with fear his fingers might act early, without the sanction of his will.

Wolf and Tom fled back their separate ways. "All hangs on timing," Wolf had said in conference. "If the slightest thing goes wrong—"

So Tom counted as he ran, each second dreading to hear the roar that would tell him Grouse's nerve had cracked and he'd jumped the gun. But there was still silence as he reached the open space where the helicopter stood, and walked out into the moonlight, trying not to breathe too hard.

"Captain sent me back." (Forty-five, forty-six.) "No trouble." He slouched, looked up casually, grinned at the guard. "C'n I come up with my brother?" (Fifty-one, fifty-two.)

The guard hesitated, then lowered his gun and waved Tom on board. "Three, four junks, what's the difference?" he grunted. The pilot turned and stared; pressed an "out" button, and reported Tom's return.

"Hi," said Alastair tensely.

"No talking," said the guard.

They sat in silence. Tom's palms were sweating, and he'd counted another ten before Fox, in accordance with the pre-arranged plan, shouted and stood up.

"Listen, something wrong!" But Tom was pushed aside angrily by the guard.

"Don't you interfere, junk—"

Fox gave a well-rehearsed moan, staggered dramatically, and fell.

"Knifed? Gangs." The guard was nervy now, turning his gun outwards, inwards.

"Let off a round, fast. That'll settle it," said the pilot. And to Base: "Rats biting. Putting down poison."

The guard jumped from the helicopter's belly, just as Tom drew the van's spanner from his pocket, and cracked it down on his neck like someone cracking a boiled egg. Then he leaped to pick up the gun. In the cockpit the pilot swivelled to find Clanger's friend's knife at his throat; and Clanger's friend pressed the button so that no sound left the cockpit.

"Freeze, chum; do as you're told, an' you won't get hurt."

A small voice from Base 20 kept repeating: "North 1, come in, North 1, lost you, resume contact." And then, in growing concern: "South 2, come in, South 2—resume contact immediately. Lost you, South 2—"

In helicopter South 2 Wolf had had to knock out the pilot, and had done the job too well.

"Cripes, s'pose he doesn't come round in time to take us up. What's that fool Grouse doing?"

"Did you hear, Jan?" asked Charlie, handing up another case of medical stores (from Bart's) that the van had brought down earlier in the day. "They've lost contact with that other one. Good for Tom."

"No one could help hearing," muttered Jan, restraining Hoppo with one hand and balancing a jar of beans with the other. "Can't we cut them off? They jitter me."

"Must know what they're up to. Leo! Could you take this thing up?"

"Maybe. But whether it'll stay up—"

"You must try. Oh, Grouse—blast it!" Wolf's tone was anguished.

Blast it, Grouse did. There was a sudden roar and then a louder one; and then, as both died away, a smaller, third. The sky above the Temple erupted into purple. Three purple roses of varying sizes hung in the air, partly obscured by clouds of dust and flame.

But instead of racing northwards to find Tom, Grouse was lying face down behind his sheltering wall, knocked colder than South 2's pilot, by a piece of flying stone.

"Base 19, Base 19." A voice from Base 20 was moaning on the air. "Come in Base 19: North 1 and South 2, square Law Courts, Thames. Blown. Reinforcements needed. *Base 19.* Are you hearing me?"

"Is that the last case? Everyone in? Now see what you can do, Leo. Someone pour something on this ugly brute's mug."

"Did you have to hit so hard?"

"Yes," said Wolf feelingly, "I did—"

It was three minutes before helicopter South 2 rose lumberingly into the air, guided by Leo's quaking hand.

And for three minutes the others in North 1 sat and sweated it out, waiting for Grouse.

"Tell this b. to start up?" Clanger's friend tickled the pilot's neck with his knife.

"Try contact with Wolf first. If you can."

Base 20 was still agitatedly trying to rouse Base 19.

Clanger's friend hesitated. "Wolf said not—not till we were well clear, then only if we lost contact."

"Damn Wolf," said Tom. "He's—"

"Hullo, Base 20," came in a new voice loud and clear. "Hearing you."

"Well, Wolf was right . . ." But Tom felt frantic, knowing he should get the heli up. " 'M going to look. You coming, Ox?"

"Bring the gun?"

"Leave it. Must hold the heli, if—if anyone comes." Tom touched Alastair's shoulder. " 'Bye, kid. See they take off if we're long. Ox?"

Ox drew his knife, and scrambled down after Tom. They disappeared in the Temple's direction, where the night was mottled with that rosy glow.

"There's South 2 going up already," muttered Ox. "See him?"

"Don't talk. May be survivors. Guns deadly. Run."

They doubled, surefooted in the scattered mounds of stone. No one came to meet them. The Temple was burning fiercely. The van had blown right across the courtyard. Other things were scattered. Ox and Tom looked away.

"Behind the wall; lying somewhere."

They searched. Haste made them overshoot. Just as Tom, half-sobbing, was almost giving up, Ox called softly: "Here."

"Dead?"

But as they touched him Grouse moved, and moaned.

"C'n you carry him, Ox?"

"Sure."

"I'll take both knives, then. You go first."

Circling with whirring blades, South 2 hovered above the spreading fiery rose.

"Can't see 'em anywhere," muttered Wolf. "Try once more."

Charlie bent over the pilot. "He's coming round. Hoppo's been sick on him, that's done it."

"Sending four. Rocketeers," reported Base 19 to Base 20.
"Good thing we didn't get in touch," said Clanger's friend.

In the darkest runnel of the home trip Ox barged straight into someone without warning. A sickening jar. He waited, coldly certain, for the laser fire.
"What's up?" muttered Tom.
"Soldier."
But it was only one of the braver spirits from Bartlett's gang, hopefully come to spy upon disaster. Before a knife-thrust could follow, Ox swung Grouse aside and Tom slipped past, half crouching, to drive one hand upward. There was a scream, a panic whirlwind of fighting arms and kicking legs.
"Get on!" yelled Tom to Ox; and waded in, enthusiastic, forgetting fear. Slice and thrust in the darkness, and in his brain one thought hammering: no one must live to tell that the helis had survived the fire—no one—

"That you, Ox? Got Grouse there?"
"Huh. Take him."
"Where's Tom?"

"Just once more, an' then off," said Wolf despondently. "Something's happened."
"We can't leave Alastair."
"Nor Tom," added Charlie, quite wholeheartedly.

And he crept the last few yards, almost beaten to his knees. Other blood mingled with his own. He hadn't strength to haul himself into the heli, but was yanked up gasping: "Pull out, quick. Mustn't lose Wolf an' the others, now."

They fled north over the city, shadows like Hercules though

not noiseless ones. It was lucky for them that no one was carefully screening the stricken land. And they were only just in time: as they went four similar shadows buzzed in from the west. They hovered over the flames and smoke, seeking but not finding. Base 20 learned that something had gone wrong: terribly wrong. Total disaster. No sign of life or helis. Only fires.

Ambushed—

Base 20 was appalled. Teach them. Rockets.

And rockets Square Law Courts Thames received. Two huge orange roses absorbed the dying purple ones, before the buzzing shadows flew purposefully westward again, their duty done.

5 § Matt and the Monks of War

The cold was bitter. Golden leaves had been stripped from the Tauber valley by east winds. The abundant apple crop had long been carted off by scarecrow women, bundled in sacking aprons and cotton headscarves, and driven by their conquerors' cruelty to prodigies of labour. The remaining walls of the medieval towns gave small protection against a tigerish autumn. Nature itself seemed to have conspired with the enemy to scourge the people of the crumbled Western Federation.

"Survival's a mere habit now," Matt was thinking, as he stood watching an old woman drive a half-starved donkey slowly ahead of her down the narrow street.

The slavemaster's long black lash curled itself around his shoulders. Matt shuffled obediently back into line, barely reacting to the pain. He had been consigned to an Anglo-German labour gang that was herded here and there to do rough manual work. They were usually quartered in straw; and on their diet—lentil porridge—many had grown sick, and weakened, and then disappeared. No one ever heard a shot.

Matt often felt it was ironic that he had travelled this part of Europe before, as a student. He had wandered across the Austrian Alps, and north from Füssen through Bavaria and Franconia, viewing the walled cities with an appreciative tourist's eye. But now that he walked barefoot over cobbled streets, and saw towers rising before him in the morning that would imprison him icily by evening, he viewed the journey in a different light. The hospitable inns in Rothenburg ob Tauber were filled with the arrogant Freaks, while Matt and his companions were locked in the icy Jakobskirche, where the sagging remains of the great woodcarver Riemenschneider's masterpiece was already broken up for firewood. Not that Matt's gang were allowed fires. In the dark he'd lain shivering, too cold to sleep, and his open hand had closed upon a carved wooden head; he had stroked it gently, sadly, thinking that it and he were victims of the same disaster.

That had been four or five nights ago, and now they were quartered in Bad Mergentheim, clearing the streets of rubble during the day, and locked into the former headquarters of the Teutonic Knights at dusk. Another freezing place, and another of Matt's gang died there. But one depressed moralist was still very much alive.

"It's a judgement on us all," he declared, with a certain air of gloomy pleasure. "Know why?" He stared up accusingly at the exquisite rococo ceiling. (They were lying on their backs in the room where the Archduke Karl once presided as *Hochmeister*.) "Laziness and love of riches, that's the size of it. Greed and sloth, in Biblical terms. We weren't found worthy to triumph over these iron people. No zeal, d'you see. What we needed was a Cromwell—a man of God. And what did we get? What we deserved, of course—some fat-bellied carpet-baggers salting away our defence funds into Swiss bank accounts. Well, at least those banks have been liquidated too."

Matt said nothing. He was only interested in keeping his aching bones together long enough to see all Freaks damned —a simple enough ambition, he thought ironically. The reasons for what had happened, and any apportioning of blame, seemed beside the point now—fruitless. As did any discussion about the growth of Neo-Stalinism and the surprising speed with which so many disparate people had fallen beneath its spell. Academic questions, irrelevant to personal survival. If only the moralist would keep quiet! He seemed to run on self-satisfaction, like oil. Matt sighed, and turned his thoughts to Jan—ghost-memory of a Jan, with long pale hair, which had looked clean and shining even when there was nowhere to wash it but some cold, muddy stream. Her laughter—he couldn't remember it: the exact cadence of a laugh or voice was the first thing to fade.

"—and now they sell our womenfolk in the marketplace. Well, we asked for it—"

"Shut up, can't you?" Matt kicked himself free of dirty straw, and stood up. No one had shackled them here—the entrance to the complex of buildings was too easily guarded. (Anyway, where could they go?) As he blundered through the door the moralist said with gloomy satisfaction: "Looking for trouble. That sort never learn."

Room after room, corridors, staircases. The place had been used as a museum, an art gallery, even a ballet school. It was enormous, barren, echoing. And the ferocious cold was worse outside the *Hochmeister's* room. Matt leaned on a splintered glass display case, and stared idly at a picture of black enamel crosses, and the remains of torn and rusty ribbons. Black crosses . . . His father talking of Messerschmidts . . . He looked again, and focused intently. So this was where the Iron Cross originated. Iron Crosses for gallantry, black crosses for aircraft; black crosses from the ancient Order of Teutonic Knights, those severe and dedicated Christians fighting for the Holy Land; those ferocious warlords subduing the far north-east which became East Prussia and caused such trouble.

Parfait gentil knights, I don't think. And then they twisted the black cross to a swastika—or was that just subconscious? Funny—I'm dying on my feet, so what can it matter to me, yet my historian side still goes working away like an automatic beaver.

Something was stuck at an angle in one corner of the shattered stand. Matt caught the gleam of metal, put his fingers in, and pulled. The thing came away easily enough:

part of an Order, the actual emblem of black enamel, chipped and damaged though still basically intact. A flicker of a grin crossed his gaunt features, and he stuck the cross's pin into the front of his tattered sweatshirt. Iron Cross for survival. What *would* Grandfather have said?

He continued his wanderings, swaying on his feet. This place was bleak, though! Enormous, harsh. Monument to a strange, heroic, often savage national spirit. Wouldn't mind a few wild old warlords on my side right now . . .

Another corridor. White, echoing. Nearby, a broken, twisting staircase. A painted knight's chest, smashed open. Matt reeled, propped himself against the wall with one hand, started cautiously upward. Never find my way back now. Never. Somewhere under open sky if it must happen. Stairs neverending—all alone though—Jan—

He was sinking, stair's edge cutting into his knees. A huge place, spinning white . . . nothing . . . eternity.

Strange, they should speak German in eternity. Good thing I studied it. Maybe that's why I did?

They were quarrelling in eternity. The German sounded fractious: "There are foreigners stabled here; he's one of them."

"A spy, I tell you. *Their* spy."

"A very half-starved spy. Does his spadework well."

"*Englisch*," said Matt sleepily, not opening his eyes. He was so comfortable—had felt nothing like this for ages: comparative warmth. Something velvety was beneath him, something furry and smelly on top: a bearskin.

He made a severe effort: "*Bin aus England gekommen.*" It was a mad dream, of course. He'd wake in the straw, a nailed boot nudging his side, the crack of a whip above his head. He'd been thinking of the old Teutonic Knights before he fainted; maybe he'd gone mad. Anyway, who cared?

He opened his eyes. A young man was leaning over him, holding a cup. No: some form of glass goblet, very fine.

"*So! Trinken Sie—*"

He put his hand under Matt's head and the cup to his lips. The wine wasn't worthy of the glass. It was rough, and stung his lips, but Matt drank deeply. "*Mosel, aber nicht spätlese*," he murmured. A roar of laughter greeted his words. But they hadn't minded, for he was being offered bread, sopped in that abominable wine. It was *kornbrot*, almost black with a bitter flavour. This time he was conscious enough not to comment, and to try apologies.

But someone interrupted with, "Our *englisch* better than your *deutsch* is, *ja*? *Englisch* speak, then."

"Usually the way," said Matt wrily. He was so weak still that when no one held him up he fell back on to the velvet. Velvet? His hand stroked it. "Not somewhere in the past, am I? All this. It can't be—*now*?"

Someone laughed again. "Naturally. This is certainly 'now'."

Matt blinked. "Not a dream world? Well, at least they're not *Alpträume*."

"*Ach*, very good. No, the *Alpträume* are outside this room. Here, we do not deal in nightmares, only—" Someone stood over him, a hand touched his breast. "So: where do you get this, then?"

Matt squinted at his chest; not wounded, was he? "Oh, that." Vaguely he recalled pinning the cross upon himself, though before that nothing, yet. "Here . . . I think."

"Think?" Several pairs of eyes watched him narrowly.

Someone muttered for the second time, "I tell you, he is a spy."

The argument broke out again, but in such rapid German that Matt lost most of it. Someone was saying it was nonsense, if he were a spy all he had to do was turn them in; someone else was determined he'd been planted on them to learn more about resistance. Matt's mind was still so weary that it all seemed unimportant. His eyes wandered over the high white-painted room; the torches stuck in iron brackets; the slit-window, carefully covered with black cloth.

"I'm—here in the fortress?"

They were too busy arguing to listen. Suddenly he felt terrified. "What if the enemy hears you? Something horrible could happen." His lips trembled. Weakness . . . He bit them, savagely, till the blood came.

There was a silence. Then the first man, who had given him the wine, said almost indulgently, "You are as safe here as anyone can be. Here no one comes any more. They see a broken stone stairway, fallen timber. They look no more. Once or twice someone—investigated has." His voice grew grim. "Then Hans some action took. Two deaths by falling— careless, *nein*? And so a fortunate bad name."

There was a movement from the man who had accused Matt of spying. Certainly, this was careless talk before him! He shuddered. He could have gone that way, too.

"You had your protection. The *Ritterskreuz*. We drink to your fortune."

They drank, solemnly raising their glasses to him. Matt, feeling absurd in the bearskin, bowed above it in reply. He was starting to sort out these new companions, and made a mental note not to run foul of a stocky Saxon with the square- headed, square-handed look of the born fighter. They were dressed in a strange selection of garments, but all of them wore somewhere emblazoned a black cross, neatly sewn in place.

"I'm lucky enough to have found a new—*deutsche Orden*?"

There was a brief exchange of glances, some suspicious.

"European history and maths were my main subjects," Matt explained hurriedly. He drew a hand across his eyes. "Seems—so long ago."

"History is—the present. We make some—a little—now. How do they call you?"

"My name's Matt Harvester."

"Surnames, we do not use. I am Walther. And these: Hans, Joachim, Ludwig, Jakob, Friedrich, Klaus—" Matt barely heard him, for his head was spinning again. A mixture of wine and weakness. He was drowsing, couldn't help it; but something was nagging at his mind.

"Labour-gang. Search for me."

"We arrange."

Now he could sleep in peace. The last he heard was Hans's voice, demanding to be given his clothes; and as he went plunging over some dream-abyss he was still wondering why they should want anything so shoddy.

When he woke again he was feeling more revived, but frozen. The black cloth at the window had been drawn aside, and the light was that of chilly dawn. He had thrown off the bearskin and lay naked. Something colder than air slid against his skin. At least they'd trusted him enough to give him back the cross, and someone had slung it on a cord. After these cruel months it was luxury to wake without blows or kicks. He thought almost shamefacedly of his comrades, and with an instinctive movement huddled beneath the bearskin.

Walther, who had sprawled dozing in a chair, opened his eyes like someone accustomed to sleep on the *qui vive.*

"*Wie geht's?*"

"It's just the cold—" Matt bit his lip again. No complaining.

Walther smiled wearily. "It will be cold until these slavers go. Since two nights we light not a fire."

"You do have them, then? That's why this room was warmer."

"Yes—And we have some food and wine. A little. We hope your friends go soon." Matt recognised an undercurrent of anxiety.

"Not my friends. And we weren't long, anywhere. We— you couldn't rescue the other slaves?" But he wasn't surprised when Walther shook his head.

"*Unmöglich.* For each vanishing, bodies must provided be."

Matt was appalled. "Someone was killed last night—for me?"

Walther raised a reassuring hand. "*Na, na!* Still peasants die of starvation—a few. So last night we arranged—your suicide! From the battlement. Who farther than your clothes looks? At detail Hans is specialist."

Matt thought that Hans's talents weren't exactly those one was taught to admire at school; and he shivered as he thought of what might have happened to himself if Walther's instinct hadn't accepted him as genuine.

"We're back in the Dark Ages," he said slowly.

"*Ja.* But I tell you, Matt—I, whose studies in philosophy and astronomy were—that all things and ages in this world of conjurors' illusions both light and dark are; though sometimes one more apparent is. You do not hide things, always, with fine living."

"It's a kinder illusion, though."

"*Ach!* Who needs illusion? We are men."

Matt's teeth were chattering. "Walther," he said, grinning, "you've reincarnated from Sparta. Anyway, I'd sooner have illusion than this bearskin's fleas." He scratched.

Walther merely yawned, and smiled. "To scratch will warm you! And, Matt, do not impatient be. When these slavers go, then comes news of how things are outside."

"But how?"

"Sleep, now. *Na,* you have many, many questions to answer, when day comes." He said it pleasantly enough, but added: "You have not passed our tests, my friend."

It was three days before Matt was passed as "clean". He was amazed at how many questions had been framed to test his honesty. When one questioner finished, another took over. Who, what, when, why ... They were specially interested in his taste for languages. French, Spanish, Italian, as well as his bad German and Pandemotic. What job had he hoped for?

"I've told you already," he said desperately, head in hands. "It's helpful. In—in research. In staying places while one researches. And why would the enemy put me where my knowledge is so weak?"

"In order that you should seem to be a convincing member

of that labour-gang, of course. Details, please, of where you studied."

"But I've told you."

"Again."

"But—"

"No 'buts'. Again."

Walther took no part in the questioning, but was always present. He was treated with a certain ceremonious respect, although he mixed freely with the others and seemed to demand no special treatment. Matt, wrapped in his bearskin— an itchy business—felt at a disadvantage. Now and then he asked for clothes, but was ignored. And when he demanded: "Have the slavers gone?" no one replied.

But on the fourth morning he woke to find Friedrich by him, holding out a bundle. He was actually smiling.

"Now you may dress. We hope they fit."

And later in the day Walther drew him aside to ask very seriously: "Do you wish to join this Order?"

Matt was taken aback. This was a bit awkward. Poverty, obedience, even military orders, now he might accept all these. But he wasn't monkly enough for some archaic vows of chastity! Not even in this hopeless situation. In England Jan could still be alive; could be . . . "I—yes; but how far—"

"We are not the knights' direct descendants, you understand. Just, we take the name for—for—" His English failed him.

"Hardcore resistance? Like under Hit—" Matt stopped. It didn't seem polite.

"Matt, my friend, you are so nice, so correct! Under Hitler, *natürlich*. You must find this modern life very difficult." Walther was definitely laughing at him, though straightfaced. It surprised Matt, who liked and admired him but had thought him humourless. Perhaps he had a different brand. "You must be more tough."

"I am tough." Matt was nettled.

"Body yes, mind no. Hans shocks you, *nicht*? But Hans is

necessary. A Hans appears, is necessary, in this type of situation. Always. Listen, your slavers have gone, and the district safer is. For you, too. If you wish it, stay; but then you join us."

"You'd trust me to leave, knowing what I do?"

"I would. Some others, no."

There was a silence.

"I'll stay," said Matt.

"Total commitment?"

"Yes. I—I think I didn't stumble in here quite by chance."

Walther nodded. He said. "*Ja*—it was odd, the *Kreuz*. We took everything we could find. Strange, we should miss one."

Matt wondered what the old monks of war would have made of his admittance to the Order: a brief promise to obey, to act only for the Order, to put its interests always above his own; never to desert or imperil it, on pain of death. (On pain of Hans, he thought.) From these promises he could only be released by three members of the Order acting in agreement, of whom the *Hochmeister* must be one. As he had long since guessed, the *Hochmeister* was Walther. When the small ceremony was over he expected to be given immediate dragon-slaying tasks. He was soon deflated.

"First order," said Walther briskly, "improve your German; it lacks. Ludwig, who was a schoolmaster, will make you a full course before you go outside these rooms." He smiled at Matt's expression. "*Ach*, you do not just join an Order—you return to school, my friend."

They also taught him to find his way about their hiding-place: its thick-walled rooms, its traps, its ancient passages leading underground. He was amazed, and they laughed at his amazement—those who didn't watch him with sullen resentment because Walther trusted him and had admitted him so quickly to their company.

His pride found it hard to accept occasional rebuffs. Once, he came on Joachim, in charge of commissariat, talking with

Heinz. "—plan a raid soon," he was saying. "It grows harder all the time. No one must ask why these supplies disappear."

"Nor who wants them," agreed Heinz. He turned, saw Matt watching, and walked away.

"You'll go outside?" asked Matt. "Can I come?" He was beginning to fret at inactivity; and verbs.

"No, Matt, no. And you should not have listened." Joachim folded his map, and followed Heinz.

A day or two later Matt was in company with Walther and some others, and asked impulsively: "What's beyond that locked door, there—at the bottom of the stairs?"

"Too many questions, Matt. Please remember you are still at school."

"*And* on probation?"

"If you like." Walther's voice was remote, chill. He turned away. "Here is Ludwig, looking for you."

"Back to school, I suppose."

"You resent it? We ask small things, at present; and your German improves."

Matt flushed. "I apologise."

Walther nodded his dismissal, and Matt followed Ludwig to the small room where they worked together. "Hitler's filthy feet," he said darkly beneath his breath.

"*Was ist?*"

"A—a sort of swearword I made up."

Ludwig burst out laughing. "Believe me, we are no neo-Fascist group! The regrettable Führer shored up Marienburg in the northeast as a show place, but the *Orden*'s spirit is far, far older; *and* attracted men like the Archduke Karl, whom even Napoleon respected."

"Napoleon could be cruel enough." Matt spoke hesitantly in case discussion wasn't in his contract. "And one sometimes feels great men are the scourge of humanity."

"Tell that to Walther—he has lively views on what really causes the scourging. And Walther himself is a great man, you know; he is so manysided. Friedrich too is clever, oh, very, very clever, a linguist, and expert in—" he stumbled over the words, shot a glance at Matt, and added quickly: "Did you know that Walther, apart from all his other skills, holds a pilot's licence too? He loves to drive fast cars, to ski—"

"He's a paragon," said Matt crossly. (*What* was Friedrich expert in? Had it anything to do with what lay beyond that locked door at the bottom of the stairs?) "But he hasn't discussed these things with me. He doesn't *talk* of anything at all. It's all 'do this, do that', like being at the beck and call of some medieval abbot."

"You should have ended that sentence with the verb."

Matt gave up. But later in the week Walther himself took him aside, and asked: "Matt—would you perhaps say you are the type to volunteer for ambulance work, in total war? I mean, more an endurer, than a fighter? One who does not really believe in resisting force with force."

"I don't like violence, certainly. What good has it ever done?"

Walther looked past him, absently. "We don't know what it does, really. You are an historian—so *you* know that all civilisations rise on the ruins of the old. Is war the frost that clears the ground for a new growth? Men have always said they wanted peace—and fought to prove it. What is your opinion: today are our enemies the new barbarians—or an embryo new culture?"

"Barbarians," said Matt without hesitation. "They kill and lie, and distort, right through. For greed. How can you build on that? At least, what you build will grow crooked."

He thought Walther was looking at him as though he had passed some type of test. "Well—these barbarians we harry. That's why we fight on."

"Yet there's so little we can do."

"We live—while they wish us dead. That's already some small victory. But if we die, we become a legend! Perhaps. It's surprising, what power some legends have . . ." Matt shivered, and heard Walther say abruptly: "I have decided.

You shall be Friedrich's assistant. He, too, is no natural fighter."

"I'm not a coward!"

"Nor is Friedrich. Nor do I think he wants you as his assistant; you must tread carefully. But the art of resistance is to use the right person in the right place." Walther sighed. Perhaps he was thinking that "resistance" was a rather grand word for this isolated cell of his Order that had bravely established itself at Bad Mergentheim, in the heart of an empty countryside regularly ravaged by their enemy.

"You don't use it to transmit, surely?"

"We listen. Or it listens. See, it listens now." A small red light was showing at eye-level.

"So it has a built-in computer. Very cunning. But how do we run it? Not on torches."

"Walther has commanded me to explain some things to you. Please examine this map of Europe."

Feeling very snubbed, Matt studied it. "You've drawn lines to—Other transmitters?" Friedrich nodded. "But you can't know they're Resistance ones, can you?"

"No. They can be fly-traps."

"So you never answer."

"Not till Walther commands."

"And if we can do this, other people may." Matt examined the map more closely. "You've taken out one, near the Ardèche."

"Very amateur. Never moved, always transmitted at the same time. An obvious code. *Kaput.* These others, they sounded innocent enough. But then I noticed something strange about them. I set the computer to work out some calculations, and this is what I had." Friedrich spread out another paper: a tracing of the map; this time, instead of lines, it bore asterisks and numbers. "A picture, perhaps, of places where people do not agree with their new over-lords."

"It looks like star constellations!" Matt frowned over them. "These numbers, they refer to times?"

"No."

"Mmmm . . . Intervals of time?"

"*Prima.*" Friedrich's manner held more warmth. "At least Walther is right about your quickness. These transmissions are regularly irregular, and ordinary enough. Yet there was something else about their pattern, built in, that I discovered: the announcers would stumble over some word and repeat it. And after that—Well, there are secret messages in the reports —and always placed immediately after the apologies for an error. The next words would carry the superimposed code. All is now clear?"

Matt groaned slightly. "What are the open and obvious sendings about?"

"Oh, just weather reports, road conditions. First in that ridiculously inflated Pandemotic of theirs."

"*Lingua Freaka,*" muttered Matt to himself.

"Then in the language of the country for which the reports are meant."

"But the enemy would know if weather reports should be coming from these positions!"

"Naturally."

"Then your scheme collapses, doesn't it?" said Matt, feeling that Friedrich's maps were worse than Ludwig's verbs. He stared down at them, and tried again: "These ordinary ones: they're enemy sendings, but being subtly bent?"

"You have it. I repeat, Matt: the messages are in the phrases, after the announcer has made his deliberate mistake. It took time—and headaches—to work it out."

"It must have done! But repeated errors would have warned anyone, surely?"

"Probably overlooked—because they're never in the first versions: those in the enemy's own jargon. . . . And even then the code's not simple—I fed my guesses into the computer, and it gave me: length of sentences, standing for good old-time morse—long, short, long. Short, short, long. All these people have to do is rephrase weather reports to suit themselves, and the message emerges."

"Lord, it's good. And no one would monitor them." Matt looked at Friedrich with reluctant respect; then frowned. "But it's too complex. You'd need an actor speaking, with a trained memory. And one who could memorise the Freaks' jargon as well."

"Freaks?" Friedrich looked bewildered, until Matt explained, and then he laughed.

"No," he said. "It would be normal enough to *read* weather reports. And—for the readings in German, French or English —to rephrase them. I should have told you that these secondary readings are certainly by natives of the countries; plainly people the—the Freaks!—trust. Ostensibly collaborators, I would guess, in that case; who would receive messages from couriers of resistance cells, and then put them out. Thus a network is gradually established."

"I'm not bright enough for this sort of caper," complained Matt.

"Walther is seldom mistaken." Friedrich handed him a paper. "Try this, it's a peculiar one."

"Crosswords too? Make things easy, don't they! Have you deciphered it?"

"The first line seems simple; the fourth could be important to us."

Matt read aloud:

> *"The forests are dark,*
> *He flies them. Water divides,*
> *Men and women separate.*
> *Banquets to share.*
> *Entrenched, without communication.*
> *Word without delay is best.*
> *The great man expanding, he who gives shelter,*
> *Lies drowned, holding the key.*

Huh! Sounds like bad Chinese poetry. And urgent. Dark forests—Schwarzwald?"

"Seemingly."

"And he's been turfed out."

"Yes. And we want his whereabouts."

"Water divides—men and women separate. Left their Rhinemaidens in the Rhine?"

"Perhaps. But it's a long river," said Friedrich solemnly. "Nothing's clear."

"Except that he'll share his foodstore with the lucky winner! Try the Danube."

"Long, too."

"And who's this great man, expanding? Sounds like a local *Gauleiter*. He ate their food—so they knocked him off. Simple. Find his corpse, and there's a marked map in his pocket."

Friedrich looked at him with a pained expression.

"You joke. Memorise this, please. I would destroy it."

Matt studied the paper for a few seconds, then handed it back. Almost casually he asked, "And nothing out of England, ever?"

Friedrich shook his head. "All seems *kaput*. Finished."

Matt swallowed. "*Kaput*. Yes."

"And unless we can link up, or break out in some way soon, we shall be *kaput* too."

"I think Walther aims at setting up a legend!" Matt sighed. "We'd plenty in England—the sleeping king who will return, etc. It hasn't helped."

"*Ach*, the Matter of Britain! We have our great Siegfried. And the even greater Charlemagne, who also sleeps until we need him." Friedrich looked smug, as if Charlemagne were his personal property. It nettled Matt, whose chosen subject for his thesis had been Charlemagne and the Holy Roman Empire—"The Charismatic Crown", he'd called it, and still remembered uneasily his tutor's sardonic comments, and his own hot defence of his enthusiasm.

"Friedrich—we all need him. And that talisman he always

wore, with the bit of the True Cross. Very powerful, it was said to be. I remember seeing it once, at Rheims. I suppose the enemy's got hold of it—and the crown. A pity—it might have helped us against these new barbarians. (We don't want a swastika anyway," he added, under his breath.)

"I've heard of that talisman, because Walther spoke of it," said Friedrich. "He has great interest in that type of thing, and he tried to find out what became of it, when the disasters happened—but it was too late. I believe someone told him it had disappeared."

"Let's hope the old Emperor rose up in wrath, and grabbed it back again. But I'm afraid he's sleeping soundly. That's the trouble with these tranquillisers—they're too efficient."

Friedrich stared at Matt blankfaced. "You'll concentrate now upon the message."

A touch of the old Teutonics, said Matt sadly to himself.

Towards nightfall he was standing on the battlements with Walther when a patrol of K'an Si Vultures shot above the Eastern horizon and hurtled overhead in six sudden silver flashes. Their ominous cigar shapes, split flight tails, and short curved-back wings were blurred to oblong streaks of light.

"They go like the crack of doom, don't they? Sometimes I think time marches backwards here—it's they that are out of place, not we."

Walther nodded. Wrapped in a black cloak, black-haired, black-bearded, he was certainly a medieval-looking figure. Down below them in the courtyard a late rose, pale as flesh, struggled to live against the December dankness. Even up here they could smell the muddy earth smells, and the coming frosty night.

"Some things will probably never change till the world's end."

"It ends for each of us so quickly."

"Don't be melancholy, Matt. We try to do something, while

we live. Your German improves already! Have you deciphered Friedrich's conundrum yet?" Matt shook his head. "Then try again. We didn't rescue you so that you could droop about the battlements looking poetic." A smile softened Walther's words.

But it wasn't till the early hours that Matt got it. He had been half drowsing when buried memories rose. Walther was asleep on the opposite side of the room. Matt trod warily between other sleeping forms, and shook him by the shoulder.

"*Himmel, Matt, was ist?*"

"Come outside. I think I've got it. Have you a map up here?"

Half-protestingly Walther followed him from the room. "A small-scale pocket one."

"That's no good. Come down to Friedrich's lair." As they descended, Matt said: "Listen; what about Ludwig?"

Walther yawned. "Asleep—if not on guard."

"No, *no*. Ludwig II, of Bavaria. Last true king in the nineteenth century, Verlaine called him. He was great, all right: inflated, certainly. And he was drowned."

Walther stiffened. "Drowned—I'd forgotten, my historian. One of the Bavarian lakes, wasn't it?"

"The Starnsee, I think. If *he* holds the key, then it's one of those fantasy places of his we're looking for."

"Hmm," said Walther. "Well, continue. Which one?"

"We need Friedrich's maps."

The cold downstairs was excruciating, but they were oblivious of it. Matt drummed with his fingers on the map. "Linderhof . . . Hochschwandau . . . It was because his maddening mother settled into Hochschwandau that Ludwig thought of building Neuschwanstein, to escape her."

"There *was* something about men and women separating," Walther reminded him, sounding more awake.

"Ye-es. But look *here*." Matt's pointing finger indicated a spot on Chiemsee. "Ludwig's last and greatest folly, his imitation Versailles: Herrenchiemsee, on the Herreninsel. And there was another island near it, with a convent—Fraueninsel. That's where the water divides, and the men and women separate, I'm certain. It's an entrenched position, all right: windbreaks of trees, and that enormous lake. I should have thought of it—I've been to both those islands."

Walther was looking at him with amused approval. "*We* should have thought of it. What it is to be a foreign tourist!"

If Matt expected acclamation the next morning, he was disappointed. Friedrich said dryly, "Good. Possible." And made a small mark on his map.

"Can't we—get a message to them, some way?"

"Walther will decide. But you know we won't transmit, from here."

"I thought, maybe—the food's so important."

Friedrich looked at him. Matt felt very small, very greedy, and not at all fitted to the Order.

A day or so later: "Where is Jakob?" he asked. "And Heinz?" He looked round him at closed faces, and felt smaller still.

"Resentful?" said Walther to him later.

"No—Well, yes . . . You see—"

"Believe me, I do. You discovered something; we use your knowledge. What do you expect—a vote of thanks? To take decisions—and go yourself?"

"At least not to be treated like a child," said Matt heatedly.

"You are thinking childishly. You don't understand the enemy's ruthlessness."

"Oh, don't I?"

"Ah—you've seen them torture?"

"Not exactly, no—"

"If anyone leaves here, Matt, for any reason, only a few of us know when and where they're going. Otherwise lives could be endangered. You find it hard to accept things without questioning, don't you? This can be strength. For us, it's your worst weakness. Unhesitating obedience to the *Hoch-*

meister was always a major rule of our Order—of all monkish orders, too. Don't tell me you're no monk—I would believe you!" Walther grinned, and the grave *Hochmeister* disappeared. He looked younger, and comradely. Matt smiled, though with restraint.

"You left your girl in England?"

Matt stared. "How—"

"It seemed likely. She wasn't—dead?"

Matt put a hand to his forehead. His crazy insistence on his own way! It seemed nothing to do with reason any more, just sheer stupidity.

"Forget I asked you—and after I warned *you* against tactless questioning."

"She was alive," said Matt wretchedly. "She—she couldn't agree with my reasoning—afterwards, I could have kicked myself, thinking how I should have stuck with her—with them—no matter what."

"So at least she was with other people?"

"A small group. Hiding. No one over twenty." Matt's eyes met Walther's, pleadingly. "Tom—one of them—called me a collaborator. He couldn't—or wouldn't—understand that I —I wanted to build resistance from the inside. I couldn't believe I wouldn't get my chance—then I landed up after all in a slave gang!"

"Well, we don't accept facts here, either." Walther's face was sombre.

"Nor do I, now! You're not regretting you took me on, since I've told you?"

Walther put a reassuring hand on his shoulder. "*Na*, Matt, *na*! There were very, very many mistakes made, by very clever men, before they—Freaks, you called them?—subjugated Europe. Our only hope is that *they* may make *their* mistakes one day, instead. What was her name?"

"Whose?" Matt was confused by the sudden change of subject. "Oh—Jan. Just the two of us, we had a code—in case we could ever get in touch—a secret word-signal, Orion, to show when messages were true." And Jan probably dead, lying in some ditch! He swallowed, and said wretchedly, "It seems pretty stupid, now." Walther would think him childish again. But Walther's sympathetic silence accepted his pain, his stupidity.

"Jakob and Heinz have gone to Chiemsee."

Matt stared, thinking: I shall never understand him! And after those pathetic confidences, too.

"Thanks for telling me."

"We had a small van. Hidden. Petrol, too. They travel by night, of course."

"They'll bring back food? I shall feel to blame if—"

Walther silenced him with, "Many things can happen, apart from a wrong guess at Herrenchiemsee. Don't think about it."

But Matt couldn't help thinking of that unique baroque palace, strange and lonely beyond its woods and patterned, melancholy gardens. When he had been there the tourists had driven in a kind of horse-drawn buggy, while alpine cows had moved gently nearby, their cowbells giving out a metallic tinkle. Perhaps those bells sounded still, clink-clinking through the pasture while desperate men talked of ambushes and armaments . . . Strange dreams, different from mad Ludwig's. Poor Jakob and Heinz, would they get lost in one?

"But Walther—on my guess you sent two men with no form of signal first?"

Walther shrugged. "Bad Mergentheim stays silent still. That is my judgment. Friedrich waits for you."

Matt's resentment had vanished. He went clattering downstairs.

Friedrich was wearing headphones, and held up a warning hand as his right moved across a page, jotting. "There—" Matt was motioned to a seat beside him, and slipped into it, picking up the spare set of headphones. At last Friedrich leaned back and took off his own, wearily.

"Routine stuff. Leave most of it to the computer."

"Right. What were you putting down, though?"

"Thought I had something, briefly, out of England."

"*England?*"

"It was nothing, Matt. A mistake. Gibberish—even just atmospherics! Now, please listen particularly for"—his pencil described an arc over north-eastern Europe—"Here—and here. Let nothing pass, will you?"

"Nothing."

Friedrich nodded and, taciturn as ever, went away.

It was a very ordinary evening's work. There seemed to be no news out of anywhere that the computer couldn't deal with on its own. Matt yawned, strove to keep awake, watched, listened, and occasionally jotted.

It wasn't till his third night on duty when he was alone again, that without warning three words came across the ether, so amazingly that at first he barely understood what he had heard.

"Golden Valley, Orion," stuttered the tiny voice again, hundreds of miles away; and was silent, swallowed up into the immensity of the night. It took all Matt's strength of mind, everything that Friedrich had dinned into him in the last long weeks, not to reply.

It couldn't have happened, anyway. He'd told Walther about Jan, and his mind was playing tricks on him, making him hear her voice. Oh, he wasn't fit for what the Order expected of him, not at all. It was good that Friedrich would be taking over before he, Matt, could start hearing angel voices singing a Hallelujah Chorus, or sloopy Soul music from the seventies! By dawn his ears felt permanently enlarged—but there was nothing more. Only endless chatter from Freaks to Freaks, intermingled with a crackle of messages from one squadron of K'an Si Vultures to another.

6 ❈ Golden Valley

"It must be nearly Christmas Day," said Alastair. "Does anyone know? Odd we've still got the time, but no one seems to have managed the date. We need some sort of Christmas to suit the way we're living now, don't we?"

"Sacrifice. You, Char—under some mistletoe, if we can find it." Tom squatted on his heels and poked at the thread hanging from her spindle. "Not much use with this, are you? Look at Jan's. Yours is full of lumps, and then so thin it breaks at a touch—see?"

Charlie sprang to her feet, dropping the primitive clay and stick spindle, so that the clay shattered from the stem. "There! I never manage the foul stuff anyhow. And after all that picking over wormy sheep, too. You try next time, Tom."

"Learn patience, Charlie-girl," teased Clanger. "I'll make you another spindle."

"Thanks, no."

"Not doing your share, Char," said Jan, firmly.

"The boys can have a go, then. I'll herd the sheep, keep watch, dig *and* hoe. I'll fight Freaks, if they come. 'M *not* going to spin and knit. Clang can teach me about electronics. I'll be his helper, won't I, Clang?"

"Know what, Fireball? You'd have felt my Mum's hand on your backside. You're spoilt," said Clanger self-righteously.

"Didn't keep you out of nick, did she?"

"Not for want of trying. You going to help Jan?"

"Not spinning any mucky thread, or—"

Clanger rose with his deceptive slowness, picked up Charlie, and deposited her on a gorsebush. "How's that for mistletoe?"

"Ow—you beast! Ow, oh, let me up, *ow* Clanger, don't."

"Going to help Jan?" Clanger bounced Charlie gently. "No, Jan, she gotter learn, an' someone gotter bring her up, even here. Make you 'nother spindle, Char, shall I?"

"Ow! I'll try—hate you, Clang!"

"That's right, make a woman out of you yet, I will. When we're married I'm not having fids of sheep tail in my shirts, am I?" Clanger nodded amiably at Jan and ambled off as Charlie rose from the gorse, rubbing her backside.

"We're going to need every bit of warmth we can get," said Jan, tactfully ignoring the defeat. "It's not been really cold yet—even up here." She glanced across the narrow sunlit valley at the hills, towering and rounded as cumulus clouds, and masking further hills towards the sea.

"Alastair spins, Char. No one respects him any the less for it, either. Anyway, Clanger's clay won't dry out at once. Why not see if you can help Bill with the heli-nets?"

Charlie made a face, but went, dragging her feet. The valley floor was pockmarked with flat white stones, oval and polished-looking, and there was a sound of rushing water from its stream. Charlie flipped a stone into it, and thought of fishing when they had first arrived; of picking nettles for soup; of whether it would freeze entirely when the snows came.

Snows. North winds howling among hilltops, grey sky sitting on them like a pressure-cooker's lid. Those old Romans must have come this way, to the Wall. History wasn't her thing, exactly, but you couldn't get away from it, up here. It was Percy country, and Arthur's, so some folks said (that was according to Bill). Looking about her she peopled the slopes with fugitives, men with wild hair, daggers—and wolfskins? Well, there were no wolves now—except the Freaks. She'd behaved like a small kid about the spinning. She'd forgive Clanger. Soon.

"Hi, Charlie. Come to help?"

She toiled up the gulley to her left, and sank down by the entrance to Bill's tiny camouflaged watch-hut. It was too dark inside for him to work there, and he had the heli-net spread out on the threshold stone while he skilfully netted rush fibres in and out with a big rough wooden needle.

"Got another needle?"

"Here. Start that end of the hole."

Charlie began to thread dead leaves along a dried rush.

"When the winds blow, the nets'll tear every day."

"Then we'll mend them every day. The helis must be hidden."

Charlie sighed. Adventure! They might as well be back at school. Tom had been foul today, refused to take her hunting with Mule and Hoppo; he'd said there were too many jobs requiring muscle for men to take on spinning too. She'd argued in vain, with no backing from anyone.

"Oh, roll on the spring! The helis won't need nets then, when the leaves are back. Why don't we make the prisoners mend them—like sewing mailbags?"

The two heli pilots were a source of headache; obviously they couldn't be set free; and the second answer was one to shrink from, though Fox and one original Skullganger were heartily for it. Fox, as Wolf said with his glinting smile, *would* simplify. In the meantime they were a nuisance, to put it mildly. They had to be fed—"Why?" asked Fox—and guarded.

Wolf had dealt with the problem by keeping them in Heli One, after its nucleo-radic equipment and self-fuelling gear had been removed. The entry hatch was secured by a booby trap which could only be neutralised from outside, although even so he felt it safer for someone to keep constant watch. Sometimes the pilots were allowed out one by one to do an hour's digging or roofing. Otherwise they spent their time playing chess with a set carved by Leo, or sleeping, or just glaring from the cockpit. The two angry, watchful faces were a sore trial to everyone. "Maybe they'll wilt and die soon," said Fox hopefully. "The b's. And they're a danger. Don't say I didn't warn you."

"We don't. Only we don't know what to do with them."

"Serpents in Eden," said Jan.

"Eden," scoffed Charlie. "You're so sentimental—and after all that's happened. You're good, too—you even like spinning, it's unnatural."

Jan had flushed deeply, thinking of her guilty secret. She, and she alone, had endangered them all, by sending out that brief, hopeless message in search of Matt. Of course it couldn't have happened if Clanger hadn't used his skills to set up the nucleo-radic heli gear on a nearby hilltop—and then fallen for her guileless enquiries about how to use it! And now Charlie was looking at her too closely, but luckily Fox distracted her attention with: "Well, what's Alastair think about our prisoners? Shouldn't they be put down, kid?"

Alastair paused in his spinning, and reflected. Charlie mightn't think it, but their gentle ribbing of his gift and insights often made him squirm. He was sometimes so conscious of helplessness, and of being almost the youngest of the party; and yet at others was overshadowed by that other, wiser self, who didn't speak, who only knew . . . And that other self had lately drawn him into an experience which still shook him when he thought about it . . . He didn't want to scare them by telling them bluntly that the testing times ahead were likely to be more than some of them could stand, and that trying to see round corners couldn't keep them safe.

Like Jan, his thoughts went to the setting up of the heli nucleo-radic equipment on the eastern hill. Clanger had carried him up there, and given him the headphones; and he'd listened enthralled until suddenly, between interchanges of Freak stations, had come a strange, distant music, which grew gradually in volume till it was vibrating against his eardrums in a way that made him involuntarily cry out.

"What's up, kid?" Clanger had asked. But Alastair had shaken his head, half-hypnotised by the strange, urgent,

wordless communication, and the power of the half-compre-
hended messages:

"—a gathering together—things of light and dark—" (Or
was it: we're gathering together things of light?)"—still too
far—power of the talisman . . . betrayal, sacrifice, have—
courage—defeat comes before—not avoidable . . . the dark
power must be spent before the turning—the turning—" And
then the sound throbbed on continuous but meaningless,
fading until it swelled again briefly as "Orion—tower of the
Zodiac" and then was swamped under a jabber of Freakish
tongues.

"Ain't never seen anyone react so violent to my work,"
Clanger had said, rather gratified, as Alastair had pulled off
the headphones, shaking, and murmuring, "Not like anything
I ever heard before . . ."

And so when Fox's voice said again insistently: "The
prisoners: shouldn't they be put down, kid? *You* ought to
know—tune in for Foxy, can't you?" Alastair had winced,
thinking the joke was too near the bone. And he couldn't even
tell Tom about the coming bad times, because Tom had
turned woundingly cold, and would probably have answered,
"Oh—try that sort of stuff on Wolf, he's your real fall guy.
I'm going hunting."

"I don't feel the prisoners are an *immediate* danger, Fox,"
Alastair had answered cautiously. "And killing doesn't always
solve things, anyway."

So the prisoners were still there, and Charlie was complaining for the hundredth time that they should mend the
heli nets.

"Best they don't even have whopping wooden bodkins like
these," said Bill, threading deftly. Charlie paused to suck a
splinter from her thumb. Staring about her at suncapped hills
rising against the gathering blue-grey, she murmured,
"December! And I saw a wild rose the other day, would you
believe it?"

"It won't last."

"No. And Bill—it's like playing dolls' houses. Or—or kids with model farms. Half-wild goats, and their disgusting smelly cheese. Leftover sheep for wool and salted mutton, and beastly gruel from those Sussex oats. And Jan loves it! We'll be having singsongs next."

"What d'you want, Char? Wolves?"

"Don't laugh. It can't go on, can it? That's what I meant. Think of snow, here. It'll be cold, and dark. Jan won't love it then, will she? It will be *worse* than dull. Jan could get sick and die." The thought of Jan dying was awful. "And Bill, one day the Freaks'll come over the hills and find us, won't they? They won't have written off this place for ever, will they? Tom says they must be north-east on the oil rigs."

"Char, this doesn't sound like you. More like how Jan used to talk."

"Jan's got stronger and I'm weaker." Charlie rubbed her gorse-scratched rump reflectively. "What wouldn't I give for a hot bath."

"Yes, you've really weakened."

"And you know what? Keep thinking of mucky poetry, too."

"Something *is* wrong. Hi—don't pinch my leaves."

"It's not so bad as most—learnt it at school. It's about that drip Arthur and all those other drips he went around with, till he got caught up with sexy Gwynnie and that did for him, poor boob. An' then he fought and died."

"You'll be just right for Clanger, I can hear Clang in every word. So what's the bit that made this deep impression?"

Charlie was staring dreamily towards the hilltops. "What? Oh—'And all day long the noise of battle rolled, among the mountains by the winter sea.' That could almost be here, couldn't it?"

" 'Fallen in Lyonesse about their lord.' "

" 'Fallen in Lyonesse'." Charlie rolled the words round her tongue, with relish. "I like that. I really do. I'd like to be someone's lord, and have them die all round me, and then go down centuries an' centuries as—"

132

"—that drip Charlie, who got caught up with sexy Clanger and that did for her, poor boob? I wonder who'd write you up, Char, and what they'd make of you—and this?" Bill swept an arm to include the valley, the leafless copse and helicopters, the dotted half-hidden huts, and a few meagre-looking sheep. "Funny, it was probably Badon they were writing up, really. And then it grew and grew."

"What's Badon?"

"Arthur's last known battle—for Celtic Britain, if he really lived. And if he did he was some tough captain, resourceful and brave, maybe a bit dishonest—there's some very strange anti-hero legend about his stealing pigs. He knew how to fight to the bitter end, though, and the Christians put the Cross of Christ upon his shoulders. Maybe it was there, but—"

"Maybe it was a little poor thin kind of life, like ours, like thin gruel! Only with something in it like a seed that grew and grew—I tell you what, that sort of thing's very strong, isn't it? I mean, look how Alastair managed everyone when they got him caught up with those old Templars."

"Alastair has a sort of greatness, I think. Wolf too, sometimes. Being human, I expect Arthur's was pretty 'sometimes' too."

Charlie felt a pang of jealousy, but generosity conquered.

"Yes, they have—and I bet that's what bothers Tom. And you know what? Hoppo's very selfish about rabbits, when he catches them! But he gives them up to Wolf, without a growl." She sighed. "He loves Wolf more than me. And that makes me as jealous as poor Tom . . ."

Jan sat spinning dreamily after Charlie left, almost forgetting to watch for sudden silver streaks on the horizon. Nice to be sitting in the sun, outside the cave—

The cave. Oh Lord, the stew! She dropped her spindle, and ran. An acrid smell met her at the cave's mouth. From shadows beyond the cooking area came Grouse's fretful voice:

"Jan, you dreamer—I called an' called, an' you just went on gawping into space."

"Couldn't you have added water?" Jan fell to her knees beside the pot and peered in at a gluey mess.

"You left the pail by the entrance."

"Oh *Lord*." She fetched it, poured in a generous supply, and sniffed. "Not really burned, is it? Shall I add more wild garlic?"

"Add yourself, before Tom kills you. The way he netted those partridges grows each time he tells it."

"So many to feed, and I have to burn the stew."

"Char would have laughed."

"But Tom's so prickly, sometimes. You all right, Grouse?"

"Fine." He had said the same thing every day, with less conviction. He had refused the greater comfort of the second helicopter, because he wanted people round him, eating, laughing, talking. Stupid to make a fuss about growing weaker, when they'd probably all be dead by spring.

But it would be good to see the spring again. It would have been fine to see the forsythia that had sprouted outside the kitchen window of the council house where he'd quarrelled so much with his Mum that eventually he'd up and left. Mum. Even to quarrel again . . .

He moved restlessly. "That was a great idea of Wolf's, to get the smoke channelled through lots of slanting holes among the tree roots—but sometimes it makes the place cold as—"

"Help you nearer the fire?"

Grouse shook his head and leaned back against the cave's wall, while Jan stirred the pot gloomily. "We ought to do some cave drawings," he said. "For folks to remember us by."

"What folks? Those Freaks won't want to remember us."

"We're crushed now, but maybe all sorts of folks every-where—"

"Grouse, these are modern times. Freaks've got the weapons."

"Look what we done already—with Wolf an' Alastair. See,

134

Freak might eat Freak! People always squabble, don't they?"

"Who cares, now?"

"I do! 'Cos I'm—Something to survive, that's what people want, isn't it? That's why they have kids—something of themselves. World to go on."

"*This* world?"

"Any world! Life, that's the thing. You ought to have a child, Jan. You an' Bill, or you an' Tom. 'Cos Char's a bit young still. A kid to fight for us."

He smiled crookedly.

Jan said nothing, but thought of Matt. She didn't want a child, not now.

The cave was a natural one, deep among a knot of tree roots on the valley's western side. Once it had had another entrance, to a pit where stone used to be quarried for the local walls; but now that side was blocked by fallen earth. At night it provided shelter, and some warmth. The fragile camouflaged huts in the open, built to act as hiding-places in daytime emergency, took only two people, and were almost as cold as living in the open. (There was Heli Two, but Wolf said: who could tell when they might need it? And if they slept in it someone might grow careless and burn it, or something.)

Wolf, Hoppo and Ox sat nearest the entrance. Wolf and Ox gnawing on partridge, Hoppo hopeful but controlled.

"There's not a single bone that wouldn't pierce your insides," Charlie told him; but Hoppo wagged and concentrated.

"This stew tastes odd; sort of smoky. Is that mixing hare and partridge?" demanded Tom. And Jan quickly mentioned Grouse's idea about cave drawings.

"We could make up a ballad too. Our history in verse, for these 'ere primitive times. Like they used to," suggested Bill. "Who's literary?"

"Ox," said Wolf wickedly. "Pride of the form, weren't you, Oxy?"

Ox chewed reflectively, and said he knew a limerick that made old Smithers turn colour like a mandril's backside.

"We don't want to be turned. What we need's something *re*-fined. Set it to a harp, didn't they?"

"We could make recorders," suggested Leo. "Something to do in the evenings."

"Who'll play one, though?"

"I can," said Tom, unexpectedly thawing. "And what about the girls? Who's got a lovely pure voice fit for a cathedral? Not you, Char, I bet. You probably sing 'Down at the old Bull and Bush' in a Russian bass. Come on, Jan—sing for us."

"I couldn't start—"

"Clanger, then. Come on, Clang," encouraged Wolf.

Clanger bashfully cleared his throat, and began an ancient pop song. After a little while, when no one was watching her, Jan joined in. And Charlie began to clap in time. Soon everyone was singing, until Mule—who was on guard—came in to demand discretion. "Sounds like some old-time pop festival!"

"We'll definitely make that ballad," said Alastair in the pause. "Everyone can do a verse or two, then we'll put it together. In case we ever need—In case, one day, we want to remember this. We can keep it going too, a record, like a diary—"

There were moans of dissent, but Alastair was firm, and— 'Kid's away again', Wolf phrased it to himself.

After that, as Clanger said, the evenings were tougher than the days: all that brainwork. He himself proved to have an amazingly good ear and memory for verse: he provided a gripping section on the Skullgang's defeat, the last battle of London, and the epic flight. Jan, who had been told to describe early meetings and first Sussex days till Matt's departure, became hopelessly entangled, close to tears.

"It's nice you're bad at something, Jan," said Charlie kindly. "Doesn't make me feel such a clot. I've done the food

136

bit—listen: 'And what was very very good, was when they found a lot of food, they never would have found a bit, if Charlie hadn't searched for it.' Isn't that beautiful? What rhymes with Hoppo?"

"Don't waste bread rubbing out, Char," said Tom. "Leave us your whole masterwork."

"Why aren't you working, anyway? Alastair said—"

"Little brother hasn't been out hunting on his feet all day long, has he?"

There was a silence. Then Jan said hurriedly: "We're all tired, aren't we, Wolf?"

"What's the kid say?"

"If Tom doesn't want to tell the part before hitching up with Char and Bill and Jan, he needn't. *I* don't care," said Alastair with an expression of hurt dignity.

"I believe he did something pretty awful, then," Charlie declared. "Bet you were a proper worm, Tom, till you turned. But we won't hold it against you—you're quite nice sometimes now. So you might try a little harder."

Tom busied himself scraping mud from the side of his shoe with a hunting knife, and then strode out into the dark. Alastair looked after him anxiously.

"I love your tact, Char," said Bill. "You're born to cement tiny communities together. Better say you're sorry."

"I'm not. What d'you make of Tom, Al? After all, he's your brother, you should know."

"Past's past, whatever happened," said Alastair, in reserved tones. "And Tom saved Grouse, with Ox, didn't he? You're a terrible little rubber in of salt, Char!"

"Don't you make more trouble in this old women's knitting party, Char," growled Clanger. "Or I'll put you in the gorse again."

Yet in spite of this occasional sniping, making the ballad made them all feel better; as if—Bill said—there was continuity to *something*. And perhaps it was mulling over past experiences that made them more adventurous again. Since coming north they'd lain low within a small circle, their contact with the outside world limited to carefully-organised hunting expeditions. So far as they knew, the countryside round them was deserted.

"Ought we to do some reconnoitring, Wolf?" asked Alastair.

"Sure. Which direction, kid?"

"Oh—all in turn, I think. Might manage to map out how much space we've got."

"We might meet Freaks somewhere, but I'll come, all the same."

"You're not at all the right sort, Jan! I'll go," said Charlie.

"Thanks, Jan," said Alastair unexpectedly. "And we'll take about four other people, shall we, Wolf? Char, you can stay with Tom and Clang and the others, and cook for Grouse. And see Hoppo doesn't follow us."

Charlie's lower lip stuck out mutinously. "Dunno why we always let Alastair decide everything, just 'cos he's got this kinky sort of mind that's—"

"That's kept us out of trouble, so far," said Wolf sharply. "Kid—let's take Ox along—he's got these fists on him big enough to slay a mammoth. An' maybe Mule too; he can help carry you."

"And Bill," said Alastair. "And—and Fox."

"'Cos he's got those eyes on him small enough to slide round corners." Charlie got up and stumped out of the cave. Daylight made her blink. She saw Tom standing idle by the stream, looking vaguely unhappy, and today she felt for him: Alastair to leave his brother behind! A sense of kinship made her aware she'd not been very kind to Tom. She ran down the hill to join him. "Tom, Tom! Shall we see who can hop those flat stones farthest up the stream?"

A reconnoitring expedition set off some days later, Ox and Mule carrying Alastair turn and turn about. Fox went ahead, covering the ground like his namesake. Wolf and Bill, with hide packs of necessities strapped to their shoulders, were both armed: Bill with an ordinary gun, Wolf with one laser, while the other had been left behind with Clanger. Jan walked with Wolf. Checking a strange urge to sing, she drew in deep breaths of air, and ran a little over the grass.

"Look at Jan being a lapwing," said Alastair, whom Ox was carrying.

"Ah, she's getting the feel of it now."

"Feel of what?"

"What I said to you in London, kid. Remember? We're the lucky ones, no more pretences. Life's not for ever, so we're going to live it now, aren't we?" Wolf sighted his gun at a lark, and lowered it again, smiling. "Seen something, Fox?" he called.

"Path forks," said Fox, returning. "One arm goes on along that stream 'mong all those rushes, an' skirts those hills to the south. The other goes on up and over. Very open."

"Well, kid?"

"Up and over—Yes. Only someone had better go on and scout for us." Alastair wrinkled his brows. "There's—" His voice trailed away.

Wolf broke into a trot, laser gun at the ready. "Follow when I wave."

"Put me down, Ox. We'll have a standeasy."

They waited. The surrounding hills were presences, the sun warm for winter, and several larks were singing valiantly, though not very high above the ground.

"Wolf," said Jan presently. And they resumed their march, with Mule carrying Alastair.

"Sure weigh a ton, kid," he said. "Must be Jan's stews."

(They're acting as if I were Char, she thought. This new sense of freedom I'm getting, they can feel it too.)

"Nothing much in this direction," said Wolf, as they reached him. "Empty, see? Even the paths die out. Want to go on, kid? There's not much cover."

Alastair hesitated. "So long as we can map a bit clear of other people in all directions, it means our valley's as good a pitch as any."

"Mere flap of a K'an Si's wings. But have it your own way," said Wolf goodnaturedly.

By nightfall they had gone up and over twice more, and Jan's exhilaration had given place to gloom over blisters and the cold. Uncured sheep fleeces were some protection but, as Mule said, the pong was horrible. They had made some sleeping bags from canvas found in one heli, and slept, or tried to, two to a bag. They had camped by a stream, and the morning brought mist, with a chill that bit into their bones. Depression was thick as the mist, but couldn't be dispersed by grumbling since Wolf now forbade too much talking.

"Could bring the Freaks right on us, if they're here. Still want to go on, kid?"

"Bit farther."

"Never find our way back, in this." Ox sucked his teeth, while Jan, aching all over, secretly agreed.

"Schoosh!" Mule held up a hand. "Listen."

There was a rattling of pebbles, and the splashing of something or someone through the shallows. Wolf pushed Jan behind him, and raised his gun. They waited. Out of the swirling mist shapes bulged and flickered. Wolf's finger arched, ready. Jan pulled at his arm. "No, *wait!*"

A shrill whinny split the air. A rough pony came trotting up the slope towards them, with a second following him uncertainly.

Ox broke into subdued laughter. "Wild animals!"

"Tame as kittens—from hunger, poor things. Look at the grass." Jan patted the first-arriving nose. "Wonder if he's broken? Make a good mount for Alastair."

"Sun's coming out," muttered Bill, rocking an eager pony off his foot. The mist was turning a dull molten colour, and suddenly started to roll away, revealing first the lower slopes and then the summits of the hills. "I'm as hungry as this chap," he added. "Come on, let's grind our teeth on Charlie's baps."

Breakfast didn't take long, with icy stream water to wash it down. And then they were on their way again, glad of movement to get them warm; while the ponies stuck to them relentlessly after being fed a bap apiece. And soon Jan was mounted on one pony and Alastair on the other, with Mule grasping its mane.

"This fellow keeps pulling to his left."

"Let him follow his nose, Mule."

"Okay, kid."

He was leading them towards a cleft at the valley's foot, and soon quickened his pace.

"Knows where he's going, all right—some old village," said Mule as the party emerged into the adjoining valley. The ponies were halted with difficulty, but no one was quick enough to grab their nostrils. One lifted his head and gave a ringing neigh.

"Devil!" said Wolf. "Tie their snouts up, someone— muffle 'em. Bill, take the laser, an' gimme Leo's gun. I'm going forward to scout."

The village was no more than two hundred metres away. The beginnings of a path joined an untended road winding between a straggle of grey stone cottages. Wolf went down the road, his gun at his hip, the tip of his nose wriggling like a ferret's. Here the mist hadn't quite cleared, and lay in tantalising ribbons across his path. Sticking out above and below one such ribbon Wolf saw a head with sproutings of grey beard and a pair of bow legs stuck into outsize gumboots. He raised his gun, and arms rose above the mist like the arms of someone drowning, and a surprisingly strong old voice called out: "Shoot, then. Been waiting for you, I have. Killer! Murderer of children!" The arms shook with strong emotion.

Wolf lowered his gun. "All alone, Gran'dad?"

"Alone, all right. Killed, they were—those that weren't

taken. Lying in the field they are up there; shallow I buried 'em, see. Couldn't do no more. You've come to finish me, I seen it in your face."

The body swam out of the mist too. Wolf and the tough old man were almost eye to eye.

"You seen funk in my face. Thought you might be a Freak—or a Freak-lover. Drop your arms, eh, Gran'pa? I'm from London town."

Two fierce eyes scanned his face, at first disbelievingly and then crinkling to an uncertain smile. "*London?* How came you hereabouts, then?"

"Ah, that's a long story, that is. Safe for me an' my friends to come into this village?"

"More of you, are there, then?"

"Six. An' we found two ponies. 'Least, they found us."

"Ah, I did hear Little 'Un neigh. Bring your friends, and welcome, my dear." The old eyes flickered, suddenly secretive, the mouth puckered. "Hungry, are they? There's no food."

Fairly well-fed old boy, thought Wolf. Scared, poor devil. "We've our own supplies."

The old man looked happier. "Tell you what I *will* share— what I kept hidden from they Freaks; I'd foxed 'em, see—lay like some dead cock robin, one eye open, staring at the sky. Then afterwards—Well, never mind, never mind—*that's* a long story on its own. First you bring your friends down to those end cottages. Little 'Un'll lead you." And he turned away, an independent, lonely figure.

Wolf trailed back, grinning to himself. "A born survivor, well-plucked," he told them, after reporting this conversation. "Want to come and see, kid? He's got something that he wants to share."

"Anywhere warm." Jan shivered.

It was unnecessary for Little 'Un to lead them, since the road ran straight past cottages till it came to the old man, waving from a doorway. They followed him in, and were met by a blast of fug and smell of spirits.

"Pickles himself," muttered Bill. "That's how he's survived. Good grief, look at that!"

"Pretty horrific," whispered Jan, shying as though she were Little 'Un; for the narrow hall, and the old man's living-room, which contained a blazing fire and a workbench littered with tools, were tastefully lined with grave monuments and headstones.

"District stonemason, Ned Harrow. Commonly called Old Ned." Their host held out a horny hand.

Wolf shook it. "Ah, we've given up full names. Here's Alastair, that's the kid. Jan, Ox, Mule, Bill—and Fox. Not a zoo, though you might think it. I'm Wolf."

"Well, Mr Wolf, it's a pity you've brought me no customers, for I've been stockpiling, you might say. Hands, they will be at it. Well, m'dear, what can I offer? Brandy, sherry, whisky? A drop of liquor, now? Champagne or port? Drop of port keeps out the cold wonderful."

"*Whisky!*" said Ox. Awestruck.

"Champagne," said Bill.

"It's so soon after bapping," said Jan.

"Spot of ginger wine? Very warming, too."

"Please."

"Mr Harrow, where did you get it all?" asked Wolf, curiosity getting the better of him. "Or how did you keep it?"

"Ah. Innkeeper, he showed me where he hid it, see. Very set on Freaks not getting it, he was. And when he—Afterwards, out I went and brought it in bottle by bottle, choosing this or that to keep me company. A man needs company, when he's carving."

He looked defensive, and Wolf said soothingly, "I'd be happy to join you in a drop of port. What about the kid?"

"Bottle of champagne with Bill," said Alastair instantly. While Fox showed a ladylike interest in sherry, discussing with Old Ned the merits of Tio Pepe versus Coronation Cream, and sniffing slightly when Ox and Mule opted for whisky.

"No one's to drink so much they start to sing," commanded Wolf, faintly alarmed.

It was a pleasant hour or two. And after he'd heard their saga, embellished here and there, Old Ned sniffed and wiped his eyes, and said Jan reminded him of his wife's young cousin, and he could maybe spare them a sack of grain, being too old to start working it himself, and another sack of little yellow apples, as well as a bottle or two of brandy, and some Spanish wine. Wolf responded by offering to send someone over the hills with dried fruit, and a sheepfleece for a warmer waistcoat. "Unless you'd care to join us, Gran'dad?"

"Ah, no. Where'd I be without my carvings?"

"And without his bottles. Maybe we'd best join him here," muttered Ox.

But Old Ned disparaged that idea. "Welcome to visit, m' dears—just now and then. Drink up, while I carry on carving —not happy without my chisel in my hand." He picked up a hammer and began tapping away at the slab of marble on his workbench. Jan leaned over his shoulder, and Alastair pulled himself up sideways from a chair, and looked too.

Afterwards, Jan said that it had given her an uneasy feeling— though perhaps it was because she'd expected to see something like "Underneath are the Everlasting Arms".

"Just let fancy rove on this one, seeing as I'd no one special in mind."

"You're an expert, Mr Harrow. That's a lovely crown," said Jan. "But why have you—"

"Ah, you may well ask. Don't know why I thought of it. Hand thinks, see, and chisel follows. That's the way it is."

Still holding their glasses, they all crowded round and stared. It was a lovely crown, as Jan had said; but it was pierced from right to left, slantingly, by a sword. A firmly-engraved zigzag line down the centre showed the splitting point.

"Gives me a kind of sad feeling. And yet hand will do it."

"What kind of a feeling does it give you, kid?" asked Wolf.

Alastair was gazing at the stone with sombre intensity. At last he pointed. "What are those scratches for?"

"Ah, that's how I work in the design, see. Seemed like something was missing, with no words up top. Stars are pretty—let's have a batch of stars, hand thought. Well, I'll be splintered! Same old set of stars Mr Wolf's wearing on his shoulder. Isn't that some strange kind of a—of a—"

"Coincidence," completed Bill.

But Alastair, staring at the design, was quiet.

"Fancy going all that way to find a mad old man carving gravestones," jeered Tom. He was whittling a stick with quite unnecessary force, using one of Fox's knives; and the knife-point slipped, and squeaked on the green wood like a protest.

"He wasn't mad—just odd," explained Jan, eyeing Tom sideways, and wondering if Wolf was quite aware of these dark, fluctuating fits of jealousy. "Anyone might be, these days. And at least we've brought back brandy and wine, grain, and apples. And one of Old Ned's ponies, for Alastair. Aren't you glad? I—he thought you'd be pleased."

"Oh, he did, did he? You thought so, anyway." Tom glanced at her, and then at the listening Charlie. He dropped the knife, which stuck upright in the cave floor, with its hilt quivering. "He's been a bit bleak since you returned. Only talks to Little 'Un, and Wolf."

"He's tired. It was an exhausting trek for everyone, you know—much worse for Alastair. I expect he was worried, too, about leaving you behind—"

"Oh, you mean leaving me alone in charge, without Wolf?"

"You know I didn't mean that at all," said Jan desperately.

And: "He didn't leave you in charge, it was equal pegging," declared Charlie. "You know what, Tom, you're always seeing insults everywhere—it's boring. But you're right about him being quiet now—sort of funny. You don't think *Alastair's* going odd, do you, Jan?"

145

"Oh no, Char! And Alastair's always been pretty odd, anyhow."

"Ah," said Charlie darkly, "but there's odd, and odder."

"You're dead right." Tom gave an angry laugh. "And it hasn't exactly helped, his being allowed to lord it over a jumped-up gangleader who regards him with awe as some sort of nutty prophet."

"You just try saying that to Wolf's face, I dare you," said Charlie, peering into a cooking pot. "And have some of Clanger's rabbit and lentil soup, to calm you down. You too, Jan. It's gone rather odd, if anything has. Almost purple. You haven't added the wrong sort of mushroom, have you, Tom—to celebrate Wolf's return?"

7 § Stronghold in Bavaria

After that night when he heard or imagined Jan's voice, Matt grew very restless. To sit day after day tracing signs on to maps chafed his spirit unbearably. It was better when some intercepted message took him racing upstairs in search of Walther; but relief would be shortlived, and soon the caged energy built again. He began to wonder if his reason would stand this place much longer. To be thrown abruptly into an almost medieval life was enough to shake anyone. Asceticism, learning, rough food, cold water, a little sour wine. It was like asking him to be the young Bernard of Clairvaux without the faith. Sometimes he thought Walther regarded him with a sympathetic eye—but afterwards he would goad Ludwig on to more strenuous efforts. Matt was forbidden to speak English at all; no one answered him if he forgot.

Days passed, and there was still no sign of Heinz and Jakob. Walther's frown became habitual. He called a council, to which Matt was eventually summoned. He looked about him, and saw a circle of unforgiving eyes. Or so he thought.

"There is no news out of Bavaria."

"That message—it hasn't been repeated, has it?" He met Friedrich's iron gaze courageously. "Perhaps it meant nothing at all."

"Perhaps we were too clever."

"You mean, I was." Sweat pearled on his forehead, and he was sure they noticed it. Were they also suspicious of him?

"Matt, we do not speak of blame, nor misplaced cleverness. Anyway, now I must send out someone else."

"To—Chiemsee, Walther?"

"To find Jakob and Heinz. We must know what's happened."

Still they were all staring at him.

"Send me. I'm expendable, aren't I?" he said, almost flippantly. And then wondered if they'd think he wished to run away.

"No one is that; but two must go, and you'll need each other's support." So it was already decided. "You could usually be mistaken for a German now. Not that it's always an advantage, outside here. German or escaped slave—" Walther shook his head sadly. "All depends on the circumstances. We send you because you've been to Chiemsee, just as Jakob had. But you may not get so far." (The words sounded very ominous, thought Matt.) "Something may have happened to Heinz and Jakob en route—or did they find the wrong people waiting there? Or—were they ambushed coming back? Anyway—it's time to act. You'll leave tonight. We've waited too long already for our own good." His lips were grimly set. "Friedrich will code a message for the pair of you to memorize." He stood up. "That's all, then. I'll see you before you go."

Matt longed to know who his companion would be; although looking round at those closed, accusing faces he didn't like to ask. But as he reached the door Walther said: "Oh Matt—it's Hans I'm sending with you. He'll have a map —remember, it must be destroyed, if necessary. He will also have the only gun that we can spare you."

Matt winced. Was that a polite way of saying that the *Orden* couldn't trust him? "Am I to carry nothing?"

"Oh, certainly." (Was *that* faint amusement in Walther's voice?) "A rucksack with your food."

Matt inclined his head gravely, and left the room. Hans, he was thinking. Well, well . . . the *Orden*'s killer. I wonder if Walther told him there could be circumstances when he should dispose of *me*?

The route to Chiemsee that had been decided on was the one already taken by the van; yet it was even more dangerously exposed for foot-travellers, with longer intervals when shelter would be hard to find. The moon was full, but a stormy sky often obscured its light. By one in the morning Matt's eyes were watering with strain, and a pulse in his head throbbed with each footfall. Hans strode on unwaveringly. Matt gritted his teeth, detested him, and was determined not to falter first.

It seemed a long while since they had seen towers of other medieval towns grim on the eastern horizon, splodges against a slightly lighter sky. He lost count of time. Each second was marked by a weary leg's forward movement. Left, right, left, right, stiff and measured as a pendulum. At daybreak Hans grunted out, "Rest", and headed for some trees. Matt followed, and sank down thankfully on soft pineneedles. His head drooped forward, and he slept.

Their journey seemed interminable. To push on, according to Walther's instructions, meant daytime travel too, but Hans was vigilant. Several ears on that square head, thought Matt. Several eyes in that impassive face. No grumble of a distant convoy, no flash of silver on the horizon, escaped him. Matt grew used to being driven into shelter, pushed into ditches, urged to run. Hans marked time by prodigious distances; and soon Matt was accustomed to the pace; but however fast and far they walked, there was still no sign of Heinz's and Jakob's van.

"Perhaps they returned another way, and are safely with the *Orden* . . ." ventured Matt; but Hans turned his large pale eyes on him, said nothing, and plodded on.

Then at last on a late afternoon they reached the very edge of Chiemsee; and suddenly Matt heard Hans draw in his breath, and followed the direction of his gaze. Close to the lakeside, slewed to the left and half-hidden by a rise in the ground, was a partially burned-out van. Matt felt a sour thickness rising in his throat. Hans said nothing. He just looked, then motioned Matt into the field before him, and drew his gun.

"Hans—*no*. S-surely Walther didn't—"

"Quiet." The blue eyes were empty of mercy—empty of anything. It was impossible to tell if he was acting under orders, or on impulse. "Raise your hands. Back, towards the lake."

Matt cursed himself for slowness. It was too late for resistance, that little black eye of death was steady on him. He felt his heart pound and his throat go dry. Where he stood now his body would fall conveniently into the lake.

The black eye never winked. Hans was backing towards the van, still covering him, manoeuvring so that he could look inside the driver's cab. He stared long and hard. Without any change of expression he walked over to Matt again, who heard the lap-lap of lake waters at his back as if they were the secretive approach of death playing at Grandmother's Steps. He licked dry lips.

"Hans—"

"Heinz is there." Hans spoke almost conversationally.

"Jakob?" whispered Matt; ashamed that he could barely speak.

Hans shook his head. The gunbarrel was close to Matt's chest. It was as though each second were already eternity. He heard his own voice as if it belonged to someone else.

"I didn't—I didn't—I *didn't*—"

He saw Hans's finger on the trigger as though in photographic close up.

There was a sudden disturbance by the lake's edge: a sound like someone's hand loudly slapping a wet sheet. The gunbarrel swivelled, and Matt acted instinctively, chopping at Hans's wrist with the side of his hand. The gun described a perfect arc and landed with a slight splash in the lake.

Matt read Hans's expression correctly, but still hesitated, although there was no going back now. Walther had called Hans the perfect killing machine. It would be like tackling a tank barehanded, and he was hampered by his pack.

The hesitation saved him. Hans moved forward lightning-swift, but his foot slipped on stones cluttering the lakeshore. Instead of executing a karate chop his right hand glanced off Matt's shoulder, and he floundered into him, swearing, correcting the thrust by a ludicrous embrace. Matt brought up his right knee. Hans yelled and doubled, as Matt twisted sideways, kicking at his ankles. He couldn't hope to hold Hans off for long—but their battleground decided things: in his automatic recoil Hans lost his balance finally and went over the lake's verge much as his gun had earlier, though with a less perfect arc. As he hit the water a second swan rose from the nearby bushes.

Matt stood staring. Bubbles rose. Then Hans's head, eyes shut, mouth open. He went down again.

Matt waited: more bubbles, and Hans's head broke water. His arms threshed up and down as his feet felt for the lake's bottom and couldn't find it. Hans, the otherwise ultra-efficient, couldn't swim. "*Help!*" The flat pale eyes were panicstricken as water closed over them again. Matt threw off his pack and dived into the lake.

"Don't panic. Float." But Hans continued to flail the water, and in desperation seized his would-be rescuer in an iron grip. Half-drowned himself, Matt tore free and managed to deliver a stunning uppercut. But a weighty, noncombatant Hans was almost as much a problem as the fighting one had been—for the bank here had a towering overhang. Matt gasped, and trod water, supporting Hans beneath the shoulders, and then began towing him along the shore.

Wish he'd drowned, the b. If it weren't for those vows I made to Walther . . .

Luck came to their rescue in the shape of an indent in the lake's shoreline, where roots from a group of alders protruded from the muddy bank. Rushes crowded thickly here, and Matt towed Hans in among them, his feet feeling for the ground. His toes touched, slipped. He struck out with his right arm, and his hand touched something half-hidden in the rushes.

Something wooden: the weed-covered side of a small boat.

Hans began to struggle again, and made grunting noises.

"Hold up! We're here." With a last, tremendous effort Matt heaved the sodden, weighty Hans into the boat; then clambered in himself, feeling limp with delayed shock. He sat taking deep breaths, eyes half closed. When he looked up at last, Hans was staring at him wide-eyed.

"You saved me."

"Yes, you fool. I can't think why."

"Heinz, Jakob . . . *You* didn't, it wasn't—"

"No."

"Heinz was my friend. You must not think that Walther ordered—But I am impulsive—" A large square hand reached out and patted Matt's shoulder.

(Impulsive, he thought. Well yes—I'd say so.)

It was like making friends with a very dangerous wild beast. Aloud he said: "Well, since we've found a boat, we'd better row."

It was amusing to see Hans shake, though as a matter of fact Matt wasn't too sure about this boat himself. Hidden in these reeds it might easily be rotten, and he could see water gleaming between its badly-caulked seams. As for the lake, being not far from mountains it should be deep. And once he and Hans were launched upon it, anyone on either side could take potshots at them.

"We'll need another oar—there's only one. I'll try to find a board, or something. Better fetch my pack as well."

The boat rocked violently as he left it, and Hans's pale Saxon skin turned paler still. Matt pulled himself out and up by means of overhanging roots. He straddled one, and worked his way along till he could grab a branch. After that it was easy, and a matter of seconds to gather up the pack. He returned, whistled softly to Hans, and threw it down. Then he went along the shore, hunting for anything that they could use. He approached a crumbling landingstage with caution, but the few neighbouring houses seemed both derelict and deserted. Among debris he found a piece of wood about a metre long, jagged and green. He wrenched it free, and went back along the lake towards the van.

Hans was peering up anxiously through the alders. Matt threw down the board, and splashed inelegantly from a branch into the reeds. He dragged himself into the boat.

"We lost our gun. Here's Heinz's. It was under his feet." He was white round the mouth, and felt like retching. Hans looked at him in silence, and Matt handed him the oar, laying the gun between them.

"I'll take first turn with this." He lowered the board's wider end into the water.

"Wait, Matt! We don't know who killed Heinz. Maybe people from the island?"

Matt shook his head. "If they were like our group, and simply thought they were being threatened, they'd not have left the van and—For anyone to see. If it's Freaks on the island—No, that's out: *they* don't need to hide. I think they just caught Heinz and Jakob nearby, and drove them into that field to finish them off."

"But Jakob has disappeared."

"Yes. And since we don't know if he was alive or dead, we'd better get to those islands as fast as possible. At least the light's bad enough now. We won't be a perfect target." He would have laughed at Hans's expression, if he hadn't been so wet and miserable himself. "Come on, man, row. Try to think of yourself as Lohengrin's ruddy swan."

But crossing the enormous lake was a nightmare. Hans shook, and splashed unevenly with his oar. Matt paddled skilfully, but his hands soon blistered. The light turned almost immediately to owl light, then to darkness. They rested on their oars, and Matt wondered dismally if they were simply going round and round, or back the way they came. It was impossible any longer to distinguish the large island of Herrenchiemsee from the shoreline beyond it, or even from the smaller and more distant Fraueninsel. He began to feel as if his eyes were crossing. Southwestward on the skyline the Bavarian Alps reared up, a blacker blackness than the sky. Water lapped hungrily around the boat. Matt put his head on his knees, and suspected that poor Hans was crying.

And then the moon rose. Ripples ran past outlined in pallor. The mountain peaks turned crystalline, and appeared to move in closer. The Herren and Frauen Inseln were easily distinguished, furred with trees, and nearer than Matt had thought. He heaved a sigh of relief, and picked up his paddle.

" 'Speed, bonny boat, like a bird on the wing—' "

"Matt—what is it you would say?" hissed Hans.

"Sorry: just my little romantic daydream."

"At such a time? You are mad."

Matt grinned to himself. These old Teutons. When there was too much to despair of, why not laugh? It didn't cost anything. Though certainly there was enough to sober anyone now—the shoreline was only a short way ahead, and who knew what marksman might be watching from the shadows, as they bobbed forward, easily visible on the moonlit lake?

He came round, and lights flared at him like shooting stars. His head seemed to open and shut as the world swayed, then steadied. A showy peacock towered over him, wearing an arrogant expression. Beside him crouched a humbler peahen.

Matt blinked, but they didn't go away. Hell, this time I *am* crazy. Wow, my head.

He lay still, and gradually the lights settled and vanished. The peacocks remained. There was something familiar about them, although not homely. Palatial. Palaces and peacocks. That's it! I have been here before.

He sat up cautiously, clutching his head, and looked around him. Simultaneously a door opened, and a tall man entered, followed by two more.

"King Ludwig of Bavaria, I presume?"

The man looked at him more haughtily than the peacock, and Matt felt at a disadvantage on the floor. He tried to rise, but his ankles were shackled to a ring driven into the peahen's tail.

"You shouldn't do things like this. It's vandalism. What will posterity say?"

No one answered. They released him and helped him up. They led him to another door and through a courtyard where other men, and one or two tough-looking girls, were lounging. For a bad moment he wondered if they formed a firing squad. But he was led onward, and so at last into a gorgeously-painted chamber with a double staircase, strangely furnished with a wooden table and some plastic chairs. Across the table Matt found himself confronting a youngish man with long fair hair, a hooked nose, and very bright blue eyes. Round him sat his lieutenants, and before him Hans, slumped in a chair, his head resting on his hand.

As Matt was brought forward, he looked up and said: "I have convinced them. Or Walther's message has."

"Good thing I didn't drown you," remarked Matt. Someone pushed him down into the next chair, and his head seemed to open and shut like an earthquake crack. He closed his eyes, and it was as though some of Wagner's dwarfs were beating on his skull with bronze hammers. "But do they convince us?" he added, rubbing at his head.

The fair man laughed. "What else do you expect, if you arrive stealthily by night?"

"We'd hardly arrive playing timbrels, would we?"

"Matt," said Hans in shocked tones.

Teutonics again, respect for authority, thought Matt. I'm always forgetting; even after my training with the *Orden*. He stared at the face before him, and decided that it was almost as remarkable as Walther's. Just so must those men have looked who ravaged England in the dark ages, and left a warrior strain behind to mingle with that of the invading Normans.

Now he was speaking to Hans. "It's good your Friedrich picked up that message. When we left the shambles in the

Schwarzwald, we thought most other cells were finished. But your two other men—I'm sorry. They so nearly reached us." He shook his head glumly, and turned to Matt, who had made as if to speak.

"You would say something?"

"Only that I don't think Jakob knew about Friedrich's findings. Walther was careful to keep some information under wraps, for those who had to know. It was Heinz who used to help Friedrich, sometimes, before I came. But he wasn't good at it."

"*Ach*—you helped? So. Well, we're fortunate that it was Heinz who was shot."

There it was. Bald and brutal. Not fortunate for Heinz, poor devil. Everybody else's lucky dip. Good training for the ego, this sort of life, thought Matt.

"And not so fortunate that both we and your friends are now endangered. This Jakob—"

"Will not talk," said Hans quickly.

The other man shook his head. "Merely a question of time. Unless he died soon." He brooded. "When we heard the shot—But we could have done nothing, only drawn attention to ourselves. Still, it would now be helpful to learn one thing: were the captors few or many, en route for the camps at Munich or Salzburg or closer home? I think we must try to examine this field now, and the van."

"And bury Heinz?" asked Matt.

A hard blue stare raked him. "And interest someone? But no." Maybe it wasn't only the headache that was upsetting Matt. He stared at the heaving floor, and was relieved to be dismissed.

"You will be taken to your quarters now. We eat at noon."

With their escort he followed Hans up the gaudily-painted staircase, thinking: How very much surprised old Ludwig would have been to see us; not to say displeased. They had been allotted a fantasy of a room, with Meissen chandeliers and ornamentation wherever it could go. Here Matt sank down on a canvas bed and stared out of the window. Between the dwarfs' hammerblows he was thinking of Heinz and the perhaps more unfortunate Jakob. Cut off. How could anyone make sense or meaning out of this strange, irrational struggle for the shards of western civilisation?

There has to be something I'm fighting for, otherwise I might just as well walk out into the lake . . . And then he thought, Jan. To be with Jan again. He stretched out on the bed, and the dwarfs' hammering lessened.

Hans was staring up at the ceiling, his pale eyes as expressionless as ever.

"What are you thinking of, Hans?"

"My parents' farm near Bückeburg."

"You hope you may get back there one day?"

Hans's expression never altered. "No longer there. It was—in the way."

Matt made sympathetic noises. "You were there?"

"No. They were." There was a silence, then Hans said sadly, "Every day still, I walk round our farm—I stand under the big *Linden*, to scratch the back of our prize-winning sow. Her name was Gundi." He sighed. "Poor Gundi."

Matt didn't know whether to laugh or cry. Jan. Gundi.

Hans was looking at him. "You, Matt. Your parents live?"

Matt shook his head. "Now I'm one of the lucky ones, because they died when I was seventeen. Air crash. I had a guardian though—a godfather; he died of the bug—Marburg X." And then, because to speak of her made her seem more real, he told haltingly of Jan: "—but I only knew her a few weeks. And she stayed in England."

"She's dead, then."

Matt said obstinately. "It's strange, but I know I'll see her again, because I must . . . And every time I think of her she's somewhere—somewhere she told me of—where she was very happy when she was growing up. She called it Golden Valley." But he certainly wasn't going to tell Hans about his extraordinary hallucination at Bad Mergentheim. Why was he even telling Hans, of all people, anything at all? He heard the Saxon say dampingly, "It's the same everywhere. All gone, like my parents' farm, and Gundi."

Matt hated him. It was incredible that he should be lying in Ludwig of Bavaria's ornate palace and telling a snubnosed Saxon killer about his girl. He curled on his side and went to sleep, hearing the dwarfs still at it through his dreams.

When he woke it was almost dark again, and the hawknosed man stood looking down on him. His first thought was, Damn, I've missed the food. The second, that he would be bawled out for unsoldierly conduct.

"I'm in command here. They call me Helmut. I wish to talk to you."

Matt followed him into the next room, feeling scruffy and uneasy. Helmut gestured towards a chair, and sat down himself. He was puffing at something that looked like a cigarette, but smelt vile. Matt refused one.

"We're crossing the lake tonight, to look for information about the ambush. One of you should guide us. Your friend isn't keen on the idea."

"Poor Hans can't swim. He's phobic about water."

Helmut gave a lopsided smile. "Oh, is that all? I imagined all sorts of things."

"Of course I'll guide you. Now?" Matt's stomach rumbled, as if in protest.

Helmut laughed outright. "You can eat before we go. Come down, now. We'll leave in ninety minutes from the old landingstage."

"Where I landed in my tourist days," ventured Matt as they left the room.

Helmut shot him a glance. "So. That's the reason your *Hochmeister* chose you for this mission?"

"One of them, I think," agreed Matt; not caring to think about other possibilities.

But in the event, Helmut cancelled their crossing at the last moment, without explanation. Matt decided the night was probably too clear for him to risk it. Instead, everyone except the newcomers was put to work on strengthening the defences. Some time during the following morning Matt found Hans drooping disconsolately in a courtyard.

"They won't let us go into the grounds alone."

"Don't they really trust us?"

"Well, there's something they won't let us see. Not yet, anyway. Defences, I suppose. And Matt, Helmut can't send food to Walther. He has no transport now. They drove theirs into the lake."

"He might renovate ours."

"You forget. He'll leave it there."

"Then we'll just have to return and fetch the others." But Hans looked even more disconsolate at thought of crossing the lake again, and Matt grinned. "He might send a message to say we're here, and get some kind of warning through about Jakob?"

Hans shook his head. "He forbids direct communication. He feels as Walther does."

Matt felt full of frustrated violence. "Then what's the use of it all? Pockets of survivors, as cut off as in the Middle Ages. And the Freaks—the enemy—are the Black Death." He beat with his clenched fists on the wall, surprised by his own violence. Just then Helmut came into the courtyard. "I'm going to tell him we *insist* on my returning to warn Walther," said Matt, and started towards him.

But Helmut was adamant. "Impossible. No one crosses till we've better cover, a cloudy sky. If your Jakob lived he will have talked, and it will be too late anyhow. If he died first, your people are no worse off." He smiled a wintry, forbidding smile.

"You'll let us go when it's dark enough, surely?"

"We'll eventually get a message through, now we know of Bad Mergentheim."

So it was all to start again: probation, surveillance. Matt could have screamed. He found himself wondering if he could possibly swim the lake; the water would be icy, too cold to allow for rests while floating.

Helmut must have read his mind, for he was laughing. "I think your *Hochmeister* unleashed you on me because he could no longer contain such a hothead." (It was the first time anyone had called Matt a hothead, and it astonished him.) "Come, I'll find you work to do—on our fortifications." And work Hans and Matt did, until they were too tired to think about the fate of Bad Mergentheim at all.

However, the next evening was more overcast, and Helmut cautiously allowed that the crossing could take place. When Matt joined him with six others they found two small camouflaged launches ready at the landingstage. He was assigned to the second one.

"*Engines?*"

"Only for surprise attack. It's oars, otherwise."

He noticed the small vicious Kreins guns mounted fore and aft, and the searchlight in the first boat's bows. So Chiemsee was not quite so medieval, either. He was placed in the stern, and given a long oar. His blistered palms stung already, but he was determined that Helmut should have no cause to despise him.

"You, Matt." Helmut was leaning towards him from the other launch. "Can you guide us in to where you found your dinghy?"

"Hope so." He wasn't forthcoming.

"You had a lucky windfall. Of course many people used this lake once, for pleasure." Helmut looked round him to see that all was in order.

"Right. Row."

They moved out across the water with roughly ten metres between the launches. With four men to each the crossing was swifter than before, though Matt's palms knew it as eternity. In the half-light he was afraid of error, and even when allowed to cease rowing and steer instead he found it hard to line up mountains and trees as he had only glimpsed them once before. He was already fearing failure when his quick eye picked out a familiar shadow lying on the water and beyond it inland the looming bulk of derelict houses.

"That's the old landingstage. Port here—the rushy bits are by that overhang."

They landed three from each launch, leaving two men to cover the shoreline with the Kreins guns. Helmut was armed and the others, but no one had given Matt a weapon, and before they left the boat a rope was fastened to his belt. He choked down fury—it was humiliating to be treated as though he were a dog which might run away, but plainly the canny Helmut didn't trust him not to escape to Walther. As he swung himself up from a branch into the field a sweetish, pungent smell met him, making him retch as before. He fought down nausea, and followed the others. Helmut was ahead, fanning out his men, and seemed to see, catlike, in the dark; but Matt stumbled, screwing up his eyes.

As they neared the van a blot of shadow detached itself from the burned-out ruin. There was a cry, a scuffle, a merging of dark figures. Someone was pinned face downwards on the grass, and in the scuffle Matt found himself thrown against the side of the van, where someone else was slumped half in and half out of the driver's cab, near poor Heinz. He gave an involuntary cry, and instantly Helmut was beside him, holding his gun against the stranger's throat, and throwing a pencil of torchlight on an upturned, bearded face.

Matt gasped out: "Don't shoot, Helmut! Don't."

"Is this Jakob?"

But an exhausted voice was muttering, "Matt—you? They've hunted us like wolves." A hand came out, groping for support. "They—got you too. All done and—over."

"It's all right, Walther," said Matt shakily. "These are friends. I tell you, it's all right."

"Destroyed," said Walther. And then again, bleakly, "Destroyed."

They stood looking down on him, as he lay exhausted on a camp bed. His skin was clammy with sweat, and blood seeped into the fresh bandage round his shoulder. After recognising Matt he had fainted, and had remained unconscious till they carried him into the *Schloss*, when he had cried out wildly, still confused. Some of Helmut's jealously-guarded schnapps poured into a cup of soup had helped the exhaustion and lack of lucidity, but Matt thought pityingly that nothing would help the look in Walther's eyes. Unable to face it, he went to stand by the window. Perhaps it had been evil chance, not good, that had inspired his brainwave about Bavaria. Well, at least Friedrich too had survived, although he had been treated roughly by Helmut's men till his identity was known.

"Tell us," Helmut was saying.

"They could have taken us out with one blow." Walther winced, and shifted his position. "One little packet from a K'an Si." He brooded; Matt thought he was wishing it had happened. "But that's not always their way, as we know by now. The whole of England could have gone like that—couldn't it, Matt?"

Miserably, Matt nodded. If Walther would only stop being kind to him.

"They're like good housewives, wasting nothing." The bearded face twisted bitterly. "If we hadn't had some warning —they'd have had the computer, everything. I'd sent out a patrol; after all, we were uneasy after Heinz and Jakob disappeared. Soldiers were spotted in a field southwards, and an armoured column standing by. One man returned to warn us —the other skirted the streets and went north-eastward, where he found more armour moving up. We were ringed." Walther put a hand over his eyes. "At least we had time to expedite Plan B."

Matt knew all about Plan B; he didn't have to listen while Walther told of deliberate destruction; of how passages and rooms had been skilfully mined in preparation for attack; and of how some essential information for any future resistance had been placed in a specially prepared canister.

"But what happened to this canister?" asked Helmut anxiously.

Walther pointed to the canvas pack they'd found beneath him in the van. "Safe. Yet it shows how dangerous it was to keep it! If the enemy had found me I was too exhausted and confused to twist the dial that should have destroyed it." His breath came pantingly, and he muttered, "Water . . ."

While it was fetched, Helmut went down on his knees to undo the pack. The canister was at the top, buttressed by an old wool jersey. He drew it out.

"Careful," said Walther hoarsely. "Let Matt. He knows—" And was silent again while Matt gingerly received the canister, trying to hide his relief that Walther evidently trusted him still.

"It was Friedrich's idea that there should be this one record," he told Helmut. "Those places where we thought underground cells existed. It's guarded like Briar Rose in the fairytale. The thorns—" he smiled faintly— "are highly explosive."

Walther was muttering, "Explosives . . . made a good show, anyway. An emperor's fireworks! We set the fuses before dawn. Once they were fired, it was everyone for himself— We'd sworn to shoot ourselves rather than be taken prisoner. We paired off then, waited till the enemy was in the courtyard —their armour made fine Roman candles. But at some cost to us—If anyone who knew about this place was taken—" He sighed, wiping a hand across his eyes. "You'll be next on the list. Perhaps you already were, once they caught Jakob. I was *Hochmeister*. I should not have survived."

Matt said quickly, "But Walther—this matters." He lifted the canister.

"Yes. And at least Friedrich wasn't taken."

"*You're* important."

"No one's more important than another, Matt. The spirit's

important. That alone—that something, the best of Germany, of France, of England, should survive. Shouldn't you know?"

"All the same, I'm glad it's you who escaped—and Friedrich."

At his vehemence Walther actually smiled. "There may be others who survived." He looked up into Matt's face, and Matt was silent. He knew how hard it was for Walther, however much he tried to look objectively on his own survival.

"Well," interposed Helmut, "somehow a mainland watch must be kept. It won't be easy, but if I can I'll put two men ashore." He left the room.

But days passed, and nothing happened that seemed to presage disaster. Whenever Matt could, he sat with Walther, whose strength slowly returned. He seemed glad of Matt's presence, although he didn't talk much.

Once Matt ventured, "Jakob can't have spoken."

But Walther shook his head. "Would he have given us away, and not Chiemsee? He would have sacrificed it first."

Matt hadn't thought of that. "Then perhaps the Freaks learned some other way, by chance, or observation. Some terrible coincidence . . ." But it was wretched, going over and over it, and at last he turned his *Hochmeister's* thoughts by cunning. "You know, Walther, Hans and I think Helmut keeps some secrets here. Hans thinks that they're some special defences—that he doesn't trust us yet, entirely. But I think it's something more—something that gives him his determination to survive; and his calm ferocity—like Fafner, guarding the Rheingold! Perhaps he'll trust you—Perhaps he'll tell you, when you've recovered."

"All your imagination, I expect; and no doubt Hans is right," said Walther; but he sat up, looking alert. "I *have* recovered—Where are Friedrich and Hans?"

"Working on the defences, by the lake."

"Never mind. Go and find Helmut. Ask him if we may have a meeting now. And first—find me my clothes."

While Walther dressed, Matt hurried off to scour the palace for the leader. At last he was directed to an office set up in one of Ludwig's antechambers, where Helmut's blond wolfish looks were as incongruous among the porcelain, gilding, and marble, as a Stone-age wolf would have been in a modern shop. When Matt found him there he was examining some papers which he kept in one of Ludwig's ornate escritoires. Walther soon joined them both, and Helmut offered him the well-thumbed and tattered papers. Together Matt and his *Hochmeister* frowned over words in a near-indecipherable script.

"You won't understand them. Try the map."

It was on a large scale and showed, eastwards of sea, a slice of coastline vaguely familiar to Matt. "These two words, here, translate as North Sea, perhaps?"

"*Prima.*"

"These marks must show where the oil rigs are. But—more than that, surely—"

"It is a city. A city in the sea."

"Off the coast of England," said Matt in a wondering voice. "Where the solar-house settlements were already. But why?"

"Oil's important." Helmut sat down beside Walther. "And our enemies try an experiment. Small slave settlements, completely cut off by water, self-supporting. North Sea oil has obviously some priority—so there they build the first one. Slaves bred in slavery, as in the bad old days of the West Indies."

"But how should you know this, here?"

Helmut shrugged, and held out his hand for the map. "You know of the Q'uo Si?"

"Smaller version of the K'an Si, with vertical take-off," said Walther keenly. "Never actually seen one."

"Well, one dropped in on us accidentally, with engine trouble. We let them repair it, and then gave them quite a shock." Helmut smiled laconically. "They had a Staff Officer on board, flying to take up an appointment. So we kept him— among other things. Poor fellow."

"You still have this plane?"

"Naturally. Though nowhere to fly it, at present."

"And no one came looking for it?"

Helmut shook his head. "We—*suggested* to its pilot that he should send a message saying he was losing height among the mountains, and the mountain lakes."

Matt thought of them with a shudder: pools of still green, between huge cup-shaped mountains. When cloud descended only the lowest ranks of conifers were visible, drenched to blackness among shreds of mist. The mountains between Füssen and Innsbruck had always made his flesh creep, they were so secretive-looking and gloomy, unlike the freestanding crystal-tipped giants ringing Salzburg and Kitzbühel.

"There are other maps," Helmut was saying, "showing other places marked for slave development. But *this* one should interest Matt." And Matt looked up, surprised at something in his tone. Old wars still unforgotten, even now? Some deep-seated nationalism, causing Helmut pleasure that Matt the Englishman should know firsthand all the humiliations of defeat?

He stared at the floor, and muttered angrily: "Friedrich and I once decided that what we needed was the perfect talisman. And *I* said—well, not the swastika."

"Matt, I forbid you to be provocative," said Walther sternly, though with a twitch to the corners of his mouth. "We're all suffering the same way now."

At the word "talisman" Helmut had glanced quickly from one to the other of them. Now: "You and Friedrich were right," he murmured, and looked as though he wanted to say more; then plainly had second thoughts, and in silence handed over to Walther some other papers from the captured plane.

"I suspect you're right, Matt, and there's something hidden here," said Walther later. "And not just that Q'uo Si."

Matt wondered if the same thought was in both their minds.

"Anyway," continued Walther, "Helmut's not a man whose confidence is forced, I think. If he has any secrets, he'll share them in his own good time."

"Time? He'd better share them soon—or he'll have to wait for the next world. Walther, he couldn't have a safer confidant than you."

Walther shook his head. "He barely knows me—but I know these hardened soldiers. What we call a *kriegsman*. I cannot press him, it would be useless. The decision will be his . . ."

Yet time passed, and Helmut's reticence remained. By night he landed two men on the mainland, where they waited in hiding to watch for possible refugees from Bad Mergentheim; but no one came, and in the end he withdrew them, and Walther's melancholy settled in as bleak as winter's fog. All work that could be done on the defences had been accomplished, and there was little enough to do when off-duty except play cards or chess; there wasn't even an adequate supply of wine, said Hans gloomily. It was impossible to black out the palace entirely, and lights and fires were only lit in one or two rooms after dark. December, which had been so freakishly mild in England, turned on its wild-boar aspect here. Icy winds blew from the mountains, with dancing bands of snow. When the winds fell, the snow descended heavily; great feathery splodges falling so endlessly that to look up into it was dizzying. Helmut was glad of the snow: it made discovery by air less likely.

One day, when Walther's sadness had grown really oppressive, Helmut offered to show the four of them over his captured Q'uo Si. He led them through the grounds to where the neat little plane was hidden behind a screen of trees, and grimaced as he lifted one corner of the snow-weighted camouflage netting. "They only have to send over a robot heli, with its radar scan, to know there's something here. But of course, they've no reason to believe there is."

They clambered up into the plane's underbelly, and Matt looked about him with pleasure; it was so different from any-

167

thing in their enforced medieval life. And yet simple; as simple as only great design can be.

"Could you fly this, Walther?" he asked, remembering Ludwig saying that their *Hochmeister* held a pilot's licence.

"With luck." Walther was studying the controls. "But navigation—a different matter. Unless one knows—Friedrich might manage that."

Helmut waved the latter towards the cockpit. "Examine what you please." Then he turned back to Walther. "My friend, I've been wondering if I should tell you of another thing that is—which is—is most important for us here." Matt had never imagined that the hawk-faced leader could look so indecisive, nor seem as embarrassed as someone discovered in a childish escapade; or was it that he was simply troubled by the presence of a foreigner? "It's rare and valuable, anyway," continued Helmut with some emphasis. "Apart from this, I don't know if we attach too much importance to what is, after all, only a symbol—" He paused.

"Symbols are most important things," said Walther. He looked grave, but Matt thought he was suppressing some excitement.

"I'm glad you say so." Still Helmut hesitated, with a sidelong glance at Matt. And just then Friedrich, absorbed in his examinations, exclaimed: "*Prima!* This is an old system, really; brought up-to-date. See, Matt—locking devices, that some rockets used; otherwise this computer settles your course—an override could change it—" His voice died away as he grew aware of Walther regarding him with deep annoyance.

"*You* were saying, Helmut—"

But Friedrich's interruption had effectively silenced the other leader. "Perhaps some other time," he muttered, looking at his watch. "Just now you want to examine these controls—And it's best not to disturb this camouflaging snow too often." And he drew Hans aside to discuss some technicalities of weapon-training.

Later, Matt saw just how furious Walther could be. His *Hochmeister's* tirade made the wretched Friedrich blench. "Now Helmut's clammed up again on his precious secret," finished Walther at last. "And if anything happens suddenly, it will be lost to us for ever . . ."

Days as snowy as anyone could remember now set in. The isolation felt more extreme, and the situation more hopeless, than was bearable. Food was short, and tempers shorter. Whatever Helmut's own feelings were, he showed little outwardly—nor any further signs of wishing to confide in Walther.

None of his assets was allowed to go to waste—he inspected arms, set watches, and gave Hans permission to arrange gymnastics. Matt told himself sourly that it was an obsessional's paradise. And all the time, in the outer world, the enemy had tightened an octopus grip more effectively from day to day. The only sounds on Helmut's receiver were the jabber of their voices, the wail of their music, and the stridency of their commands.

On the sixth of January—Twelfth Night and Epiphany, remembered Matt—there was such a freeze-up that it seemed probable ice now stretched from Herrenchiemsee to the shore. Although Helmut sent no one to examine its extent, he redoubled his watch.

On January the seventh Ludwig came staggering across the ice, a blot of shadow seemingly blown from out the heart of a blizzard. He collapsed a few metres from the shore, and would have died there if a faint rift in the falling curtains of snow hadn't revealed him to one of Helmut's guards. Matt, Walther and Hans sat with him by turns throughout the night, plying him with Helmut's precious schnapps when he awoke, and hearing his frantic mutterings with grave disquiet.

At midnight Matt joined Walther by the window. "An attack—doesn't it sound as if one's on the way?"

"Unless he's reliving Bad Mergentheim. Fetch Helmut."

Towards dawn Ludwig roused enough to recognise them, smile on seeing Walther, and gasp: "They're—going—take—Chiemsee—out."

"That's certain?" Helmut leaned forward anxiously, and the flickering torchlight made his beak of nose stand out in sharp relief as a grotesque shadow on the wall.

Ludwig dragged a hand across his forehead. Matt could barely recognize his former teacher in this half-starved wreck. "I was with—I—" He fell back and closed his eyes.

"Try and rouse him—it's urgent."

But the only answer to their coaxings and, finally, to their cruel and desperate shakings, was an exhausted babble that made nothing clear. Till at last Helmut said, "It's no use. We'll know nothing more till he's slept," and went away to check that everyone was alert and at his post.

It wasn't till almost noon that Walther and Matt went in search of Helmut, and found him in his private antechamber, working out an arms allotment with one of his lieutenants.

"Ah! He's spoken?"

"You permit?" Walther sat down at Helmut's desk, and drew a pad towards him. "Yes. After Mergentheim he went southwestward, like this—" his pencil stabbed at the paper— "and after three days he was picked up, but managed to pass himself off as an escapee from a labour gang. It was simple, since two had just left that neighbourhood. They sent him to what remains of Munich, where he was given work, cleaning and cooking for warders in the gaol. Not that there were many to slave for, with so few prisoners." Walther grimaced. "On his first day he was mucking out an empty cell when someone was brought down after questioning, thrown in to die there on the floor. The enemy is so insolent now, there was no hiding anything. Ludwig was treated as though he had neither eyes nor ears. So he was able to help the man a little, before he died. His name was Lothar. Franz Lothar."

Helmut made a sudden movement.

"Yes—Lothar. He had broken under questioning, and Ludwig said he was glad to die. He was with you in the Schwarzwald, wasn't he, before you had to scatter?"

"Unfortunately." (Not even, "Poor Franz", thought Matt. What a stone the man is.) "He was our expert in the enemy's jargon, as Friedrich was for you."

"They only picked him up about the time they caught Ludwig, or we'd all be dead by now. He'd kept successfully on the run till these heavy snows came, when he made a last strenuous effort to reach you here. Disastrously. Lothar told them about Chiemsee."

"Did he hear—air attack? Rockets?"

But one must admire him, thought Matt. Not a tremor in that voice, no flicker of dismay in those strange eyes. His own stomach felt like unset jelly.

"It seems a squadron of K'an Sis was expected to fly in, any day. But Lothar thought the Colonel favoured an alternative: armour, if the ice would hold; or snowshoe troops, with lasers. It seemed the man wanted all the information he could salvage, but was in no particular hurry, the weather being what it is. They're not only arrogant, but lazy: owing to the general slackness, Ludwig managed to break out that night."

There was silence, while Helmut stared into space, his fingertips feeling the table's surface, like a blind man's. Matt had the oddest feeling that he would never speak again. But at last he gave a great cry like a wounded hound's.

It startled his hearers so much that Walther leaped to his feet and stood staring.

"*Kaput!*"

And "Done for, done for, done for" the words echoed from wall to wall and along the adjacent gallery of mirrors. The following silence seemed unbreakable. At last Matt said timidly, "Couldn't *we* break out first? Now?" But as if in answer the snow slapped softly at the windows.

Walther put out a hand and touched the other leader's sleeve. "Defeat is bitter," he said, from a full heart.

That night the snow cleared; stars sparked frostily from a black sky. It seemed ominous to Matt, who stood by his window looking out. Walther had been summoned by Helmut, and had been gone some time. There was no sound anywhere, not even of men talking.

"A fine night on which to die," muttered Hans.

It was strange, but everything in Matt still refused to believe it.

"Perhaps it will be tomorrow."

"Perhaps. If I were their Colonel, I would say tonight. What a target we must be."

"Why, there's Orion." Matt felt ridiculous pleasure. "My childhood friend." And Jan's, he thought. Does she watch him now in Golden Valley? Does she?

It was as if his thought sparked off everything that followed.

There were hurried footsteps, and Walther entered, carrying a small, square, wooden box as though it were very precious.

"Helmut has a mission for us," he said abruptly. "Where's Friedrich?"

"Playing chess!"

"He would. Fetch him, Matt." Walther crossed to Ludwig, and took his hand. "Are you any stronger?"

Ludwig tried to raise himself, but fell back again, panting. Walther's expression was grave, and almost imperceptibly he shook his head. Their eyes met, and in Ludwig's was a look of pained acceptance.

When Matt returned with Friedrich, Walther said: "We are leaving. Four of us." And Ludwig caught Matt's eye, and tried to smile.

Walther's face was so grim that they didn't dare to question him. "Get your things together. You, Matt, take the canister."

It didn't take them long, and as they hustled to and fro the strangest fantasy occupied Matt's thoughts. They were being driven out like the scapegoat. Helmut would be sending them towards the enemy, in the hope of convincing them that Chiemsee was already abandoned—

He wasn't aware of the exact second when Helmut joined them, hurried and abstracted.

"Ready now? Your rations are downstairs, Matt and Hans must carry them." He stood looking down on Ludwig, and then said in kinder tones than Matt had ever heard him use, "Your friends are leaving you. But whatever happens, you'll be in good company."

They descended the staircase, with Walther still holding the wooden box. Helmut threw over his shoulder, "My scouts have reported movement on the ice."

It was eerie, that departure. Each man they passed was already at his post, and to Matt it seemed the way was lined with faces of the dead, a farewell from the portals of Valhalla. Once outside, Helmut and Walther set such a pace that the others could barely keep up with them. They floundered through thick snow, with Helmut urging them on impatiently. His contained violence and Walther's silence intimidated them, and they didn't dare to ask about their destination. Some hideaway, perhaps, for a mere few, which Helmut hoped might be overlooked. Yet why choose them, the newcomers to Chiemsee?

They came to a familiar band of trees. Neat and ready, beneath its camouflage jacket of netting and snow, stood the Q'uo Si.

Helmut must be crazy, thought Matt.

"Help me remove the netting."

They swore, tangled the stuff, got drenched with cascades of snow, heavier now than it had been before. Once the plane was cleared, the five stood confronting one another, their background the trees of winter, and the dark.

"Good luck," said Helmut. He appeared unmoved, but his tones sounded more guttural than usual. He touched the wooden case. "You will protect that?"

Walther smiled. "The correct answer is: with our lives."

Then Helmut smiled, and shook his head. He looked younger, and vulnerable, and very sad. Matt thought again of Valhalla. With only a wave of the hand, and no words of farewell, Helmut turned, and plunged off between the trees.

"He wouldn't leave his men." Walther looked even sadder than Helmut had. Perhaps he was thinking of those he had had to abandon at Bad Mergentheim. All of them were thinking of Ludwig, but there was nothing left to say.

Walther turned towards the plane. "We'll be rejoining him, if I can't get this off the ground. Up with you, quickly."

"Where are we going?" asked Matt at last, as he obeyed.

"With luck, to England. And luck we shall most certainly be needing, the whole way."

8 § The City in the Sea

"It's like the take-off of a multi-millionaire's toy," said Matt. "Smooth and safe."

"Wait to say things like that till we land again."

The Schloss was already another toy below. The lake was a white curve, with jigsaw-patterned edges. South-west there were many crawling dots upon the ice. Then Herreninsel and Fraueninsel dropped away beneath a wing, and streamers of cloud took their place. Walther seemed happy enough handling the Q'uo Si; and Friedrich was quietly examining a map.

"Walther?" ventured Matt.

"Mmm?"

"Where in England?"

"North, I think. Or even Scotland."

"You mean—you don't know?"

Walther shook his head. "Helmut wants the contents of that box taken as far away as possible. Saved, of course, if *that's* possible. And if not, destroyed."

Matt was dying to ask him if Helmut had told him what was in it. But he had learned better than to question Walther further when he wore that abstracted, slightly grim expression. Instead, he murmured thoughtfully: "Golden Valley . . ."

"What's that?"

Rather hesitantly Matt explained; and then blurted out the story of the Orion message that he'd picked up at Bad Mergentheim. "It could have been hallucination," he ended doubtfully. "But anyway, it sounds as good a place as any; far north, and isolated." He couldn't believe that Walther would take him seriously, but the latter seemed interested.

"We could try. Can you find it on the map? Give it to him, Friedrich."

Matt's heart seemed to give a lurch, and his hands were clumsy with excitement; but he found what he was looking for, and marked the map in pencil. Friedrich glanced sideways at it, made some swift calculations, and handed Walther the result. A light beamed up on the control panel, winked twice, and settled to a steady glow of green.

"If I've done that correctly we're locked straight on course now. If. Or we may hit the North Pole."

"Unless something else hits us first."

"What height have we now?"

"Nearly thirty thou'. Look down, Matt. That should be Würzburg on our right."

"Already?"

"Already."

A little while later Friedrich said, "We passed the border. See the coastline ahead? It's altogether too clear for my liking. Their defences must be sleeping."

"Cripes, we've got speed on."

Friedrich twirled a dial, and suddenly let out a groan. "Fool that I am—wasn't properly tuned." He pressed an intercom. button, and from his receiver a jabber of voices broke querulously on the air.

"What's this about?" asked Walther.

"Asking us to identify ourselves. Sound threatening. Must be the thirtieth time of asking. What shall I tell them?"

"Say we're on patrol from Munich."

Jabber, jabber.

"And now they want our identification number."

"Tell them the real one," said Matt. "That'll fox them."

"No, don't. Give the first two initials and a different number."

Friedrich obeyed. There was an ominous silence, and then some crosstalk as two stations discussed the unknown plane.

"*Ach, Himmel!* They're sending up an El-agent."

Walther nodded grimly. Matt's stomach felt tauter still as he asked: "What's that, when it's at home? A rocket?"

"Something like it," said Friedrich over his shoulder. "Only instead of blowing us it'll latch itself on and 'read' us: crew, course, if we're carrying explosives, or any metal." He shrugged expressively.

"I thought Helmut could be making a mistake," murmured Walther; he touched the wooden box by his side. Matt's heart thumped. *He* was thinking of the carefully-placed explosives in the canister by Friedrich's seat.

A few seconds later the plane shuddered and bounced, wings dipping from side to side.

"That's it."

There was a rapid stream of electronic pippings.

"Chatty little fellow," said Matt. "Think it's taken colour of hair and eyes?"

Once the El-agent had finished reporting there was a short ominous silence; then the steady green light on Friedrich's control panel flickered and went out.

"We're being taken off course—I think."

Golden Valley, thought Matt, clutching his knees. Too good to be true, anyhow.

"Yes," said Walther. "We're starting to descend. They've got some sort of very sophisticated ground control going. There may be a way to combat it, but I don't know it. Look."

Top right of the control panel an orange light was glowing.

"That'll be the override course."

Matt stared at it hypnotised: a small angry presence, like a hypnotic orange bee. Hans was being sick.

"Friedrich, can you work out where this course is likely to land us? Are there enemy airfields marked in this code book Helmut gave me, from those papers? Have a look, will you—we might as well know the worst."

Friedrich took the little book from Walther, examined it, and after a moment shook his head.

"There may be . . . But it's an impossible task, so quickly. Even for me."

"We're not heading back towards Chiemsee?" asked Matt.

"No. And with this speed we'll be coming down quite soon."

"I hope not. That's the sea."

"Hold on—what's happening?"

The plane vibrated violently, and then was thrown around as though caught in a whirlpool. Hans was sick again. Luckily their seatbelts were fastened, or someone would have been hurt. When the plane righted itself the green light shone once more; the orange was still there but failing, flickering like a candle flame.

"Their override's breaking down—"

They watched, fascinated, hardly daring to hope. The green shone steadily, but the orange hadn't given up. It flashed on and off.

"Listen," said Friedrich. "They're puzzled, too."

Now and then the plane was shaken again, convulsively; then both lights faltered and went out, till the green reappeared, alone.

"Extraordinary interference," muttered Walther. "Kind of freak storm, perhaps—no, that's impossible. Whatever it is, it's put out our *wunderkind* behind. Paralysed it, somehow."

Hope grew stronger.

"But why hasn't it put us out too?" asked Matt.

No one could answer him.

"What are they saying now?"

"I can't make sense of it at all. Not a word clear."

"Drunk," muttered Hans.

"Or a dialect of some kind. Not like their jargon, though. Funny; almost seems I could understand it, but—it's retreating, isn't it—No, just listen to this, now."

There was a distant-sounding murmur, which was more

like wordless song, rising and falling, and then swelling clear.

"*Are* they words?" said Friedrich. "I thought I got something then about 'time—your time, not ours'—but it keeps fading just when—If we were farther north already, we might have got it clearer."

"I thought I was getting words, too," said Matt. He felt confused, fearful that he might be hallucinating again. Last time it had been Jan's voice. Now it was music, giving him words about a Great King, and Orion.

"The Freaks are very worried now, at least," Friedrich told them. "They sent up another El, and it promptly went off course. We're still riding straight home on your target, Matt."

"The sooner we find our destination . . ." muttered Walther. "Matt and Friedrich—are you wearing your chutes? Here— one of you take this." He touched Helmut's box. "You, Friedrich. Matt, have you that canister safe?"

Matt's stomach turned over. "Yes—But isn't Hans going to jump?"

"No," said Hans, positively.

"Still holding; and must be nearly there, now. Feel the loss of height?"

"Ears and stomach churning," said Matt; and then, "Why the chutes, anyway—won't we land in the ordinary way?"

"If we can. If there's any more overriding, I'm going to drop you both out."

"You'll need me, Walther," said Friedrich.

Walther shook his head. "Don't argue. Hans is too sick to jump."

"We could throw him out! Abandon plane—all four."

"Only two chutes," said Walther simply. And Matt knew he was determined not to be one of the wearers. Not after Bad Mergentheim.

"Walther—"

"It's an order."

They were silent. Hoping. Hoping. The green shone steadily.

"Very near, now," said Friedrich.

After all, thought Matt, and: *Jan.* Unable to believe it could be true.

"Low enough to drop you, if—"

A dial needle flickered and fell. There was a shudder, and the plane seemed to stand still in mid-air, an unpleasant illusion. Simultaneously the green light died, and a fresh orange glow shone from the control panel.

"Caught," Walther's tone was dead. "Open that chute hatch. Prepare to jump."

"Something may happen again, and—"

"Out you go, both of you. Quickly."

Everything seemed to be going at enormous speed.

Impossible, Matt was thinking, I couldn't—And yet there he was, with the plane's underbelly seeming to fall away beneath his feet, and Friedrich following him out and down. They were too close together, but their luck held, and they were clear.

It was a terrible sensation. Matt was temporarily deprived of will and reason. The drop itself seemed to be eternal. Imprisoned in the viewless winds—but they didn't hold him, only let him slip downward through cloud till he lost consciousness, to open his eyes once more swinging above the earth's curve, with the pale flowering of the chute as his one delicate support. His hands felt numb, but he still clasped the canister. Above the swaying circle streamers of cloud chased each other; between them the stars shone clear. There was no sound except the creak of his harness. The Q'uo Si carrying Walther and Hans to their fates was already far away on its new course. He looked down. Nothing but obscurity, hummocks, and eastwards a black plain which might be the sea. Strange to find himself alive. Strange to see England all darkness when airflights had always brought him in over rivers of light. Uncanny . . . And immediately he saw below him a pinpoint of light, which flared and vanished. He blinked. Imagination? Some way to his right another pale circle fell, turning in the wind.

Now the earth's surface was moving rapidly to meet him, the curved horizon flattened, became the rim of a black bowl into which he fell. Were those mountains cutting out the stars? Would he hit a tree? A lake? Fear in the stomach. Cold metal in his hands.

He clutched the canister, thinking, Oh Jesus! I'll go up like a bomb. His numbed right hand felt clumsily for the cap, and gave it a quick double turn. Neutralize it, if it wasn't already. Strange, he couldn't remember. Perhaps I've activated it. Cold panic. Still here, though. Feet drawn up for landing, roll over. Was that right, or—

It was.

And how I find my way out of this—He rose, staggered, fell again, enveloped in the chute. He had lost the canister, his face was pressed into rough wet grass, his legs trailed among pebbles in the running water of a stream. He was breathless, dizzy, yet somehow exultant.

Fantastic—back in England! Smell the soil . . .

"We're here," said Walther grimly. "Feel it?"

Feel it they did. It was like descending in a lift-shaft—faster and faster, stomachs plastered to the ceiling. The orange light on the flightboard winked and went out, and was succeeded by a steady purple glow. On the dials needles flickered and swung.

Below, shreds of cloud drifted between them and a calm and moonlit sea. Still very small from this height the sea-city lay like a cluster of globules scattered among the oil rigs. At one point the cluster was quite dense.

"That's where we'll land," said Walther. And then, "We've done all we could." Defeat is bitter, he'd told Helmut; further comment seemed useless.

"What's that greenish glow?" asked Hans hoarsely.

They came down in the centre of it: a small floodlit square with beams trained on them from every quarter. The plane shuddered as they landed, and Hans let out a sigh.

"At least it's the ground."

"My poor Hans."

The silence and the greenish glow persisted. For a while nothing happened, and it was impossible to see beyond the blaze of light directed at the plane. At last a ramp was run out, propelled by figures in white helmets and boiler-suits.

"What's up now?"

There was a metallic clunking from the plane's tail end.

"The El's being dismantled, I think," said Walther. All the delays, boredom—and the fear—reminded him of his first flight: if only it would start; if only it would never happen.

"Here's a second ramp now." Walther touched Hans on the arm. They looked at each other, and took deep, steadying breaths.

It was like Airport Munich Two, that most modern of flight-ports, but with a difference. There, they'd handle your baggage for you and move you smoothly from the revolving ramp straight into your plane or—more expensively—your spacehopper. Here you were the baggage, passed silently from hand to hand; examined, tattooed on the left wrist, placed separately in small cells where lights blinked, recording discs spun, an unseen watcher used discreet eyeholes, and a soothing voice questioned, questioned, leaving time for answers.

Walther was determinedly silent until the voice, in almost accentless German, remarked conversationally: "So then you left Chiemsee with these other three—Hans, Friedrich, Matt?"

"I said nothing!" Walther broke into a sweat. His unseen interrogator laughed.

"Didn't you? Look there." His chair was suddenly revolved so that a screen came into view where needles had drawn signs and symbols as on a heart-machine. The bland voice proceeded to read it off aloud, converting the symbols into: "—then Helmut became anxious, that was, that was, yes, it was the last meeting, never tell enemies that, they don't know anything, how's Hans holding out, wish I was setting out with him again, did Matt and Friedrich land all right, wonder if Helmut's dead, must be, Chiemsee."

"Quite an interesting piece of thought recording, yes?" Walther was quick to recover from the shock.

"You'll get nothing more out of me." He began to concentrate feverishly on other subjects, anything, gardens, roses, flowers, verse, '*Bist du bei mir, geh' ich mit Freuden, zum Sterben und zu meiner Ruh.*'

"*Mit Freuden?*" asked the watcher; and laughed.

There was a silence, and the chair revolved again. Walther sat tensely where they'd strapped him. He had thought the electrodes attached to his head and body were part of some old-fashioned system of inflicting pain, which he must resist. But there was no need here for pain. On this little isolated sea-kingdom the most modern of all methods was in use.

Behind him the voice said blandly, "Simple, yet reliable."

"I can screen my thoughts from you." A rash boast.

"Is that so? We can knock out your concentration."

"Tortured people don't think. They scream."

"Your outlook is so out of date. It's quite amusing. Tell me —when you were outside, did you notice some people wearing black?"

"Yes. Men and women. Working."

"You saw nothing unusual about them?"

"No—except that some wore different-coloured armlets."

"Did they look sad, depressed, anguished—as if anyone had hurt them?"

"No." Walther gave an involuntary shudder at the recollection of constant smiles: each slave's face set into almost childish serenity.

"A good slave is a happy slave. Our motto here."

"You beat them into it, I suppose."

A sigh. "We're experimenting with ways of founding a perfect society, where inferior people do the work promptly and with no resentment. Happiness is merely part of the programming. With our specially researched methods there's not the slightest need for rebellion." The voice paused, then addressed a second invisible presence. "All right, send him in."

Walther heard footsteps behind him.

"Go round in front of him. Let him see you," commanded the interrogator.

It was Hans who stood there, already dressed in black with a white armlet. His pale eyes wore a tranced look, and on his lips was a placid smile. He stared at Walther as though he didn't recognize him.

"Hans!" said Walther urgently. "What is it—what have they done to you?"

Hans remained silent, still smiling.

"Answer your friend," said the interrogator. "Tell him how you are getting on." The tone was benevolent, almost paternal.

"Everyone is pleased with me."

"We're glad. I hope you're happy with us too?"

"So happy."

"Tell your friend Walther why you are so happy."

"An obedient slave is a happy slave. It is good to be here—such important work to do. All the world-cities will benefit. It's a privilege to work for such results. There will be no hunger, no rebellion. Everyone who works will revere his master, and love him, and would die for him."

"We're specially pleased with you and Walther, Hans. Tell him why we're so pleased."

"The masters are pleased because we brought them their valuable plane. Because I told them how Matt and Friedrich left it."

"Yes, you've been most useful to us. And now you may go."

184

Walther closed his eyes, in order not to see Hans's ignominious departure. He knew, though, that they would read his despair as if he'd shouted it aloud.

"A simple collar—you noticed it?—and a few electrodes. Almost primitive. Nothing our scientists pride themselves on, though in a few years . . . But you're feeling distressed, no? So let's speak of something else: from our Rocket-El we know the course you were following; and from your friend something of why your two men jumped, and what they carried— though no details of the contents. You will tell us this—also," the voice sharpened—"why we temporarily lost our hold?"

Walther was quick to seize on the last question.

"It puzzled all of us. It was like—like being seized by great hands, and rocked in mid-air. It was outside my experience. If I'd been at work in some observatory—" He stopped, then continued, "I was a student of astronomy, and worked for some months with one of our greatest astronomers. He might have known what caused such a disturbance."

"Interesting. We have an observatory. Strange activity has been reported lately, so—Which astronomer?"

"Heinkelm."

"Heinkelm—Indeed."

There was a silence, while Walther wished he could see a graph of his interrogator's thoughts. At last the latter said: "Mm—I wonder. Would you care to see our observatory?"

What trap now? thought Walther warily; and the other man laughed.

"You're so amusing. No trap. Perhaps we might gain something, from a fresh viewpoint. Perhaps we might be grateful. Perhaps you might even—enjoy it. Tell us everything you can, and I'll take you there. You might—work there, mm? Freely."

"Free? Not as some sort of programmed robot?"

"A robot cannot do research. You would be supervised, of course."

Walther said: "Take me there. If I can help you to understand the interferences, I will. And—*afterwards*—I'll tell you all you want to know."

There was a faint click as the scanning mechanism was switched off. Walther heard footsteps approaching his chair. Afterwards, he was thinking. A gambler's chance. But anything could happen between now and that afterwards. Friedrich and Matt, I'll do my best for you.

"A remarkable achievement."

"We have the labour, you see," said Walther's interrogator.

They stood beneath the dome of the Radiscope, on the Earthspot of the revolving floor. The black cylindrical walls, some forty metres apart at their widest point, were dull and empty on three sides. On the fourth pulsed a galaxy. The interrogator spoke briefly into a microphone, and a selected part of the galaxy was immediately enlarged to cover a wide area of wall, and then to flow around them, as though they were heading through it in a spaceship.

The interrogator was gratified by Walther's expression. "You've not seen one before?"

"Nothing so advanced." The astronomer in Walther was delighted; the prisoner dismayed. These people—No doubt they'd be establishing their world civilization, no matter of what kind. Matt's and Friedrich's escape mission now seemed a folly of follies.

"You see, we scan in depth, pinpointing the target—so."

"Beautiful."

The patterns shifted. Jupiter's moons moved in like dancers, and Saturn's rings spun nearer, then retreated.

"Home ground."

"You were scanning when the disturbances happened?"

"I'll see the reports. Wait."

A word into the microphone. The walls gleamed dull and black. The touch of a floor button illumined a panel at their feet, and a tape flicked across it.

"It was just some routine check of the northern hemisphere. One a schoolboy could have understood."

"And?"

"And the radi-scanner in the scope went mad. Our operator thought it had developed a fault, however improbable. None was found." The man's foot touched the button again, and the panel light faded away. "Time-checks show it happened just when we lost control of your—our Q'uo Si."

"On the plane's radion we heard some sounds too. Like a few words—or some sort of singing. You keep radi-records here?"

"Not detailed ones for a mere routine scan."

Walther felt acutely disappointed. "What a pity."

"Now we'll show you a similar scan." A few words into the microphone brought the whole panoply of the northern hemisphere into display.

"*Wunderschön.*"

A slow, strange circling began. Walther blinked. It wasn't the revolving floor, which was stationary. The turning of the stars made him dizzy.

"Can't you steady them?"

The interrogator spoke into the microphone again, but nothing happened. Only the circling became faster and faster. "Not another fault?" he shouted.

High in the wall of the cylindrium a door opened, and a man looked down and shouted back, angrily and—to Walther—incomprehensibly.

The giddy dance went on. He felt as if he were reeling away into space, slowly swinging towards one constellation which drew him as the magnetic north draws a compass needle. Or it was moving in on him, stretching out to cover the whole surface of the cylindrium. He saw Orion's familiar belt of stars, close and closer. At the same time as the light from Betelgeux and Rigel pulsed more compellingly he grew conscious of soundwaves beating against his eardrums, growing in volume, high, hypnotic, meaning somehow conveyed through the rhythms of a wordless song.

"You are still too far away—You must hold to the Great King's treasure. Hidden are the ways—"

Hands to his forehead, groping at meaning, Walther felt as though he spun indefinitely in space.

"Not flinch before . . . Deliverance . . . do you understand?"

Walther was unaware that he was shouting: "*Make the message clearer.*"

The sound and light grew till he felt as if it absorbed him into itself.

"The ancient tower in the zodiac."

Tower? What tower? This observatory couldn't be called a tower.

And then there was a sudden jarring which shook his entire body. He was struggling to stand upright.

What happened? Exhaustion . . . Did I faint? It was like the aftermath of a titanic wrestling match. While he stood, drawing shuddering breaths, he was suddenly aware that the interrogator was lying sprawled across the floor. Simultaneously a door behind him burst open, and two men came running in, jabbering excitedly in their distress. They ignored him, and bent over the fallen man.

Walther felt as though he were in some extraordinary dream that had also heightened his perceptions. He noticed how the unconscious interrogator's foot was just touching one of the floor-set control buttons. The star-patterns on the wall had faded till all was dull and black. He looked about him wonderingly, and back at the figure on the ground. So—*he* tried to fight it! Didn't the fool realize how dangerous that could be, in a place like this?

"Your interrogator is—er— He suffered a black-out, in the observatory."

Walther nodded gravely. He was back in his cell, but not strapped to that abominable chair; so it was safe to think, at present. If only he had managed to escape, he might have thrown himself off the top of the observatory; but there had been no chance.

There was a pause. Evidently this new man was examining his notes.

"I see you were taken there because you worked with Heinkelm."

"Yes."

"And there were one or two outstanding matters which we wished you to clear up."

Walther didn't answer. He was thinking: What luck, his German's terrible. That means we'll have to wait for the other one—if he recovers. Mustn't show I speak English.

There was a rustle of papers. "Well, we will leave those matters now. The two escaped men will eventually be found, no doubt. We will discuss your working for us here. As a privileged case you would have relative freedom."

"No need to spell it out."

"Spell?" The man sounded perplexed. He said pompously, "Confinement to the observatory and surrounding quarters. Incidentally, we are making a fine water-park there. Most pleasing. Outside, we should treat you like anyone else."

Walther thought of Hans.

"We offer you a chance to prove your worth for our superior rule. When the observatory system—er, failed, we were interested to see that you were unaffected."

So no one had noticed that the first interrogator had tried to jam it—more luck, thought Walther.

"These—disturbances are very odd."

"You said the system failed."

"Possibly, possibly." Walther felt that he was being looked at darkly. "If you're not helpful, we can always reconsider your case."

"You'll force me to help you."

"But we can't harness your intuition to work for us. At least, not yet."

Well, that's something—and I too should like to know more

189

about these peculiar disturbances, thought Walther. The Great King's treasure . . . Could that be Helmut's treasure?

And: If I co-operate enough, could it help to keep these Freaks' minds off Matt and Friedrich . . . and what they carried?

"I shall be interested to do all I can," he said.

9 ⚘ Reunion

Early on the night of Chiemsee's destruction, Jan climbed the high hill eastward of Golden Valley. It was growing dark, and very cold, but luckily the heavy snows girdling the Continent had missed the north-east of England. Lately the skies had been overcast, but tonight they were so clear that the stars blazed furiously, and almost seemed to be approaching. She was two-thirds of the way uphill, and could see Orion wheeling above her, Betelgeux blazing at his shoulder and Rigel at his foot.

Jan, staring, stood entranced. Easy to see why primitive cultures worshipped heavenly bodies. Orion, Great Hunter, chase those Freaks from the earth . . . Strange imaginings one could allow oneself at night! Yet why shouldn't stars be heavenly messengers—or at least mysterious influences, good or bad? Orion, you're good, you remind me of Matt, let him have received my message . . .

It was just then that she heard a whisper of sound from the south-east—a sinister vibration of the air. Oh, no: not another of them—

Orion—Hardly with her volition, her right hand moved, and some brandy spilled from the clay cup's rim on to the earth. A libation.

Half-laughing, half-ashamed, she pursued her way uphill.

Clanger had his listening post in a hollow just over the summit's brow. It was protected from the east winds by sheep hurdles and brush, but even so they found out every crack and corner. The little retractable mast that he had built swayed to and fro; she could see its whipping motion as she neared it. Clanger was crouched in the entrance, blowing on numbed fingers.

"Hi, Clang!"

Clumsily he pushed back his headphones. "Hi, stranger! Late, aren't you? Brought my nosh?"

"Cold rabbit, bread, apple, goat cheese."

Clanger pulled an ungrateful face, just visible by the brilliant starlight. "Cold to the cold."

"And brandy. Old Ned's special, from Wolf."

"Good girl. Give it here, quick."

Jan peered at him anxiously. She'd grown first to tolerate Clanger, and then to like him. In a decaying civilization he'd been a thieving and violent misfit, but under primitive conditions he'd proved to be one of the strongest of them all. Resourceful, cheerful, a born survivor and perfect scrounger and constructor. If there was a minor problem Clanger always seemed able to cope with it. No one else had known how to make passable soap, or plasters for Jan's chest when she had bronchitis (mustard from the Sussex foodstore, thick on a pad of sheep-wool). He was—so Bill asserted—the perfect type of early nomadic man, plus nucleo-radic genes.

"Had a boring time, Clang?"

"So-so. They've not used much English in ten days. Got a good notion of where they're speaking from, that's all." Clanger's fine teeth tore at the rabbit leg. He wiped the back of his hand across his mouth, licked his fingers with relish. "That was good, that was. Like a nip of brandy?"

Jan shook her head.

"There's been some sort of muck-up somewhere. Lot of pipping, an' flurry." Clanger picked his teeth, reflectively.

"They don't—sound nearer?" A tinge of Jan's old fear showed in her voice.

"They're in the sea."

"*What?*"

"Yah. Yell, isn't it? Reckon they've something going for

them, out there. By the oil rigs. 'Least, *I* don't reckon," said Clanger philosophically, " 'cos it takes learning, that does. Bill an' Leo worked it out—an' then Wolf gets Wolfish with one of our ruddy prisoners, in a manner of speaking, an' learns a bit. Seems they'd plans for a solar city state, cut off, slave run. Experimental stuff, see? Slaves born to slaves, never let 'em off their island; no reading, no learning. Just teach 'em to obey an' worship Freaks. Nasty future stuff."

"Cruel," said Jan.

Clanger stretched out a hand to her. "Well, that's enough." He shot her a quick look. "See what you make of this: got a lot of crackle on tonight; like you get with sunspots."

"Oh Clang! Sunspots! You're just trying to distract me. This time of year?"

"Heh, sun don't run by our time, does it? Too blazing big. This were something different, see? Seemed almost like it was meant. An' jamming! Real vicious jamming, it was. Or something. Then nothing."

"Just Freaks again, I suppose."

"Don't think so. Tell you for why—each time there'd be one hell of a lot of squeak-squeaking; like Freaks throwing fits getting the wind up somehow. That's what I guess. An' once or twice someone giving tongue with even worse mumbo than theirs. Funny sort of sound, almost singing. Couldn't block it off, I couldn't, even if I'd wanted to. An' then it was as if I'd know what it was about." Clanger wrinkled up his forehead like a puzzled gundog.

"Did you hear a plane?" asked Jan. She couldn't take this singing seriously. (Clang hallucinating, all alone here?) But planes, like helis, were all too real.

"Dunno. Can't seem to remember one. I thought—" he laughed, self-conscious—"some bloke said, 'your time's not our time' an' 'the Great King's tal—talisman'. What's that, anyway? But I couldn't have understood, could I?"

Jan looked at him anxiously, thinking of the strangeness of hills by night, the loneliness.

"Like Char to come up and keep you company? She's wild for star-watching."

Clanger's laugh was entirely normal; ribald and reassuring.

"Stars? Growing up a bit too fast out here, I reckon."

"Oh."

"Send her up, though—if you're sick of her down there. I c'n cope." Clanger chuckled. He read doubt into her silence. "Tell you, she won't get out of hand with me. Not yet! S'funny, Jan. Reckon you've somehow cut off since that Matt of yours scarpered. Pity. Could do with a woman, here—"

Jan started to scramble up. She'd had trouble before—though never with Clanger. But in the Temple, or the Valley, there'd always been other people close at hand. Now she was suddenly very aware of Clanger's stifled violence, the aloneness, a primitive fear. He laughed again. Out of the darkness his hand gripped her wrist, pulling her towards him. Caught off-balance she fell forward, groping to save herself. Clanger's rough jersey was against her face, half-stifling her. His other hand was entangled in her hair.

"All this comradeship stuff's not up to much, is it?"

Just then they heard Charlie's resonant tones hailing them from somewhere close at hand: "Clang! Jannie! It's only me."

Clanger swore. His arms relaxed and Jan struggled free, calling softly, "Char. Don't make such a row."

Charlie's fleecy rabbitskin helmet, visible by starlight, bobbed over the brow. In a moment she was scrambling into the hollow beside them. "Brought you another apple, Clang."

"I said you needn't come." Jan pushed back her hair, and pulled her sweater straight. She could almost feel Charlie's suspicious stare, and Clanger's sardonic grin. "Come on, we're going down."

"We're not. I've only just come."

"You both get out an' stay out. Had enough of girls up here, see."

"Why, Clang, whatsa matter?" Charlie peered into his face. "Had a row with Jan?" Her voice quickened with interest.

"Oh—bet you tried some sexy business. You are stupid, she's *fixated* on Matt, didn't you know? You'll just have to wait for me."

"Not waiting for no one. Told you to get out, an' meant it." Clanger turned his back on them and replaced his headphones. After a moment Charlie accepted the rebuff and followed Jan downhill, muttering, "Funny how life's just the same everywhere, isn't it?"

"Is it?"

"Well, even Arthur had trouble, didn't he?"

"Oh Char, it wasn't all that!"

"Well, at least I'll be fifteen *next* December . . . Did you hear a plane, earlier? I thought—Look, there's Orion."

"Yes, I did. And I've seen him," said Jan shortly. "And do look where you're going."

But she was still troubled as they stumbled downhill; and not just about the plane. Fixated on Matt, as Charlie put it, she'd not given much thought to anyone else's feelings. Had Leo, Tom, Wolf or Bill felt as irritated by her unawareness as Clanger? And what, in these abnormal times, was the age of consent for a rapidly ripening Charlie?

Then, more naturally, she began to laugh.

"What's it now?"

"Nothing. Just wondering if it's my fate or yours to be future mother-goddess to the tribe."

They reached the bottom of the valley, and followed the stream in the direction of the cave. The water's babbling was loud in the stillness.

"Clang's freezing up there, he'll have to come down soon," said Jan, as they picked their way among stones and tufts of grass. Suddenly Charlie clutched at her. "Jan! Somebody coming!"

"Don't, Char! It's only Wolf—and Leo. What's the matter, Wolf? Why've you got that gun?"

"Didn't you both hear that plane go over?"

Jan had been trying to pretend that she hadn't. Her stomach somersaulted. "Yes, we did."

By moonlight Wolf's features were pinched, ferocious. There was a look about him that Alastair would have recognized.

"It's trouble," said Leo. "We think."

"Where's Alastair?"

"In the cave, with Grouse an' Fox."

"Tom?"

"Heli-guarding. With some others." Wolf's tones held the careful neutrality that they always had when he spoke of Tom. He hoisted the webbing sling of a laser gun over his shoulder, and nodded to Leo. "March."

Charlie grabbed at his arm, but he shook her off. "Go join the kid, can't you? *Leo.*" They slipped away into the half light. Hoppo came bounding out of the shadows, and followed them. Jan noticed that they moved almost as silently as he did. She turned towards the cave.

"Come on, Char."

Inside it Alastair was playing at knucklebones with Fox, by a doused fire. Grouse was sleeping, propped against the sloping wall. Such tension as there was showed only in white faces raised towards the entering pair.

"*What* about this plane?" asked Charlie breathlessly. "There's been others, so why the—Surely Freaks couldn't have seen anything, could they?"

Alastair finished his throw, and calmly inspected the result. "Leo was on watch, thought he saw something drop. Chute, maybe."

"One parachutist wouldn't make sense." Jan felt cheered. (More night hallucinations, that was all.)

"But if he saw one, there were probably others."

"Where—"

Alastair's head jerked vaguely south-eastwards. "There, up the other end. So there could have been—" He left the sentence unfinished. " 'S your throw, Fox."

"There's no one on guard," said Charlie indignantly, stripping off her rabbit cap.

"You do it, Char."

"Not me. I'm fruz. Did you have to let the fire out?" She held her hands over the damp, warm ashes.

"Wolf said."

"I'll go." Mule picked up a wooden, weighted cosh, and sidled past them.

"Jan, could you take a look at Grouse?" said Alastair. "Bill seemed worried about him, earlier. He keeps falling asleep."

Jan's stomach did another somersault, as she groped her way to Grouse's side. His pulse was threadlike, bumping now and then beneath her touch as though his life were trying to escape between her fingers. His forehead was cold, and sweating. He twisted his head away and mumbled something without waking.

"What did he say?"

"Back with his mother, I think."

"Ought we to wake him?"

"What good would that do?"

"Maybe give him something to drink?"

"I think it would be better not," said Alastair. "*Much* better not."

There it was. Much better not.

Poor Grouse, thought Jan. He did want to see the spring . . . Then she remembered that none of them might see it. Her stomach was turning over like something on a spit. She must, she must escape from this place of forced and unreal calm— She jumped up and stumbled from the cave. Charlie's "Jan— don't! Come back" floated out into the dark behind her. Mule looked up, startled.

"Here! Whassup?"

But she paid him no attention, either, and ran on through the cold wet grass. The brook was down on her left, and the sound of its gentle, inexorable flow was calming; she slowed to a walk, aware that Wolf would be angry with her, yet reluctant to go back. She stood and listened; there was no other sound, anywhere.

Alastair did say "up the other end". But if I just follow the brook a little way—

And why should Wolf tell me what to do?

Now she felt oddly peaceful. It's like some old TV film. Nothing real can happen . . . Orion blazed in the sky away beyond some stunted thorn-trees. A sheep was bleating in the fold that Bill and Leo had constructed from ancient hurdles. There was what she called a night smell, as cold and thin as wet leaves trailing in cold water, or bark of trees after rain; as sweet as clover crunched beneath passing feet.

She had wandered a little while, still in this state of withdrawal, yet keeping instinctively to the streambed, when her right foot struck against something too large to be a pebble, too regular to be a rock. The newly-risen moon was just then hidden behind cloud. She knelt, to explore by fingering what she had found. It was cylindrical, not very long, metal—Her heart lurched, she withdrew her fingers as if stung. Springing up, she landed off-balance and ankle-deep in the streambed. The water was icy. She gasped and floundered. Something was clutching at her, dragging her down. She bit off a frightened squeal.

The moon sailed out from behind a cloud, and showed her the chute floating like a giant water-lily. She was entangled in its cords and the abandoned harness.

Oh Jesus! Leo was right. They're here. And I'm alone.

She stood shivering. Mustn't splash. Suppose that thing goes off?

Now the moon and starlight posed a threat. She felt herself snared against the stream's bright surface, as if tethered for the kill; the more she tried to free her ankles the more the wet cords twisted and clung. Her water-numbed fingers slipped uselessly on her skin.

Mustn't panic. Pull myself ashore . . .

Against combined drag of stream and chute she accomplished it, gathering up part of the billowing, wet mass. On the muddy bank she slipped and fell, turning her ankle, grazing her elbows, and kicking the metal thing, which gave out a clang. She began to cry, from mixed exasperation, fear and pain, and the chute itself took on a nightmare personality: enemy, octopus, malicious weight winding itself about her to hold her helpless for the kill.

A few metres off a shape rose against the sky, and a husky male voice whispered, "Friedrich?"

Jan froze.

The head moved, listening; the figure bunched into a crouch. Moonlight glinted on a knife-blade. She made a small sound like a trapped hare's cry.

The bunched figure launched itself forward. Her neck, stiff with terror, was extended as if she were offering herself for sacrifice. Moonlight and fear together blanched her face. The falling knife-blade was deflected to grate on the pebbles of the streambed.

"*Jan?*"

She couldn't swallow, couldn't speak. I'm mad—I must be, if I think it's—

"Jan! Darling, it's all right, it's me. Don't shake so, it's all *right*, I tell you—"

Matt's arms were tightly round her; she could barely breathe, but at least this form of suffocation was a better death than being knifed.

"You're freezing, it's like kissing an icicle ... What were you doing in that stream—dance of the seven veils?"

She laughed, weakly. "Your chute. It caught me. Matt—you're sure it's you?" She touched his shoulder. "It can't—how could it be?"

"Long story." He raised his head, to listen intently. Nothing. Only the stream babbling as before. His glance fell on the canister.

"Clever girl, you found it. Like a water-spaniel!"

"Is it important? It looks—dangerous."

"It's important, all right. If anything is. There's something else. I wonder—" He listened again, holding her.

"Help me get clear. Who's Friedrich?"

"German. Dropped with me." He picked up the knife, and began sawing at the entangling cords.

She bit her lip. "Who—dropped you?"

"Friends." He moved slightly away.

"I didn't mean—"

"Couldn't blame you, could I?" He dug with the knife; the point slipped, and she said, "*Careful*."

"Sorry. I was wrong to go, Jan. You were right. It was worse than anything you could have imagined. But I got away. Tell you later."

They were both silent, while he worked the cords free. At last she stood up, shivering. Matt stood beside her, and put his arm round her. She knew then that they were so bound to each other beneath the surface of things that explanations between them were unnecessary.

"Are the others all right—Bill and Char?"

"And Tom." She felt him stiffen. "And—oh cripes! Wolf and Leo!"

"Who?"

She clutched at him. "If they find your friend first—they've got lasers. Leo saw you fall and—oh!"

A second shadow was confronting her. "What you doing out here, Jan? And who's this?"

"I—I came out, that's all. And it's Matt."

"Matt?"

"Yes—you've heard us talk of him."

"Freaks dropped him?" Leo's tone was sharper than hers had been. The laser covered Matt with its wicked-looking eye.

"No—friends," she said firmly.

"Friends. With *planes*?"

"We had helis, didn't we? You've just got to take him on trust."

"Not got to do any such thing, have I? Keep your distance,

mate. Wolf's got another of 'em, up the hill, Jan. Hoppo found him."

"We took you on trust," she said, with spirit.

"Didn't come somersaulting from the sky, did I? This other fella's hurt. Sounds foreign—said he came with someone else. Wolf sent me to scout."

"That's Friedrich," said Matt, relieved. "Not badly hurt, is he?"

"Arm. Fell on a rock." Leo looked from Jan to Matt, uncertainly. "Come on, better join them."

Matt picked up the canister, and Leo took a hurried step towards him, saying, "Hey, that looks—"

"It's all right; you can carry it—I'll bring the chute." As he began gathering it up, Matt asked anxiously, "Friedrich— has he got a wooden box?"

"He'll have one soon enough if Wolf's laser goes off," said Leo tartly. "You just keep on the trot ahead of me, chum, so's I can see you. Wolf's not going to be too pleased with you for roaming, Jan. Does the kid know?"

10 ❧ The Talisman

"Let's have a look at your Walther's wooden box," Alastair suggested, in the early hours of the morning, when much of Matt's and Friedrich's story had been told.

Someone had rekindled the fire, and bottles of Old Ned's wine had been broached in honour of the occasion. Even Grouse sipped some, and then slept again. Hoppo lay pressed up against him, as though instinctively aware that Grouse needed the comfort of his furry warmth. Matt and Wolf sat on opposite sides of the fire, watching each other's faces beyond the meagre flames. Matt, his arm round Jan, was alternately wondering what Wolf and Walther would have made of one another, and worrying about the latter's fate. And Wolf, who didn't so much think as let his adventurer's antennae rove, was sensing what Matt's arrival might mean in terms of this settlement's ongoing.

Something beginning, but something ending, he put it to himself. Big change coming. He sniffed danger, like a tingle in his knife, and yawned luxuriously. Walk on the abyss, maybe. Well, that's life—good, too. Softness is one helluva bore. Char'd agree. Hope Fox wasn't right about those heli pilots— One thing, must see the kid's okay. And his sharp anxious eye lingered on Alastair's absorbed face.

"Friedrich?" said Matt tentatively. "What do you think?"

"We were to guard it with our lives—so Walther told Helmut, and he didn't joke. How can we guard it, unless we know what's there?"

"Carried," said Wolf.

"Yet Matt and I know the enemy at first hand" ("So do we all," muttered Fox, bristling) "and we know their methods. It is best, no?—if only two or three should look."

"Right," said Wolf briskly. "And we can't keep old Fritz here out—can we, kid? So that's the kid, Fritz—"

"Matt," said Jan firmly. "It's only here because of him."

"And Wolf. Wolf must stay," said Alastair. "And that's all."

"Me, please, me!" begged Charlie.

Wolf rolled his eyes heavenwards. The firelight turned the whites orange and lent him a wild-animal look. "Out you go with all the rest, Char. Wakee, now—everybody out."

"Into the *cold?*" said outraged Charlie. "And I'm worn out, anyway."

"Nothing would wear you out. What about Grouse, though?"

There was a slight pause. Then, "Grouse stays. Naturally," said Alastair softly. "Good thing Tom's guarding the helis tonight with Bill—he wouldn't like not seeing." He sounded anxious, and Wolf reassured him with, "It's fine, kid; nobody'll tell."

"Hope it's fine." But Jan thought Alastair sounded unconvinced. She caught Matt's eye, and rose to shepherd out Charlie and the others.

The four remaining with the sleeping Grouse and Hoppo sat staring at the wooden box: a very rough affair, put together hurriedly and nailed down by inexpert hands. Wolf drew out a knife and began to use it as a lever. Matt and Friedrich bent forward eagerly, while Alastair held his breath. When the lid shot up he extended a hesitant hand.

"Go on, kid. It won't bite. We hope."

"It's hard—got things like stones, and—" Alastair's fingers groped gingerly among soft wadding, and withdrew, holding something hard and heavy.

"*Du lieber Gott!*" exclaimed Friedrich; and addressed Matt fluently in German.

"What's old Kraut say? Looks like he's going to have a fit."

"He's recognised it. You're sure, Friedrich? I've seen something rather like it, but he says this is the most precious part of the Holy Roman Empire's regalia—the Crown of Charlemagne. From Vienna. This really is the most astonishing thing," said Matt slowly. "I wonder how Helmut managed to get hold of it?"

Everyone sat staring at what Alastair held, while the rubies, sapphires and other stones gave out a gentle radiance in the dying firelight. And at last Wolf whistled softly. "Holy Roman whatsits! Mustn't let Freaks get hold of it, must we? It's a sort of—a sort of a—"

"Symbol," said Alastair. "That's what it is, a symbol. But the crown was split, wasn't it? Split means—division. Perhaps it causes one. Yet the stars were there, for protection. That's what Old Ned put, anyway. On that gravestone."

"Old Ned?" Matt stared. "Gravestone?"

"Pay no attention," said Wolf soothingly. "You'll get accustomed. He's like this, sometimes, aren't you, kid?"

"How fantastic. That's *something*, isn't it?"

"Char," said Alastair, outraged, "out you go."

But Charlie came forward and slipped to her knees beside the fire. "What's the point? I'm in, now. It was freezing out, and the others have gone off to tell Tom and Bill about Matt." They stared at her speechless, as she put out a fingertip and ran it over the jewel-encrusted gold.

"What we need here's Clanger," said Wolf, with a grim wolflike snarl. She paid him no attention, but took Alastair's hands and placed them on the crown. "Go on."

"Stop it, Char—only the anointed wore it," protested Alastair; but did as she told him, almost as if he couldn't help himself.

"*Ach, nein*," said Friedrich; but that was all.

"Now you don't look like yourself."

"Like what, then?"

"Dunno—but it certainly suits you, kid," declared Wolf;

and then told Charlie, harshly, "Heard, didn't you? Kid said out you go. What you stopping for, then? An' don't you go telling *anyone* that you seen this, see? It's you we're thinking of—too. 'S dangerous."

"Don't push her, Wolf." Alastair saw that Charlie was looking upset. "Go on, Char: we're putting it back in its box, anyway. You can do it, first."

She took it from him and reluctantly began rumpling up the packing.

"Why—there's something else here, too. 'S a chain, I think. *And*—something else—"

She withdrew her hand, and everybody gasped.

The firelight drew colour from the dangling pendant as it had from the jewelled crown.

"*Cripes!*" said Wolf inadequately. And to Matt: "what's your chum say—that part of the Holy Roman whatsit too?" for Friedrich was muttering again in German; he seemed to have temporarily lost his English.

"No. He can't think why Helmut had it with the crown."

"Just worth saving, p'raps." Wolf grinned.

"Here—let me have it—"

Charlie obediently swung the pendant across into Matt's outstretched hand, saying, "What's that huge blue stone?"

"Sapphire. Two of them—set back to back." Matt's head was bent above her find.

"But there's a thing in the middle," persisted Charlie. "Something stuck there, sort of. Rich, isn't it, though? All that gold, 'n coloured stones—pity they spoilt it with that middle thing, though."

Matt was silent. He had seen this before . . . shaped like a pilgrim's flask, two huge oval cabochon sapphires forming the centres of the swelling sides; the surround of gold, filigreed, set with gems and pearls; a rectangular neck containing another jewel, a ruby or almandine . . .

"Matt?" Alastair was watching him, wonderingly.

But Matt was faraway both in time and place: a bored

seventeen-year-old, lounging behind his godfather in the resplendent cathedral, while the talk went backward and forward, backward and forward, between him and the *Archevêque*, in precise, knowledgeable French.

"Pay attention, Matthew," his godfather had said suddenly. "Here's one of the great Treasuries of Europe which the *Archevêque* himself kindly shows us, and you stand there with your mouth open—doubtless dreaming of some football or pop idol."

Matt had moved forward reluctantly to stand between the two old men. Something was expected, so: "What's that?" he'd mumbled gracelessly, pointing. And then they'd told him; while he'd fidgeted, suppressed yawns, wondered why he'd ever chosen history as one of his subjects, when the day outside was so sparkling fresh and the girls at câfé tables so inviting—A gaudy, dead, and superstitious thing he'd thought it then; and now here it was, giving out mysterious beams of blue light, whole and entire, escaped from the decay and ravagement of Europe. Enough to make anyone superstitious. And Char had said "—pity they spoilt it with that middle thing."

"It's Charlemagne's jewel," he told them slowly. "He always wore it: one of the most famous talismans in history. And that 'thing', Char, is a bit of the True Cross. If anyone really had a bit, it was Charlemagne. It was buried with him at Aachen—but Otto the Great ordered it to be dug up again. It's a wandering piece—always in the forefront of history. Napoleon grabbed it once—but it ended up in the Treasury of Rheims." He looked hesitantly at Friedrich. "No wonder Helmut and Walther risked so much for it—it's a survivor! And wherever it goes, civilisation seems to fight its battles, and survive as well."

For a few minutes there was complete silence, except for Grouse's uneasy breathing.

Matt held the talisman aloft. Firelight caught the centre stones, and a flash of blue seemed to light the cave.

"Strange," murmured Alastair dreamily at last. "Imagine all it's seen—battles, triumphs, its own burial and resurrection."

"*And* the converting of the barbarians," added Matt the historian.

Charlie was nursing the crown on her knee. "Look," she said, "these stones too—don't they give out a sort of strange light?"

"Firelight," said Wolf firmly. The conversation was getting too airborne for his liking.

"No, Wolf—something more shining. Luminous," said Charlie, proud of the right word. "And *mysterious*."

Wolf gave a sudden bark of laughter. He couldn't have said why, exactly. Maybe it was the thought of kings on their thrones, and then kings as common dust. Or maybe it was Char, the sturdy foster-child nobody had wanted, holding an emperor's cherished jewel in her grubby hands—

"It's lovely, that pendant," said Char suddenly. "Better than Auntie's costume jewellery, any day. Can I wear it?"

Friedrich looked outraged. He took the pendant from Matt, held it between his palms, and kissed the centre stone. Everyone else felt very English.

"I s'pose you're one of those odd Catholics," said Charlie tolerantly. "Well, *I* don't mind."

"It's holy, Char," said Alastair.

"Yes—and a king's ransom we got here," said Wolf. "So, now then, Fritz—hand it back to her. No, Char, you can't wear it, you little twit. The sooner it's back in its box the better. An' I'll nail the lid down, good an' proper."

Friedrich reluctantly gave back the pendant, while Wolf stood up to search for his stone hammer. His shadow blocked out the firelight, and the crown's colour died as Charlie placed it tenderly within the box.

"Oh Wolf—I can't see—"

"She will be careful—" begged Friedrich, as Wolf moved out of the light.

"Tight fit, but—There." Charlie pressed the packing down, and rose with a self-satisfied air. "All *right*, Alastair. Now I'm going."

He looked up at her with an expression of inner amusement. "You'll tell no one what you've seen?"

"What d'you take me for?" She pulled her Eskimo-style sheepskin jerkin higher round her throat, with a theatrical shiver, and stepped out into the night.

"Clanger. *Clang*—"

"Not you again?"

"I say—I've got a secret. Want to share?"

"See I'm going to, like it or not." Clanger pushed his headphones up, and stared resignedly at the pale blur of face looking in.

"Well, to start with, Jan's Matt's back—with a Kraut."

"*What?* Yah—nearly caught me there, Char."

"Oh *Clang*. It's not a joke. I swear it. He jumped. From a plane."

"You're serious?"

It took a while to convince him, as well as to disentangle Charlie's flow of disconnected and excited words. When she'd done, Clanger said: "Don't see this Matt counts as a secret, Char. I mean, he's large as life—can't hide him."

"'S not that. It's—Can I come inside with you while I'm telling you? Oh Clang, I just love it up here—if I lean against you we'll both be warmer, won't we?"

Next day the rain poured down, and the hills were shrouded in mist. A strong scent of drenched, crushed bracken filled the cave.

"It's as miserable inside as out," said Jan dismally.

No one paid her attention. Alastair crouched sad and white-faced by the smoky fire. Tom leaned scowling against the rocky uneven wall. Bill, who was sitting beside Grouse, thought that whenever it was bad weather the cave looked like a slum. There were bodies everywhere, a stench of dirty clothes, and barely room to move. It was often a time when boredom and frustration brought forth rows; but never before had there been such a monumental one. And all, as Wolf now said mildly, because that fool Fox couldn't keep his muzzle shut. Why hadn't Jan stopped him?

His remark made things worse. Tom brought his fists out of his pockets, and they were clenched as though he would fight anyone. His whole body felt so taut with hurt and anger that he was on the verge of violence. He would have liked to start shouting and clobber Wolf, or batter Alastair against the wall until he begged for mercy. And all the time, inside him, was a sense of weeping, of being outcast, as miserable and constant as the rain outside.

"Don't, Wolf," said Alastair.

"'Don't, Wolf'," mimicked Tom. "Who came to London, to get you out?"

"I know, Tom. I'm sorry."

"Look, Tom, you needn't bully your brother," said Matt. "There's only five here—no, four—" he corrected himself hurriedly, "in the know. For everyone's safety. Would have been better if no one else had even known about this box and canister in the first place."

"Better still if Fox hadn't told *me*?" asked Tom, dangerously quiet. "Alastair?"

"Wolf didn't mean it to sound like that. Did you, Wolf?"

"Not if you say so, kid."

"That makes everything quite clear."

"Tom, you're boring. It's *pathetic*," said Charlie. "We all know you're jealous of everyone round Alastair, but—"

"If someone doesn't throw that child out of this cave I'll go raving mad," said Tom, looking as if he might. "This is a straightforward issue between me and my brother."

"No, it's not. No, it's not." Wolf also spoke quietly, but his sharp chin jutted. "'S group thing, if it's anything. But what the kid says goes, for the group, see? And what the kid says,

I'm backing, see? And old Kraut here—sorry, Fritz—he brought the ruddy thing down, so he got his vote. The kid an' Fritz says better only four knows, an' four it is. An' four it stays." He gave Charlie a warning look.

Tom's smile was unpleasant. "That's interesting. Because I'm going to have a look inside that box."

"Do be reasonable, Tom," begged Bill. "They won't let you." The box was on the floor, beyond the sleeping Grouse. There were several people between it and Tom, including Wolf and Leo. He hesitated, and all might have been well, if Charlie hadn't laughed.

"*Char*," hissed Jan; but it was too late.

Charlie rolled out of the way, and grabbed at Hoppo's collar as Tom launched himself forward, violence breaking, transferred from thought into muscle, hatred for Wolf expanding from seed into full plant of fury. As he leaped he snatched up a brand from the fire. Sparks went scattering round his feet. For once Wolf was taken by surprise. He tried to roll clear like Charlie, and nearly succeeded, but the brand slashed him across his forehead, redhot and agonising. Most people would have yelled; Wolf was on his feet in silence that terrified. No one saw his hand move, but the knife was there.

"Wolf, no!" cried Alastair.

The mark burned on Wolf's forehead, but it was nothing like so angry as his eyes. Tom felt almost paralysed by the result of what he'd done.

"No?" questioned Wolf softly.

Matt made as though to take his arm, but thought better of it when Wolf turned his face towards him. A small circle cleared rapidly round Tom and Wolf, who confronted each other by the fire. The only sound was Grouse's sobbing breaths as he lay huddled on his pile of skins.

"Oh Wolf, please," begged Alastair, in a voice wobbling with panic. "Tom, say you didn't mean—You don't know what Wolf can—Please, Tom, say—"

"Be quiet, kid," said Wolf, "an' keep out of it."

"A knife against this?" asked Tom, sounding scornful, but inwardly quaking.

"You chose your weapon, chum. But drop it, an' find yourself a knife. We'll fight fair. Go on. Counting fifty."

Wolf began to count.

"Fair," said Tom with bravado. "Fair enough—for you. I've no knife on me, and you know it." He dropped the brand back upon the fire.

"Fox. Give him yours."

"Now, Wolf—" temporised Fox; but at a glint from Wolf's eyes he capitulated. Tom gripped it nervously, thinking with sick horror of knife-scars, and wounds under such conditions. The blistering scrawl of red across Wolf's forehead seemed to fix him with a third and furious eye. But Wolf himself suddenly laughed, a rasping and contemptuous sound.

"Big mouth. Couldn't stick a pin in a baby's bottom, could you? Go on, say you were a sod, and to the kid too, an' we'll forget it."

"Look, Tom, I don't mind, truly," said Alastair. "And Wolf —Wolf wouldn't, if you—"

"Your friend Wolf! Common gutter fighter." And Tom made a thrust with Fox's knife in the clumsy, amateur, ferocious way he'd used successfully against the Junks. But Wolf was no Junk. He almost danced aside, yet with such economy of movement that he landed in just the right place to bring his arm forward, slice the blade of his knife along Tom's, press downwards, and send it twirling out of his grip, far into the shadows beyond the sleeping Grouse.

Everyone gasped. It was only a second or two, and yet it seemed to them as if everything happened in slow motion. With horror they watched Wolf's knife hand move upward and the blade hover like a humming-bird before Tom's throat— then descend more like hawk than humming-bird. There was a ripping sound; Tom's leather belt was neatly slashed in two, and his trousers fell around his ankles, leaving him half nude and wholly ridiculous.

Wolf laughed.

"Don't you tangle with common gutter fighters, laddy, not quite their weight, are you? An' just you learn to fight clean in future, you middle-class bigmouthed mouse! Now out you go an' do another night on heli-watch, and let's see if that nice cold rain out there'll cool you down." Wolf made another of his lightning movements, and Tom, almost weeping, found Wolf's right hand gripping his jersey neck and Wolf's punishing left in the small of his back, urging him out into the night.

"An' don't no one go out after him," said Wolf, on the threshold, "nor take him food. Not even you, Jan—he's got to learn once an' for all that the kid's a bigger potato than he is, an' I'm the next size down."

"He'll hate you for ever, Wolf," said Alastair dolefully. "You don't know Tom."

"After that little game, I think I do. And don't you fuss yourself, kid, see, he's not worth it. Once he's thought the matter over, he's going to see light."

But Alastair, staring into the fire, didn't answer, and could only shake his head.

The day of pelting rain gave place to a night of storm such as they hadn't seen since they found the valley. It raged all night, making such a roaring in the trees above the cave that talking was impossible. The wind only dropped when it was grey dawn inside the cave—the light came filtered through sacking screens to join the feeble glow of a tamped-down fire. Grouse, with Hoppo at his feet, was coughing and restless in the smoky atmosphere. Jan lay close in Matt's arms, happy as she'd not been since that awful hour in her home. Charlie snored like a puppy in the heavy sleep that succeeded her indignant tears, after Wolf had told her off blisteringly about her tactless laughter. She hadn't even stirred when Leo had slipped from the cave a little earlier to relieve Tom from heli-watch.

Alastair was miserable. He lay on his stomach, looking into

the embers and feeling not only a general sorrow that crushed him as if the cave had fallen in upon his back, but also his own personal misery about Tom. The grey ash curled and fell, and a small cavern of brightness was suddenly swamped and went out. He prodded it with a stick, but it wouldn't light again. He was thinking how cold and hungry Tom must be, if Ox, who'd been also on heli-guard, hadn't shared his rations with him. Tom would have hated to explain to Ox . . .

Tom. Poor Tom. Always jealous, guilty. Sometimes over-protective, sometimes cruel . . . Wolf should have let me send someone to fetch him in, he'll think I don't care. Wolf . . . I should have reminded Wolf of how Tom rescued Grouse, how he helped get everybody out of London . . . came to find me. Wolf's always done what I wanted. Till last night.

In his mind's eye he saw Tom returning caveward, trudging through dead bracken in the dawn, filled with wounded bitterness and hatred. And choking humiliation. Other people might feel able to live it down . . . But not Tom. He's too proud.

Another cavern of brightness was overwhelmed by ash.

His eyes pricked, red-rimmed from sleeplessness and staring at the fire. It was going out. Alastair couldn't bear to look at it. His thoughts were relentlessly drawn back to the day when Clanger took him up the eastward hill, to the nucleo-radic hut; and to those strange messages about the defeat that was coming, and the courage that would be needed. But why should a row with Tom be connected with those things?

Shall I wake Wolf, and talk to him about them? I never told him—didn't want to worry him . . . Yet perhaps it's time—

But Wolf's sleeping face wore an implacable expression.

No. Not wake Wolf . . . not yet. Poor Tom.

He won't return, thought Alastair suddenly. *I* wouldn't. This sense of total, crushing blackness. Of foreboding.

Outside, Mule—on cave-watch—cried out. A sacking screen went over with a crash, enveloping the nearest sleepers. Everyone sat up, staring, and Hoppo woke in a flurry of barking.

Leo stood in the entrance, wide-eyed and out of breath. His words stammered, wouldn't come.

Wolf was on his feet as though he'd never slept.

"Tom?" cried Alastair; cursing his own helplessness.

"Ox—he's there semi-conscious. Keeps moaning someone hit him—Tom, I think."

"Tom!" cried Alastair again, with terrible certainty. (Remembering: betrayal.)

"Yes—and the prisoners, they've gone. And Heli Two, with all its nucleo-radic gear. And —I reckon!—Tom as well."

The land below was hidden in grey mist; but the dawn was splendid above the first cloud layers. Streamers of ragged gold and pink floated past. Tom, staring from the heli window, didn't appreciate them, and barely listened to what the second heli pilot was saying to him.

"What?" he asked dully.

"You'll be rewarded," the man was saying. "Co-operation is most valued."

Tom flinched. "We're not going south?" He looked out of the window again, at the newly risen sun.

"No—we've been in contact with our superiors. We've been diverted straight to our nearest headquarters. Offshore, where the English oilfields are. A modern experiment, quite interesting, they say: a city in the sea."

11 🎜 Fallen in Lyonesse

It was a cold dawn for their already frozen spirits; and a colder one for Grouse, who died gently, sleeping it out. It was Wolf who drew the sheepskins over him, and stood looking down, not pityingly, not even sad, but thinking: he's the lucky one, after all—and just when the luck's running out at last. He returned softly to the ashes of the fire, and sat down, closing his eyes, to brood over what Alastair had told him, finally, of his awesome experience on the summit of the eastward hill.

Kid should have told me, even if it was depressing. To think of him carrying that burden, all by himself. Courage— he's got that, all right. Seems like we're going to need it. Maybe there won't be defeat—but the kid's never wrong; he was puzzled though—Seemed to think it was a dark-before-the-dawn type of thing. Wolf sighed, equally puzzled by the words Alastair had repeated to him. Then he smiled. "Tower of the Zodiac"—what the hell's that? Trust the kid to involve us with something so improbable—

And Wolf dozed, the light animal doze of fighters before battle; while uncertain daylight gradually penetrated the cave.

Jan didn't doze. Nor did Matt. They lay in each other's arms, beneath a pile of skins; oblivious of people round them, and the sword of Damocles. Disaster seemed to attend their meetings, whenever the circle of their lives touched. They were as fated as lovers in some legend, but they didn't think of it. Jan touched Matt's face with her fingertips, and smiled to herself, tracing the outline of his mouth with one finger.

"Oh, Matt . . . Oh you."

Charlie overheard their murmurings, and sat up suddenly. Clang! No one had warned him. He was due down at noon today, but anything might have happened by then. Maybe he'd hear something up there, but—She groped cautiously for her shoes; and her hand touched that canister Matt had brought, and lingered on it. Matt seemed to think it so important . . .

When she slipped from the cave Hoppo followed her, alert for rabbiting. Fox, who was on duty outside, grabbed at her arm, but she shook him off.

"Wolf said warn Clanger." And she was away, with Hoppo in pursuit. Fox looked after them with misgivings. Wolf would probably skin him, but it was no part of his duty to leave here. Particularly now.

With the fire out, they ate a meagre breakfast.

"Montrose's men did well enough on oatmeal," said Bill; but no one smiled.

"Well, kid—shouldn't we have left?" asked Wolf.

"Char and Clanger haven't come down. How could we go without them, anyway?" put in Jan protestingly. Matt took her hand in his.

"I'll skin that Fox," growled Wolf. But his heart wasn't in it—someone else would probably do the job for him. He glanced up at Alastair.

But Alastair was staring into the fire's ashes, and eating his food very slowly, as if he found it hard to swallow. There was a long pause, while everybody watched him. When he looked up his eyes were very wide and dark, and he spoke so quietly that Wolf asked: "What, kid?"

Alastair turned towards him. "We could go to Old Ned's, I suppose—but Tom knows about him, and—Freaks would come looking for us. They'd kill Ned, and—Someone could take Friedrich's box there, but . . . Well—same thing."

"Just get out, then—and keep going? We've always kept ahead of them so far."

Alastair hesitated. "Now that—Tom's gone," he said in a low voice, "they're going to know too much about us, aren't they? Matt and Friedrich dropping by chute. That box. Our numbers. We'd only be hunted down. So we'll stay. Oh Wolf, we must, anyway. Because that's the way it's got to be. This time."

There was another lengthy pause, till Wolf stood up suddenly. "*Right*—That's it, then. Now we've got to—" he swallowed—"give old Grousey a—you know—"

"And decently," said Jan, using words from the past. "The heli copse? Be pretty in spring—ground's easy there, too, because of the beech mast. And there mayn't be—much time." She gripped Matt's hand more tightly. "Oh, I'm glad— I'm thankful now that Char's not here."

"Don't you go, Wolf," said Alastair. "I—I feel like talking."

Wolf gave him a quick, bright glance. "Let Jan an' Matt go then; with Leo and Bill. An' Mule—Ox isn't feeling quite so good, just now."

When they returned, there was even more tension inside the cave. "What's up now?" asked Matt, as he began searching through the sheep fleeces and debris beyond the fire.

"Fritz and his damn box," said Wolf laconically. "He's sort of mourning over it. Won't let anyone touch it. What you hunting for now?"

"My canister. It's gone—must have rolled. It was here all right early on."

"You and Fritz, you're a pair. Your ruddy canister, and his English."

"Wolf wants to send someone off alone with the box—run till they almost drop, then bury it," said Alastair.

"And? (I've looked there.)"

"And Fritz isn't playing," said Wolf. "Pretends he don't hear, an' sits making noises like a naughty little Kraut. See what you can do."

After a brief exchange in German, Matt reported, "It's since Tom—Sorry, Alastair! He—well, anyway, Walther told Helmut we'd defend it with our lives, so that's what Friedrich wants to do."

"No wonder Hitler lost the war," said Wolf. "Don't adapt, do they?"

"He doesn't want the box to leave the cave. He's sure the cave's as good a place as any for hiding it. In the roots of that tree."

"Don't think so. Would be too easy for 'em, kid."

Alastair gave a sigh. "We shouldn't really stop Friedrich doing what he wants. But they'll certainly get everything out of Tom, he's not strong enough to—And nor is anyone else, under questioning."

"Just as you say, kid. Still, what's *your* real feeling about the thing?"

"Oh Wolf! I can't always know, can I? You could be right, but—" Alastair looked at Friedrich. "It's his, isn't it?"

There was a pause. Then Wolf nodded. "Right. Made yourself clear, kid. Now, supposing Fritz wants to fight, what about Jan and Charlie?"

"Resistance is going to be pretty useless," put in Bill.

"It will only make things worse," agreed Alastair.

"I still can't find it," Matt was saying desperately. "You don't think Charlie—It could explode."

"*Char*! Oh Matt, I do wish she and Clang would come on down."

"It's a pity she didn't take that box," muttered Matt, giving up the search. "All right, Friedrich—it's agreed; hiding-place is here." Together they pushed the box out of sight between the roots.

"First place they'll look," complained Wolf, watching with narrowed eyes. "Oh, well. Got all the guns out, now? Stamp on the fire, Foxy. Someone better go an' look for our two truants soon." He glanced down at Alastair. "What's on the mind, kid? Still say, no resistance?"

"There will be," said Alastair. Bleak.

"Right—but don't fancy waiting here to be trapped. Come on, everybody out. Down to the sheepfold, lay up behind the hurdles there. Leo's got one laser, I'll take the other."

As they began filing from the cave, Alastair held out a hand. Wolf moved across to help him up.

"Wait, Wolf. Just stay a moment. Here."

Wolf sat down beside him, and stared at the flattened grey ashes of the fire. He sighed and leaned back against the cave wall. When he half closed his eyes the cave itself seemed to vanish, and he might have been sitting alone with Alastair in the ruined room near Paul's.

"Feels like quite a time . . . " And then, as Alastair looked a question, he added, "Wonder what happened to old Hercules."

"Flown, I expect. Like us."

There was a pause. Still Alastair didn't seem disposed to talk. At last Wolf said, with a jerk of the head towards the hidden crown, "Still seems to me that someone ought to take that thing and run."

Alastair looked at him thoughtfully. He knew that stubborn, fighting look on Wolf's face. He sighed. "Maybe it's what I felt, earlier. But Friedrich—And now it's so late, Wolf, isn't it? Maybe it can't make any real difference. Either way. Not to what happens now."

There was a heavy silence. Wolf broke it with: "Something you wanted to say, was there, kid?"

"Oh well, just—Thanks, Wolf. Thanks a lot."

"Nothing to thank me for," said Wolf, a bit huskily. "Looking back, never had such a time in my life. Never know how lucky you are, do you? Till it ends."

"Ends?" Alastair was also looking at the place where the fire had been. "That fire could be relit."

"Don't you start talking in riddles, kid."

Alastair smiled at him rather sadly. "I'm not. I don't want it to end here, Wolf. Really I don't. Yet—this time—that's the way it's got to be."

"So we've just got to take it. You were always right, kid. But they were good days, all the same." Wolf looked into Alastair's face and thought he saw there, fleetingly, the same expression that he himself must have worn earlier that morning, looking down on Grouse. For a moment a blur of darkness came between them, rubbing out Alastair's features as if the sun had suddenly gone down. Then the light returned. Wolf drew his hand across his eyes as though to clear them.

"Well, kid! Which of us is it going to be?"

"You ought to come on down, Clang. Please."

"'M waiting. Not due off yet, am I?"

"It's all changed now. Oh please, Clang!"

"You go down, Char. There's maybe something I'll hear. There's been a lot of chatter—mostly Freakish jargon. An' crazy disturbances—specially since you came up here."

She rolled over resignedly on to her stomach, and peered through tufty grasses at the valley floor below. She began to bite her nails.

"Nails is disgusting," said Clanger severely. "Worse than usual. Like a dog's, been burying a bone."

"Don't be auntie-ish." But she spoke absentmindedly, concentrating now on the eastward valley.

"*Clang*—I think—"

"Uh-huh?"

"Here—Hurry!"

Clanger raised his head. He stared.

"Jesus! Already!"

They came over the hilltop in a steady, ordered stream. As the column moved downwards its van was obliterated by shreds of lowlying mist, but on the skyline the dark dots advanced outlined against the white glare of morning.

"Ants on the march," said Fox disgustedly, peering from behind a sheep hurdle.

Jan interlaced an arm with Matt's. Their pulses beat together.

"Don't fight. No one must fight," he was saying. "It's useless." His eyes were on Wolf's laser. "Wolf, they mustn't—Have you told Ox?" For Ox, recovering, had taken over the second laser from Leo, and was crouched with Mule and others behind boulders farther up the hill.

"Wish Char were here," mourned Jan softly. "And Clanger."

The ants advancing through the mistline were ants no longer, but distinguishably human. Two small track vehicles accompanied the column.

"*Wolf?*"

Wolf made no reply. He was glaring at the advancing men, teeth clenched.

"Bastards!" he said at last, between them. "Well, they're not getting back their other heli, that's for sure."

Up on the hilltop Clanger and Charlie had almost torn his equipment into its component parts, and were feverishly stuffing them down the various holes of an unused rabbit warren, long earmarked for such an emergency.

"Can't—get this—down *here*," panted Clanger. "Something stopping it."

"Try another."

"Char—you put something down—already?"

"Why—yes, I did. Something that—Look, Hoppo's digging —got to tie his jaws." She used a piece of rag which had served her for a handkerchief. "Hurry, Clang. We've got to be with Jan—and Alastair. And Wolf—"

"Hang on a minute."

Arms interlocked, like Jan and Matt, they lay on their stomachs to peer over the hillbrow at the scene below. And so were the first to see pallid flames lick upward around Heli One, and explode skywards into orange sparks and a thick trail of smoke.

"Good old Mule." Wolf licked his lips in satisfaction. Alastair turned his head, and saw the heli-fire. When he looked at Wolf his eyes were slightly reproachful. And sad.

"Sorry, kid. Just couldn't let them get away with everything."

Alastair held out a hand to him. And then Jan, watching, saw an odd thing happen. Wolf took it, hesitantly. Their two figures blurred and darkened before her eyes, seemed to grow larger, were shot through with sparks of light. She blinked, wondering if her sight were going funny. And later on could never tell just *what* she'd seen, exactly, only speak of it vaguely, with some awe and a little fear. They might have been figures from the past, or from the future; not Wolf and Alastair as she knew them now, just presences. She wasn't even sure what clothes they wore.

Then everything looked clear and normal again, and for a second she thought Wolf bent his forehead to Alastair's hand, in the old gesture of fealty. And then suddenly he turned, to run from the precarious shelter of the hurdles, carefully shielding his precious laser gun from the enemy's watchful eyes.

"Bet Wolf ordered that," said Clanger in satisfied tones. From this height the heli-fire was a mushrooming bloom of black and orange among the trees.

"Oh Clang, look—Wolf!"

And they watched as Wolf ran steadily uphill towards the cave, and the column's van halted on the opposite slope, though its rear continued to wind on down, like a snake coiling itself to strike.

"Jan, Jan—" cried Charlie hysterically. "We gotta *go*."

"Wait." Clanger's arm across her shoulders held her down. "Can't do nothing now, Char. Too late."

Wolf had reached the cave mouth, and nothing had happened. He was inside for what seemed a long minute, but was only seconds. When he emerged again he was carrying

Friedrich's box, and swift as a wild animal was doubling up beyond the cave towards the hills behind. He was among the trees now, and out of their vision, and still the enemy did nothing.

But his impulsive action triggered off another. For Ox was standing up, visible above the sheltering boulders, staring after Wolf. His gun was clearly visible as well.

He was the first to fall. The snake's head puffed out daggers of light, soundless, lethal, and Ox went bowling head over heels, like a shot rabbit. But someone else crawled after him, grabbed up his gun and, standing, directed it towards the enemy. One valiant little stream of light flickered across the intervening stream, and died, overpowered by the return.

Charlie was weeping, Hoppo was trying to lick her, impeded by the rag. Clanger held her face downwards on the turf. "Don't look, Char. Don't—"

There was a heavy thud! in the valley below, and the boulders rose into the air, lazily, like flying birds. Black dots were running about helplessly, fell, crawled, fell again. Clanger couldn't look away, although he wanted to. How many—who?

Behind the sheep hurdles no one knew what had happened since Wolf had disappeared from sight, and Matt had grabbed hold of Friedrich to stop him following. They heard one or two thin, wailing cries, like gulls, and the thud as the boulders disintegrated. That was all. Now they saw nothing, heard nothing, till one of the track vehicles raced past them on the right and lurched up the hill's flank in the direction Wolf had taken, disdainfully ignoring them. Jan heard Alastair give a little moan, and saw sweat start on his forehead. His eyes were wide, unseeing. There was a strange look of exaltation on his face.

"Alastair?" she whispered.

"Hush, Jan," hissed Bill, crouching beside her.

On the hilltop Clanger, still shielding Charlie from the sights below, followed Wolf's flight and the pursuit. Wolf emerging from trees, Wolf zigzagging, Wolf running low like a lapwing, Wolf pulling himself up a vertical piece of scree, hand over hand, but hampered by the box. He had thrown away his gun. On the lower slope the snake lay coiled, completely still.

Momentarily the vehicle was halted by the scree, too steep even for its gripping treads. Then as its driver hunted sideways along the slope, seeking for ways up, Wolf reappeared on the hillbrow above, running outlined like a Greek athlete against the sky. It was Clanger's last sight of him. Someone was standing in the track vehicle, holding what looked like a long thin black rod, with a bulge at its tip. A streak flashed from the muzzle, and Wolf flung up his arms and turned slowly on the skyline, and then went over the hillbrow in a dizzying, beautiful dive, like an Olympics swimmer going off the highest board.

Clanger held Charlie's face pressed down into the grass. Tears were running down his cheeks.

"What's happening, Clang, what's happening?"

"Nothing. Nothing, Char. Oh God—it's all happened. It's over."

The track vehicle was still hunting slowly upward; it paused beyond the brow; returned. The driver was laughing. A second soldier held the box negligently beneath one arm.

A coil of the snake had flowed across the stream, and surrounded the sheepfold. Clanger could see hands raised in the air. Someone was lifting Alastair on to a hurdle, his right hand was up, shielding his eyes. There was no merciful mist to hide any of it. And away beyond the trees the helicopter was burning brightly.

"Jan? Matt? Alastair—and Wolf? Oh leggo me, Clang," moaned Charlie softly. Beside her Hoppo was whining in a puzzled way.

Clanger took his hand from the nape of her neck, and she sat up, wiping grass seed off her cheeks obsessively.

"Alastair's alive. Wolf—" Clanger stopped. "Don't know which of the others."

"Oh Clang, hold me. Feel so sick."

Very high above them, a lark began to sing.

It was late afternoon before the snake left the valley. There had been a good deal of coming and going during the day, with crannies searched and huts razed. The soldiers were destructive for the pleasure of it, as soldiers often are. They pillaged the cave, and then tossed grenades into it, causing such a blast of earth and stone that Little 'Un, grazing placidly by the stream, was hit by flying pebbles and went snorting away up the valley. The prisoners were tied and taunted, and no one bothered to do anything about the still forms dotted here and there, sightless on the grass.

Throughout the day Charlie lay beside Clanger on the hilltop, fiercely clutching his hand, and moaning at intervals, "I want Jan. Oh Clanger, I want Jan."

"Shoosh, Char, shoosh," said Clanger inadequately.

When at last the column began to move off in the direction from which it came, a small bunch of prisoners, half-hidden by the marching soldiers, were plodding near its centre. Matt and Bill could be seen carrying Alastair's hurdle, and Jan following them, head drooping and hands tied. It was then that Clanger said irresolutely, as though he'd been arguing with himself, "Dunno . . . ought we go with 'em?"

"*Follow* them?"

"Yah. Or—give ourselves up, like. Be with the others then, wouldn't we? Shouldn't split the group, maybe."

"Clang . . . Wolf wasn't there. Couldn't see him, anyway."

"No." He avoided her eyes.

Charlie didn't ask. She knew, now. And she felt nothing, immediately. Except finished. Barely human. Not even hungry or thirsty any more. She tried to think, but thoughts jumped from one thing to another, overlaid by lurid pictures of what might have happened down below. She half wanted to know, half feared to. Clanger was saying, "Seems like they got the Kraut's treasure box, all right. 'Least, Wolf saved it from that grenade."

"Was that when—"

Clanger nodded.

She sat looking at the grass. Her face was swollen from crying. She put her hands on Hoppo's back, and it seemed strange he was alive and warm. She pressed her head against his flank.

"Think what—Matt said about the Freaks. Mightn't keep us with the others, might they? Might they, Clang?"

"Maybe should take you to Old Ned," Clanger was muttering.

"But he didn't want us there, anyway . . . And I want to be with Jan." She untied the rag slowly from Hoppo's jaws, and he licked her hand.

"So it's not Old Ned. We gotta follow, then. Like to take— Wolf's gun, though. If no one else did."

"Wolf . . . "

"That's right."

Charlie began to cry again, but Clanger paid her no attention. Already he was looking round him with a survivor's eye. She remembered how they'd found him after the collapse of his gang. It gave a fleeting sense of comfort.

"Things hidden here is best left, now."

"Yes, Clang."

"Think we'll go down, Char, once they're out of sight. An' see what's—what, down there."

"Yes, Clang. Anything you say."

When the two of them and Hoppo reached the valley floor, the sun was still a bright gold ball seemingly poised on the hill-brow where Wolf had died. Mists were rising from the stream-bed. They drank the icy water, and Charlie's teeth began to chatter, not only from the cold. Clanger led her towards the hurdled stockade.

226

"You take a rest, Char, while I look round."

Inside the sheepfold they found Jan's homespun woolly jacket. Charlie snatched it up, and rocked it against her face.

"Oh, poor Jan—she'll freeze."

"Put it on. It'll warm you. An' wait for me."

But after a while she couldn't bear the aloneness, and crept out to follow. She found him returning from the direction of the scattered boulders, looking grim, with Hoppo whining at his heels.

"Char!"

"Let me come with you now, Clang. 'S worse, imagining."

Clanger thought that it mightn't be, but nodded; he guessed he couldn't stop her.

The sun had dropped behind evening clouds when they found the laser gun beneath the scree, hidden in long grass. Charlie stumbled on it, or they would have missed it.

They found Wolf where he had fallen. He lay full-length, eyes open, as though staring at the sky. His features were set, but peaceful, as though he knew that he had done his best, and now it was out of his hands—which lay flung out on either side of him, palms upward, as though welcoming a guest. Clanger looked up at the sky too, and saw stars pricking out already in the deep blue of the approaching night. Hoppo shivered and whined, and lay down beside Wolf's feet.

"There's no mark on him, Clang. Except this one—Here. Only his jersey looks all scorched." Charlie's voice was husky. She knelt, picked grasses, placed them in the open hands. "It's from us," she said. " 'Fallen in Lyonesse.' That's what it said, didn't it? And that's for the others too. 'Fallen in Lyonesse about their lord'." Clanger looked on helplessly, worrying about her words. If Char was going crazy, he didn't see how he could cope. Not alone.

"He looks so—quiet." She kissed Wolf on the forehead, smoothing it with her hands. It was cold as stone. She was crying again. She seemed to have been crying all day.

Clanger stood there stolidly, saying nothing. His responsibility for Charlie was weighing heavily; it was as though Wolf, lying so near, yet so remote, was laying some charge on him which he felt inadequate to bear.

"He was a quiet one, always," he muttered at last. And at that moment something caught his eye, some movement down in the farther valley: a pattern of dark forms weaving slowly upward; hard to see at this distance, and by this light—And instantly he knew what he must do, as if Wolf had told him, spelling it out loud and clear.

"C'mon, Char. We're going. There's something—someone, down there."

"Where? Could—could it be the others, Clang? Some of them?" Even as she said it she knew how ridiculous it was; but she was still in that strange state when it's hard to believe in the cruelty of what has happened, and a faint, irrational hope persists that some part of it can be undone.

"He—Wolf got farthest. Maybe the Freaks circled us, though. Think we'll follow Jan, an' Matt. Better go, than be grabbed."

She touched Wolf's forehead again, with one finger, and stood up. "All right . . . I'm so tired."

"Yah. Must get you food—maybe there's bits we can scavenge, but—Freaks've got it, mostly, now."

She looked at him steadily. "Suppose there's someone wounded—Ox, or—"

"When Freaks done a job, they done it. I had a look round, see? Mule's there. Couldn't find Leo or Fox. Or anyone could be that Kraut. Prisoners, maybe. C'mon, Char. Fast."

"It's not right to leave Wolf alone, like this."

"Ain't alone. Better than being buried. Got the stars, hasn't he? An' the hilltop—Wolf liked hills." His arm was round her, urging her away. They were both so shocked and exhausted that neither noticed Hoppo was still lying flattened in the grass. "C'mon, now," Clanger was saying. "Else we've seen the last of Jan, an' Matt, an' Alastair, for ever."

Hoppo looked after them, whining deep and pitifully in his

228

throat. But they had forgotten him, and they had left Wolf lying there alone, and he was so fond of Wolf. He crept a little closer, and put his head down on Wolf's ankles, and lay there guarding him beneath the stars.

Old Ned had felt restless for a few days. Lonesome like. Kept thinking of young 'uns over the hill, and if they'd run out of wine. Damn it if I don't take 'em two or three bottles for a little celebration. Seeing as the stone's finished. And maybe I'll take it over, for that Wolf to see. That kid, he was right struck with it. Pretty I made it, with those stars. Spot of chat won't do no one any harm, now nights are longer.

He laid down his chisel, and went outside. In his valley, with its lower western horizon of smaller hills, the sun was still on high, a fiery orange crossed by bars of blue cloud. Darn me if it's not barred like a pretty bird's wing, he thought, as he chirruped to his pony. It flung up its head, whinnied, and came trotting over to him.

Old Ned's age was telling on him, in spite of his sinewy toughness and air of being pickled like a walnut in good alcohol. Once he had wrapped the stone in canvas, it was a struggle to get it on to the pony's back. But he managed, and lashed it there with old straps and bits of rope. He put some provisions into a sack, with four large bottles, and swung it over his shoulder. Then they set off together, he and his pony.

It had taken Alastair and the others a day's march to find his village. It took Old Ned an extra day. So he reached the first slopes of Golden Valley's western hills on the late afternoon of the disaster. Here everything was already grey with misty shadow, although behind him the sun's rim was bright as a copper twopenny piece, just slipping below the peaks of the lower, inland hills.

Staring upward and ahead of him, Old Ned saw some movement on the skyline. But then he thought, maybe it was only a bit of a bird; and my old eyes are none so good, these days—He urged the pony on, for the air was chilly, and his imagination already reached forward towards companionship and the sharing of wine.

Now hup! with you, fella! Nearly at journey's end—

Journey's end; but it was Wolf's journey's end they stumbled on, high on the hill crest. Hoppo rose growling from his vigil, and the canvas nearly slipped from the shying pony's back. Old Ned quieted it, and gentled Hoppo in his countryman's soothing voice; then he stood gazing pitifully down. More enemy work . . . Like at my own place, seemingly. The poor young 'uns . . . That Wolf as bold as brass, and so pleasant with it; and so successful in his cunning, you'd think he'd have 'em outwitted, so you would . . .

He was uncertain what to do. Unwilling to go on, unwilling to go back without learning what had become of his other young friends: that Alastair, whom they'd called the kid; and that girl, so pretty, so like his late wife's cousin. And all the while he was noticing things: the marks on Wolf's sweater— seen that before, I have—and the grasses, still fresh from picking, laid lovingly in the palms of his hands. Some of them young 'uns was here lately, but daren't stay, seemingly. That's bad. Flown like birds, they have. But the more he looked on Wolf's silent form, so lonely on the ancient hilltop, the more everything in Old Ned revolted against the idea of leaving him. Not decent, that isn't. And there's my old stone, like as if I'd brought it here specially . . .

Wait though, Ned lad, he told himself cannily. Could be there's danger still—then I'd best be making homeward . . . But somehow this idea, after his coming upon this sorry ending to dreams of a companionably happy evening, was not appealing.

Might as well be hanged for a sheep as a lamb, they do say—

He had trouble lifting Wolf tenderly on to the unwieldy canvas pack, and more trouble with the pony, which objected strongly. But at last they set forward again, this time accompanied by Hoppo. Delayed as they were, and so laden, they only began moving down into Golden Valley as Charlie and Clanger were leaving it by the other end.

The sun was lost, but afterglow and starlight revealed the desolation in the valley: splintered boulders, broken sheep-fold, razed huts, and blackened cave-mouth. The animals had scattered, and Little 'Un was nowhere to be seen. There were none of Old Ned's friends to greet him; those who were here would never rise again. In the copse at the valley's head the heli fire still gave off its ruddy glow. All this Old Ned saw, and accepted—for he was a good age, and had seen it all before, or most of it.

But—he thought—there's something still to do.

Wolf's earlier orders had prepared some of it already. By the copse Old Ned halted the pony—which was anyway reluctant to approach the fire—and tied it, and took Wolf gently into his strong old arms to lay him down beside the burning heli. Hoppo stood near, quivering. Old Ned gathered up twigs, and dried leaves and branches, and built them round Wolf like the walls of a Viking ship. He took a stick, and brought fire from one place to the other. And when he had seen it well alight, he stood for a while honouring the dead who must have fought so well. Finally he unpacked the stone that he had carved, and set it up close by, ramming one end deep into beechmast, and leaning the head against a tree. The sword, the carved split crown, Orion's stars, were well illumined by the growing fire.

Too old and tired I am, to do this for more than one of you, my friends. So let him be the one for all . . .

Slow and saddened he started to retrace his steps. Hoppo trotted, a gaunt shade, at his heels, and Old Ned turned to fondle the wolfhound's ears. "With young 'uns, were you? Come along o' me, then. Reckon that's what you're intending, any road." The pony, relieved of its double burden, followed peacebly enough.

They regained the hillbrow when Orion was blazing high above Golden Valley, with the clear January brightness of his starry belt and sword shining down upon the little leaping flames of Wolf's funeral pyre. The mighty hunter was spread splendidly across the heavens, far, far above the pitiful darkness of the earth. Old Ned nodded grimly to himself, thinking that it was a strange thing to remember how he'd drawn that very same pattern of stars upon his special stone.

Beyond the eastward hill, Charlie and Clanger were crouched in a disused quarry, eating such bits and pieces of food as they'd salvaged from the wreckage of the settlement. For some while they had been too tired and upset to speak. Now Charlie said: "*And* we've lost Hoppo, too."

"He'll follow."

In the darkness she shook her head. "No . . . Think—he stayed—with Wolf."

"Don't cry again, Char," said Clanger hastily. "Wear yourself out, you will."

"Oh, Clang . . . Does it matter?"

"Yes, it does," said Clanger stoutly. "On your feet, an' fight. That's all there is to it. If I learnt anything from Wolf, an'—an' the kid, that's it, see. Mustn't never give up."

"You're brave. You're braver than I am."

"'M stronger. Makes the odds. Here—kept this bit of bunny for you. Speaking of that, just what you been shoving down that rabbit hole by my radic hut?"

"Well—if I don't say, only one of us would know if—if we were—well—questioned."

"Rather that one of us weren't you, though." Clanger sounded definite.

"Perhaps I ought to tell you, anyway. In case—something happened to me. And then you and—and the others, needed it. Though you couldn't really, I suppose . . . " She heaved a sigh. "Tell you, shall I, Clang?" She leaned forward to breathe the information in his ear, as though the enemy were listening.

"You did well, Char," said Clanger, when she'd done. "Freaks don't know what they're up against, not with you still

232

at large. Matt would be pleased as anything, Kraut too. An'—
an' Wolf would've been proud of you. Now, on your feet." He
put his arm round her, and pulled her up. They stood close
together, looking towards their lost valley, and familiar Orion.

"Jan's special stars, those are, remember?" Clanger told
Charlie comfortingly, as they began their weary plodding in
the wake of an enemy who was leading them north-eastwards,
away from Golden Valley towards the city in the sea.

HERE ENDS THE FIRST STAGE OF
A QUEST FOR ORION